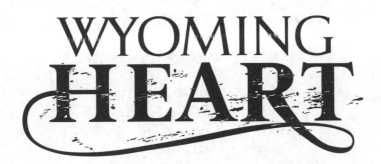

DIANA PALMER

WYOMING HEART

HQN™

ISBN-13: 978-1-335-14635-9

Wyoming Heart

Dear Reader,

Cort Grier showed up for the first time in *Lawman*. His second substantial appearance was in *Undaunted*, where he flirted with my heroine.

I thought he was a complex character even then, and I wanted to write about him. So here is his story.

He's at his cousin's ranch in Wyoming pretending to be a poor cowboy. He meets his cousin's female friend, who hates him on sight when he ridicules her for liking to knit and read romance novels. He doesn't know that she's a successful novelist who researches her books by going out in the field with a group of commando mercenaries.

Expect fireworks when they discover the truth about each other, LOL.

I really enjoyed writing this book, although I must confess that it took paths I didn't dictate along the way. I hope you enjoy it!

Your biggest fan,

Diana Palmer

For Robert
Who keeps our computers and printers going,
even when they don't want to!

CHAPTER ONE

Cort Grier was disillusioned with life. He owned a huge Santa Gertrudis breeding stud ranch in West Texas. He was thirty-three now, in his prime, and he wanted to have a family. His father had remarried and moved to Vermont. His brothers, except for the second youngest, were all married with families. He wanted one of his own. But every woman he thought might be the one turned out to be after his money. The last one, a singer, had laughed when he mentioned children. She was in her own prime, she told him, and she had a career as a rising star. No way was she giving that up to live on some smelly ranch in Texas and start having babies. She wasn't certain that she was ever going to want a child.

And so it went. Women had been a permissible pleasure for many years, and while no playboy, he'd had his share of beautiful, cultured lovers. The problem was that after a time, they all looked alike, felt alike, sounded alike. Perhaps, he told himself, he was jaded. Certainly, age hadn't done much for his basically cynical nature. He found more pleasure these days in running the cattle ranch than he did in squiring debutantes around El Paso.

The ranch was a bone of contention with prospective brides.

Every one of them enthused about his vast herds of Santa Gertrudis cattle, until they actually saw the ranch and realized that cattle were dusty and smelly. In fact, so were the cowboys who worked with them. One date had actually passed out when she watched one of the hands help pull a calf.

Not one of his dates had liked the idea of living so far from the city, especially around cattle and hay and the noise of ranch equipment. Park Avenue in New York would have suited them very well. Perhaps a few diamonds from Tiffany's and an ensemble from one of the designers who showed their wares during Fashion Week. But cattle? *No,* they said. *Never.*

Cort had never liked the girl-next-door sort of woman. In fact, there were no girls next door when he was younger. Most of the ranchers around where he lived had sons. Lots of sons. Not one female in the bunch.

The point was, he reminded himself, that the kind of woman who'd like ranch living would most likely be a woman who'd grown up on a ranch. Someone who liked the outdoors and animals and didn't mind the drawbacks. He probably shouldn't have been looking for a bride in the high-rent districts of big cities, he decided. He should have been looking closer to home. If there had been anyone closer to home to look at.

He'd had a brief encounter with a pretty young woman in Georgia, during a visit with Connor Sinclair, a multimillionaire who had a lake house there. The woman's name was Emma, and her zany sense of humor had interested him at once. It was one of the few times he'd been paying attention to what a woman said instead of how she looked. Emma was Connor's personal assistant, but there was more than business there, or he missed his guess. Connor had separated Cort from Emma with surgical precision and made sure there were no more opportunities for him to get to know her. Not too many months later, he heard from his brother Cash Grier, who was a police chief in South Texas, that Connor had married Emma and they had a son. He'd actually thought about going back to North Georgia and courting her, despite her testy boss. That was no longer possible. He balanced Emma against the girls with diamonds in their eyes and greedy hands who'd filed through his life. He'd felt suddenly empty. Alone. The ranch had always been the core of his existence, but it was no longer enough. He was in a rut. He needed to get out.

So Cort had decided that he needed a holiday. He'd called a fourth cousin in Catelow, Wyoming—Bart Riddle—and invited himself to help work around the ranch incognito. He explained the situation to his amused cousin, who told him to come on up. If he wanted to ruin his health digging postholes and chasing cattle, welcome.

He also had another cousin in Carne County, Wyoming— Cody Banks, who was the local sheriff—but Banks lived in town and didn't own a ranch. Cort wanted to get his hands busy. But he had plans to visit with Cody while he was in town.

Bart met him at the airport, an amused smile in his dark eyes as they shook hands. "You own one of the biggest ranches in Texas and you want to come up here and be a cowboy?" Bart asked.

"It's like this," Cort explained on the way out of the airport. "I'm tired of being a walking, talking dollar sign to women."

"Oh, if only I had that problem," Bart sighed. He stuck his hands in the pockets of his jeans. "I'm older than you, no pinup boy, I budget like a madman and I'm not housebroken." He chuckled. "I guess I'll live alone with a houseful of dogs and cats until I die."

Cort glanced at him, his suitcase and suit bag in one hand and a carry-on bag in another. "What happened to that local veterinarian you were going around with?"

He made a face. "She moved to Arizona. With her new husband," he added.

"Sorry."

Bart shrugged. "Fortunes of war," he said. "I'm giving up on women. Well, not all of them," he added. "I have one who's just a friend. Kind of like a baby sister." He smiled. "She's a writer."

"We have a lot of writers back home," Cort mused. "Hopefuls. Not a published one in the bunch,"

"This one is very published. Her latest book actually landed on the *USA Today* bestseller list."

"Not bad. How about the *New York Times* list?"

He shook his head. "But it's early days yet. She has the talent."

"What does she write?"

"Romance novels."

Cort made a face. "Drippy, oozy, sugary stuff."

"Not exactly." They reached Bart's big black pickup truck. "Climb aboard. I think it'll get us home. Halfway, anyway."

Cort made a face. "What do you do with this thing, herd cattle?" he asked, noting the dents and scratches.

"It goes all sorts of places. I have another one that looks a little better, but it's in the shop. Had a slight malfunction."

Cort stowed his gear in the boot and climbed in beside his cousin and closed the door. He reached for the seat belt. "What sort of malfunction?"

"It accidentally got slammed in the passenger door with a tire tool."

Cort blinked and stared at his cousin, who flushed. "It what?"

Bart's lips made a thin line as he cranked the truck, put it in gear and peeled out of the airport parking lot. "That's a long story."

"I'll wait with breathless abandon to hear it," Cort replied with a chuckle.

He looked out the window at the passing scenery. Wyoming was a lot greener than Cort's part of Texas, where there was sand and desert and sharp mountain peaks and salt. The ranch was in an area that got a little more rainfall than its surroundings, so at least he had the semblance of good pasture. But Catelow looked as if it had more than its share of rainfall. The pastures they drove by were lush.

"Nice forage," he remarked.

Bart chuckled. "Expensive forage," he corrected. "We don't get a lot of rainfall here. We depend on snowmelt, and we haven't had as much snow in past years as we'd like. But if you've got enough money, you can pamper your cattle. This guy—" he indicated the ranch they were passing "—has millions. He has ranches here, in Montana, and even a big property in Australia. Name's Jake McGuire."

"I know him," Cort replied. "We met at a cattle convention in Denver about three years ago."

"He's a good guy. Always trying to help people." He sighed. "I guess if you've got enough money, you can have forage and do charitable things as well. I wouldn't know."

Cort's dark eyes smiled. "You do all right," he returned.

Bart shrugged. "Well, I do know ranching. I just can't quite wrap my mind around budgets and billing."

"You need to marry an accountant."

"Oh, chance would be a fine thing."

"You never know."

"I have to stop in town and pick up some supplies on the way home, if you're not in a flaming hurry?" Bart asked.

"Not at all."

"Won't take a minute. I just need a few salt blocks."

"I'll wait in the truck, unless you need help loading them…?"

Bart shook his head. "The Callisters took over the feed store. McGuire owns it, but they lease and run it. They've got some hefty men who help with the supplies."

"Callisters. The Montana Callisters?" Cort asked.

"The very same. The youngest son, John, married a local girl, Sassy, who used to work in the feed store. They have a son. Gil,

John's brother, and his wife and kids still live on the headquarters ranch in Montana."

"That's not a ranch, that's an empire," Cort chuckled.

"It sure is. Not to mention that Gil's wife is the goddaughter
of K. C. Kantor."

"The millionaire who made his money as a merc, fighting in
wars all over Africa," Cort recalled.

"It's an interesting family. And we're here," he added, pulling up in front of a feed store, just off the main street that ran
through Catelow. "I'll be back."

Cort sighed as he looked around. He lived in a smallish community near El Paso, which looked a lot like this except there
weren't so many green trees and no giant fir trees like the ones
all around town. Lodgepole pines, he recalled from reading
about Catelow.

He needed to stretch his long legs. He stuck his creamy Stetson over his black hair and slanted it over one light brown eye
as he got out of the truck and walked up onto the sidewalk.
He drew the eyes even of older women. He was tall and rangy,
but powerfully built with long legs and narrow hips and broad
shoulders, a physique that would have looked right at home on
a movie lot. He was handsome, too, in a rugged, outdoorsy way.
He had a way of looking at a woman that made her feel as if she
was the only woman on the planet. And when he wanted to,
he could be charming.

He glanced down at the dust and leftover cattle poop on his
expensive hand-tooled leather boots. They needed polishing.
He'd worn them out into the pasture to look at a sick bull just
before he'd left for Catelow. *Sloppy*, he thought. He should have
changed them for something cleaner.

"I never thought we'd have our own shop right here in town,"
a young woman with blond-streaked brown hair in a tight bun
was saying to a slightly taller woman as they came down the
sidewalk. "All sorts of exotic yarns, just right for knitting…"

"Knitting," Cort scoffed.

The plain woman looked up at him with big brown eyes in a pleasant but not really pretty face. She wore no makeup at all. *Shame*, he thought. She might not look half-bad if she tried to look attractive. Nice mouth, rounded chin, pretty complexion. But she dressed like a bag lady, and that tightly pulled-up hair wasn't at all appealing.

The dark brown eyes were openly glaring at him as their owner looked up, a long way up the rangy, muscular body to the lean, tanned face under the cream-colored cowboy hat. "If I had boots as nasty as yours," she said in a soft but biting tone, "I wouldn't be so insulting about another person's choice of hobbies."

His eyebrows arched. "Do you rock, too?" he asked pleasantly.

She frowned. "Rock?"

"It goes with knitting. Chairs? Rocking chairs?" he taunted.

The glare got worse. "I don't sit in a rocking chair to knit!"

"You can do it standing up?"

The look, added to the suggestive velvety tone, brought a scarlet flush to her cheeks. She started to come back with something even worse when she was interrupted by her name being called.

"Mina!"

She turned. Bart came down the sidewalk grinning. "Hey, girl!" he teased.

She laughed. It changed her whole face. She looked much more interesting now to the tall cowboy who'd been insulting her.

"Hi, Bart," she replied. "I haven't seen you since the church picnic!"

"I've been keeping a low profile. You know, so all the women wouldn't embarrass themselves mobbing me."

The brunette beside the one who was talking to Bart laughed.

Bart looked down at her with a smile. "You can laugh," he returned. "I know the men mob you. I've seen them do it, you gorgeous brunette, you."

She laughed again. "Stop that, or I'll tell my husband you're flirting with me."

He held up both hands. "Oh no, please don't," he said at once. "I don't need John Callister looking me up with his shotgun."

"He wouldn't dare," Sassy Callister retorted. "He needs a new breeding bull and he likes the look of yours."

"I noticed." He grinned. "Thank him for his patronage, in advance. Oh, sorry, I forgot to introduce you. This is my cousin from Texas, Cort Grier."

"Nice to meet you," Sassy said with a smile and a nod.

The other woman didn't smile or nod.

"This is Sassy Callister." Bart introduced the brunette. "And this is Mina Michaels," he added, indicating the woman with the glaring brown eyes.

Neither Cort nor Mina spoke. They glared at each other even more.

Bart cleared his throat. "Well, we'd better be getting out to the ranch. Cort's just flown in from Texas and I expect he's in need of some rest."

"All that flapping. Are your arms tired, then?" Mina asked.

He glared at her. "Aren't yours tired from all that knitting?" he drawled back. He gave her a hard look, taking in her lack of makeup and the dowdy dress she wore. "I guess a woman as pitiful looking as you has plenty of time to knit, for lack of a social life."

She stomped on his booted toe as hard as she could.

He cursed and glared harder.

"That's assault," she said helpfully, dripping sarcasm. "I'll go turn myself in to the police right now!"

Cort opened his mouth to reply and his expression indicated that it was going to be something toxic.

Bart, who knew his cousin's temper very well, caught him by the arm and almost dragged him around. "We have to go now. See you later!"

★ ★ ★

"You shouldn't have saved her," Cort muttered as they got back to Bart's pickup truck. His high cheekbones were ruddy with temper. "What a damned, unpleasant, ugly woman! I should have had her arrested for assault. Wouldn't that have wiped that smirk off her face?" he added. His foot was a little sore. She'd been wearing boots, too, he recalled suddenly. Odd, for a city woman to have them on. Maybe they were in style. On the other hand, what would such an unattractive woman care about style?

"Now, now, she's not so bad…"

"I'd rather we never spoke of her again," he interrupted, and gave his cousin a look that said he meant it. "The other woman, the nice one," he emphasized, "she's married to John Callister, you said?"

Bart wanted to tell him about Mina, about her past, but he realized he'd get nowhere. At least not right now. "Yes. Sassy's well-known here in the community. Her mother had cancer, but John got her treated and she continues to thrive. The family adopted a little girl who'd worked for an employee who died, and she lives with her adoptive mother as well. They're a fine family."

"Mrs. Callister seemed pleasant."

"She is. And Mina…"

"Please," Cort interrupted. He drew in a breath. "That's about all the unpleasantness I can manage for one day. And the damned woman *knits*, can you believe it? I wonder if she knows which century this is?"

Bart held his tongue. He could have answered that remark, but it was just as well to save it for later. "How about a nice cup of strong black coffee?" he asked instead.

"That sounds good."

Bart grinned. "I splurged on a pound of Jamaican Blue Mountain coffee." He glanced at his cousin, who was grinning from ear to ear. "Yeah, I know," he added on a chuckle. "It's your favorite."

"And you just became my most favorite cousin," Cort returned with a laugh.

"No surprise," came the drawling reply.

They sat around the small kitchen table nibbling on a pizza they'd picked up on the way home and drinking the delicious coffee Bart had fixed for them.

"This is really nice," Cort said, glancing around at the modern, clean kitchen with its blue curtains and appliances.

"I love to cook," the other man said. "So I've got pretty much every device known to the culinary arts."

"I can't boil water," Cort sighed. "There was a notable surplus of women in our lives after our father kicked our model stepmother out the back door."

"I remember," Bart said. He shook his head. "Amazing that a man as smart as your father could let a woman like that take him over lock, stock and barrel."

"I guess love can be pretty inconvenient." He fingered the coffee cup. "Our father alienated my brother Cash, so badly that even after our stepmother left, Cash wouldn't speak to him. He wouldn't speak to Garon or Parker or me, either, because we sided with the mercenary woman." He shifted in the chair. "We live and learn. Garon went up to Jacobsville, where Cash is police chief, and made peace with him. The rest of us followed. We're still wary of each other, but we're making progress."

"Cash is a legend in law enforcement," Bart pointed out. "Ask our cousin Cody Banks." He laughed. "Cash was even a Texas Ranger for a while, until he slugged the acting officer in charge."

"Stuff of legends, my brother," Cort agreed, trying not to feel smaller at the comparison. Cash had done things the rest of them had never even dreamed of. He'd been a government assassin, a merc, a military man, a Texas Ranger, a cyber expert for the San Antonio DA's office. And, above all that, he'd married one of the most famous actress/models in America, Tippy Moore, the Georgia Firefly. Cash and Tippy had a daughter and a baby son, and seeing them together was an experience. After all the years, they were still like newlyweds.

"You're quiet," Bart remarked.

Cort smiled. "I was thinking about Cash's wife and kids. Tippy really is beautiful, even without makeup, wearing jeans and a sweatshirt around the house. God, he's a lucky man!"

"Yes, he is. I've seen photos of her. Gorgeous woman." He sipped coffee. "What's Garon's wife like?"

"Quiet," Cort said, but with a smile. "She's gentle and supportive and a wonderful mother to their son. She almost died having him," he added softly. "She had a bad heart valve and didn't tell anybody, least of all Garon. He went almost crazy when he found out. They married because she was pregnant, but Cash said he had to get Garon drunk enough to pass out while Grace was in surgery, and then in ICU. They didn't know if she'd come out of the operation at all. The pregnancy was a big complication, and Garon had just saved her from a serial killer who had a knife at her throat." He shook his head. "Garon said he paid for sins he hadn't even committed during those hours at the hospital."

Bart grimaced. "Poor guy."

"Our dad's still a rounder," Cort told him. "Well, he was. He was in Pensacola a few months ago, chasing a widow who liked motorcycles, when a former newspaper reporter tripped over him and knocked him down. Apparently, he was instantly over his head. He married her two weeks later and they moved to Vermont, to be near her family."

"Well!"

"Parker says he's not getting married for years and years. He's got two girlfriends. He's hoping they'll never meet," he added on a chuckle.

"What about you?" Bart probed.

Cort drew in a long breath and finished his coffee. "I don't know," he said after a minute. "I've had my pick of beautiful, rich women. They all had one thing in common."

"They couldn't bear the thought of life on an isolated, smelly cattle ranch, no matter how rich its owner was," Bart guessed, and sighed. "That's been my luck, too. Not that I'm that rich—I'm just comfortable. But women who come out here don't ever come back." He frowned. "Well, that's not quite true. One did. But she's like the sister I lost when I was a boy," he added with a sad smile. "There's no spark, no romance. She's just nice, and I like her."

"Maybe that's what I need," Cort said sardonically. "Someone to be my friend and listen to my complaints when estimated taxes come due."

"Miracles happen every single day."

"So they say."

Cort dreamed that night. He was dodging rockets, covered with dust, flat on his belly in it behind a wall, his heartbeat shaking him as he waited to see if he was going to die or not. He was back in Iraq, thirteen years ago, in the Army fighting insurgents.

Beside him, a younger soldier was praying. Nearby, another was cursing as every shell hit.

"I hate rockets!" the cursing soldier burst out.

"Not too fond of them myself," Cort replied. "Where's our sniper? We need to take out that position."

"McDaniel? He caught some shrapnel in the chest," he replied, indicating a form under a blanket. "Poor guy."

Cort's lips made a thin line. "Where's his rifle?"

The soldier found it and handed it to Cort.

"That's going to be a hard shot," the man told him solemnly. "He's got the high ground and he's got plenty of cover." He indicated the position, where movement could just barely be seen among some trees in the dim light of dusk.

Cort loaded the high-powered rifle. "No problem."

He stole around the side of their position, going very slowly, making no sound. He was a hunter. Every fall, he brought home at least two deer for the dinner table. He loved venison stew. Nobody made it like Chiquita, nicknamed Chaca, who'd cooked for the men since Cort had been a little boy.

When he found a place that gave him a good view of the mortar and its operator, he hunkered down and rested the stock of the rifle on the broken wall that ran around the perimeter of the bombed-out blockhouse where he and the other soldiers had set up camp.

He took slow, deliberate aim at a spot he was certain the insurgent was occupying. Sure enough, seconds later, there was the faintest glint of light reflecting off metal. Cort smiled as he pulled the trigger.

There were no more rockets. Cort hadn't seen the result of the shot, but he was pretty sure he'd wounded the enemy soldier. He put the rifle down and caught his breath.

"Nice shot," another soldier said.

He smiled. "Thanks. I hate being bombed when I'm trying to sleep."

"Tell me about it!"

The conversation, and his actions, had been real. But the dream suddenly morphed into a nightmare. There was a woman nearby. He couldn't see her, but he heard her screams. She was begging someone to stop, to leave her alone. Cort searched for her, but all he could hear was her voice in the distance. "I'll never marry!" she was sobbing. "No man will ever have power over me again!"

He wanted to tell the shadowy woman that unless she lived in a cave, someone would have power over her. A boss. A stubborn friend. Doctors. Lawyers. Power came and went. It never ended. But he couldn't find her.

She was crying softly. "They said it would get better with time, but it doesn't get better. It will never get better!"

"What will get better?" he asked.

"Life."

He opened his eyes and the ceiling was above him. Bart's ceiling. Bart's house. He sat up in bed and drew up his knees so that he'd have a place to rest his forehead. The dream had seemed very real. The woman had sounded as if she were being tortured. He wondered why her voice sounded so familiar. He wondered who had hurt her.

Well, he reasoned, it was only a dream, after all. He lay back down and went back to sleep.

They were working out on the ranch, branding calves, when one of Bart's part-time cowboys rode up.

"There's going to be a party for that friend of yours who writes," the cowboy told Bart. "And get this—they're going to have it at the Simpson mansion. How's that for highbrow? When she was in school, the kids of the family who lived there used to throw rocks at her when she went by toward the school bus stop."

"She's had a hard life," Bart agreed quietly. "It's nice to see her getting some recognition, finally."

"What sort of party is it?" Cort asked.

The cowboy chuckled. "The sort where anybody's welcome," he replied. "So I guess I'll clean my boots and see if I can find a clean change of clothes, and I'll present myself to the single ladies present!"

"Good luck with that, McAllister." Bart grinned. "You'd do better to pin fifty-dollar bills to your shirt and go date-fishing at a mall. You are a disaster when it comes to women."

"I noticed," the cowboy sighed. "But then, miracles happen

every day, they say. I'm waiting for mine with both hands out-
stretched!"

"Uncomfortable posture," Bart returned.

"What's a little discomfort in pursuit of love?" the cowboy
said with a laugh.

"When is this mythical party?" Bart asked.

"Saturday night."

"I'll bring my cousin," Bart told him, indicating Cort. "A
night out will do him good."

"It won't do me any good," McAllister said in a sad tone. "He's
prettier than all the rest of us combined. I reckon the pretty ladies will trample us to get to him." He pointed at Cort, who
laughed uproariously.

Mina Michaels, meanwhile, wasn't laughing. She was dreading an upcoming party that she was being forced to go to. A
lot of people wouldn't even recognize her as an author, because
she wrote under the pen name of Willow Shane. The hosts,
the Simpsons, were kind people who read her books, so she felt
obligated to go. Besides, many of the local citizens who'd been
so kind to her would be present. Her life had been a hard one.
It was better now that she lived alone at the ranch that her father had owned. He'd left her mother when she was nine, and
her mother had a rich boyfriend who kept things going at the
ranch afterward.

The rich boyfriend, however, eventually got tired of Anthea
Michaels. She found a married man and seduced and then blackmailed him into keeping her up. Men came and went in the
house all the time Mina was growing up. She saw things that
turned her stomach. Her mother thought it was hilarious that
she was shocked. She chided Mina about her stupid morals and
her infrequent trips to church whenever Mina could get a ride.

Despite the boyfriend who paid the bills, her mother had slept
with a lot of other men, including a boy Mina had a painfully

fervent crush on. She'd cried for days. The boy was too ashamed afterward to even speak to Mina, and of course, all the kids at school knew what her mother had done. Her mother chided her about it long afterward. It amused her that she'd taken away Mina's one chance at puppy love.

Cousin Rogan Michaels had taken on the responsibility for the ranch soon after Mina's father left. He hired and fired cowboys and kept the livestock healthy. But he wouldn't give Anthea one penny for her lifestyle. He did give her money to spend on Mina. Of course, Mina never saw a penny of it, or even knew about it, until after Anthea was dead and gone.

Anthea's married boyfriend's wife finally found out about the affair and threatened to leave him. It seemed that she had the money, and her husband was taking it out of their savings account to give to Anthea. So that was the end of that gravy train.

But soon afterward, her mother had brought home a man who promised to help pay the bills. He turned out to be not only a liar, but a raging alcoholic. Her mother seemed obsessed with him. Mina hated him on sight. He spent weekends getting drunk on whiskey and pills. He went from weekends to every day, and her mother tried to sell off the livestock—until Cousin Rogan found out and threatened litigation and charges of attempted theft. So Anthea quickly decided not to pursue that plan.

She started drinking heavily, too, and locking herself in the bedroom with their new houseguest most nights and sometimes all weekend. She was crazy about the drunk, whose name was Henry. He didn't work, but he made a good job of turning Mina's life to hell. She'd complained about him, just once, to her mother. Henry had beaten the hell out of her and dared her to go to the law about it.

Mina, bruised all over and hurting, took the dare, feeling that her life couldn't be any worse than it already was. She was sixteen and sick and scared to death of Henry. So a sheriff's deputy, a newcomer to the community, had come out to the house to answer Mina's call.

Mina's mother got to him first. She swore that Mina had fallen down the steps and blamed it on poor Henry. Her teenage daughter didn't like her mother's boyfriend, she said. Mina called him names and threatened to have him put in jail on fake charges all the time, she added. Anthea cried and sounded so convincing that the sheriff's deputy believed her and went away. Afterward, Mina caught hell. Henry left more bruises on her, along with a few lacerations from the edge of his belt. Anthea didn't say a word. She poured herself and Henry another drink.

Cody Banks, the sheriff, read the deputy's report. He didn't buy Anthea's explanation. He kept a watch on Mina. But he couldn't catch her mother's boyfriend in the act, and Mina's mother wouldn't have testified, anyway. It would be Mina's word against Henry's, and Mina's mother had already spread it around town that Mina was a terrible liar.

Life had been so hard. Mina didn't do well in school because she was shy and withdrawn and bullied. Her home life was even worse. Her only escape had been her writing, a secret she shared with very few people. From the age of thirteen, writing had obsessed her. Cousin Rogan had encouraged her. Her mother wasn't told, ever.

Mina didn't date, so she was ridiculed by the other girls. Only one of them, Sassy, had been kind to her. It was why she and Sassy were such good friends. Bart had met Mina when her mother had got her a job after school in the local restaurant as a waitress, to help bring in money, because her mother and her alcoholic boyfriend were too stoned to work. Despite Cousin Rogan keeping the ranch up, there was no food without money, no utilities, either. Her mother had made threats when Mina protested that she didn't want to work as a waitress. They were sickening threats, and Henry smiled at her while they were made. She didn't protest again. Henry liked to try and fondle her when her mother wasn't looking. Not that her mother would have cared. She'd hated Mina her whole life. Mina had never known why.

Mina's little paycheck took care of groceries and the power and water bill, with nothing left over. Mina gritted her teeth and studied hard so that she could graduate and get away from home as soon as possible. She would have thrown herself on Cousin Rogan's mercy, but he'd spent a couple of years in Australia, in partnership with the local cattle magnate, McGuire, working on their big cattle station there. He had a man assigned to act as foreman of the ranch in his absence, but the man was cold as ice and Mina was as nervous of him as she was of Henry.

Bart was kind to her. He took the place of the brother she wished she had. He was encouraging, and optimistic. He reminded her that she was almost old enough to graduate and then she could get away from her mother and her mother's awful boyfriend. He'd help, he added, anyway he could. It had really touched Mina, whose life had been a daily torment.

Then, when Mina turned eighteen, just days before she graduated from high school, her mother's boyfriend, high as a kite, drove the two of them out to a local bar in the country to buy more liquor. On the way, he ran the car into a telephone pole at a high rate of speed and killed them both instantly.

Mina felt guilty for the relief that overwhelmed her. She and her mother had never been close, and since Henry had moved in with them, nothing had gone right.

She had Bart to help her with the funeral arrangements and finding an attorney to help with the administration of the estate. Luckily, Mina's cousin Rogan had come home from Australia about the same time, and he was a tower of strength. He was outraged when he heard what Mina had gone through, and sorry that he hadn't been near enough to help. He took care of everything and set Mina up with a computer and enough money to keep the ranch going while she did what she'd dreamed of all her life—write books. He'd read some of her work. He was convinced that she'd go right to the top. He was the first person who'd really believed she could. Well, he and Bart.

Mina's life was better, after the funerals. She had horrible memories about the past few miserable years, but she put one foot in front of the other and went ahead in spite of her pain.

Her cousin had a ranch of his own, much bigger than Bart's, and he'd been keeping the Michaels ranch going for several years, with men and money that Mina's vicious mother couldn't touch. The men he'd had on the ranch answered to him, not to Anthea, so the ranch stayed solvent. Mina learned from him how to buy and sell cattle when she was barely in her teens. She used that knowledge after graduation to help with expenses. The cowboys were patient with her and helped teach her how to keep the ranch going in Cousin Rogan's absence. One of them, an older cowboy named Bill McAllister, was her part-time foreman. She learned a lot from him. He'd worked on ranches all over the West, and he knew ways of doing things that saved both time and money. Her friend Bart was one of his other employers. The little profit that she managed from her efforts was more than enough to pay the utilities and grocery bills and even give her a little extra to spend on clothes. She loved cattle.

But what Mina wanted to do more than anything on earth was to be a writer. She loved romance novels. She was also crazy about soldiers of fortune and people in law enforcement. She found a way to combine those preferences and put them into a book. The first one she tried to market wasn't well received. She put it away and tried again, slanting the book more toward romance than hard fiction. And she made her first sale.

Two years later, after her graduation, Mina was selling novels and garnering praise from reviewers and readers. Her old-fashioned attitude and small-town slant on life, besides the realistic action scenes, gave her a unique voice that went over well with her reading public. She'd attracted a group of mercenaries through a friend who gave a copy of her book to its leader. The group adopted her and taught her all about covert ops, even taking her on missions with them. She achieved a realism in her novels that made them stand out, especially when her research group was known.

It was like a dream come true, especially considering what her life had been like. Her cousin Rogan was proud of her. So was Bart.

So now at twenty-four, Mina was selling novels to a major publishing house and she was hitting bestseller lists. Her latest novel, about a gunrunner who reformed, had made the *USA Today* bestseller list. She was hoping that it would move to other lists as well. Reviewers had been kind. She had a bright future.

It was just that her past haunted her. That mean cowboy who was staying with Bart made her angry every time she thought of him. He was handsome and attractive and looked as if he knew more about women than she did. He made her uneasy, because she knew she'd be fair game for such a man if he turned up the heat. So she was going to avoid him like the plague. Because she was never going to let a man into her life. She knew what men were like from the ones her mother had brought home, especially Henry. She knew that when men drank, they were dangerous. She'd had quite enough of dangerous men. Well, except for her tutors, she mused.

CHAPTER TWO

"But you can't go to a party looking like that," Sassy wailed as she studied Mina. "You just can't! Mina, there will be society people from all over the county at the party. You have to look the part of an upcoming, successful author!"

Mina bit her lower lip. She was wearing a simple black dress, very modest, with black pumps. But her hair was in its tight knot and she wore no makeup at all. "Sassy..."

"Look, just let me improve you. Only a little. Please? I brought my makeup kit with me..." She stopped and looked repentant.

"You planned this. You didn't just happen to stop by," Mina accused, but gently.

"Yes, I did," Sassy confessed. "I don't want you to be gossiped about. And you don't want that, either," she added firmly. "'Willow Shane' has to look good for her readers!"

Mina's mouth pulled down at the corner. "I suppose I've had enough gossip to last me a lifetime," she agreed. "Well, I guess..."

She stopped because there was a hard knock at the front door.

She went to answer it. There was an older cowboy standing there, one who worked on the ranch part-time as her foreman.

Mina shared him with Bart, who had the same sort of financial issues she had. Neither of them could afford a full-time foreman, but Bill was perfect for the job. She smiled. "Hi, Bill, what is it?"

He had his hat in his hand. He grimaced. "Sorry for the interruption. Oh, hi, Mrs. Callister," he said, nodding at Sassy, who nodded back. "We've got a fence down," he continued. "Damned...darned bull ran through it to get to another bull. They had a real bad fight and the young bull's crippled. May have to be put down. I need permission to get fencing materials at the hardware and call the vet to look at our bull."

"You have permission for both. Tell them I said it was okay." She grimaced. "It was Old Charlie, wasn't it?" she asked with a sigh. "That will be the second young bull he's crippled. I'm afraid this is going to be the last time. We can't keep a bull who's that aggressive. He's showing his age, too."

He sighed. "I was afraid you'd say that, Miss Michaels. You're right. It's just, well, I've got sort of attached to Old Charlie..."

"Then take him home with you," she said suddenly. "You've got several cows of your own and you lost your bull. You can have Charlie. That will solve my problem and yours, too."

His face brightened as if it was facing sunlight. "Miss Michaels, that's the kindest thing...thank you!" He hesitated. He knew her financial situation. The bull was a purebred Black Angus, from a known bloodline. "You know, you could sell him for a good bit of money..."

She smiled. Her face changed. It was pretty when she smiled, but she did it rarely. "Bill, if I sell him, I'm putting some other poor rancher's livestock at risk. What if the new owner got mad and sold him for beef?"

Bill grimaced.

"So we're not doing it. You take Charlie home with you, and you're welcome. Okay, go get the part-timers started on that fence. I have to go to a party in my honor," she said with a grimace. "Mrs. Simpson is giving it. She's read my latest book,

SPECTRE, the one that's on the *USA Today* bestseller list, and she wants to introduce me to some people."

"I was invited, too," Bill said, flushing. "Guess I'll show up later when I get the fence fixed. And I'll bring the trailer for Charlie in the morning, if that's okay."

"That's fine. I'll see you at the party, then."

"Nobody will dance with me, but I'll go drink punch and eat finger sandwiches anyway," he chuckled.

"I'll dance with you, Bill," she said gently.

He flushed more. "That would be kind of you. Otherwise, I guess I'd just be a wallflower."

"Me, too," she laughed. "But you're the only man I'll be dancing with."

"So now I'm really flattered." He knew about her past. Most local people did.

She didn't mind Bill knowing. He had a soft heart. What a shame that he'd never found another woman to appreciate it. He'd lost his wife and daughter to tragedy. He drank infrequently and Mina was fetched to get him safely home. He'd follow her out of a bar like a lamb.

"Party starts at seven," she added when Bill started to leave. "If the boys aren't finished by then, leave them to do it and come on over to Mrs. Simpson's house, okay? It's Randy and Kit working today, and they're trustworthy."

He brightened. "Okay. Thanks again." He tipped his hat and walked off the porch, his spurs jingling.

Sassy turned back to Mina. "Okay, chicken," Sassy said. "Sit down and be improved. You might attract a nice young man."

"I don't want a man, young or old," Mina said quietly as she sat down in a chair and let Sassy go to work on her. "I don't want a man at all, ever." She crossed her arms over her chest as if she felt a chill.

"Not all men are like your mother's boyfriend," Sassy said

gently. "Or like that horrible man who tried to paw me when I worked at the local feed store."

"But how do you know what they'll be like behind closed doors?" Mina asked miserably. "Henry yelled. He always yelled before he hit me. I had so many bruises. I had to always wear long sleeves and long skirts or slacks to school so the bruises wouldn't show. And he said he'd kill me if I told."

Sassy put a gentle hand on her shoulder. "You should have talked to that nice psychologist in town."

"I can't talk about private things to people I don't know," Mina said miserably. "I just can't."

Sassy took a long breath. She didn't know what else to say. So she went back to work on her friend.

The result was stunning. Mina looked like a different woman, even with just a touch of makeup and her hair long around her softly tanned, bare shoulders. She looked fragile. Breakable. Lovely.

"You'll break hearts tonight," Sassy said with a smile.

"Not on purpose. Are you coming?"

"Yes. John, too. And a few other local people."

Mina's eyes blazed. "Bart's coming, but he's bringing that friend of his along. I don't like the man. He's rude and arrogant, and he looks at me as if he could see my underwear…" She stopped and swallowed, hard. She hadn't meant to let that slip out.

"He's a rounder," Sassy said, confirming her suspicions. "I don't know him, but John does. He met him at some cattle convention he went to before we married. He says the man collects women like a car collects pollen in the spring."

"I guessed that already," Mina said, the remark about Cort Grier at a cattle convention going right over her head. She was looking at herself in the mirror. Except for her big brown eyes, which wore an expression of perpetual sadness, she looked almost pretty. She was shocked. She'd never taken time to do makeup.

She hadn't wanted to encourage any of her mother's boyfriends, at least one of whom tried to get her mother to let Mina do a threesome with them. Her mother had laughed and given Mina a sardonic smile. Mina had hidden outside in the woods until the man left. It was one of many experiences that haunted her.

"Bart will make him behave," Sassy promised.

She let out a long breath. "Do I have to go?" she asked miserably.

"Yes."

"Okay. I'll drive myself to the guillotine, then."

Sassy laughed. "It's not going to be that bad. Really. You might actually enjoy it."

"I might learn to fly."

"Spoilsport."

"I'd rather groom my new horse." She smiled broadly. "He's a palomino. He's absolutely gorgeous! I named him Sand." Her eyes were dreamy. "His last owner died. They said he'd been grieving, but when he saw me at the auction, he came right over to the fence and lowered his head. I knew he was mine. I couldn't afford him but Cousin Rogan bought him for me for my birthday."

Sassy laughed. "Your cousin is one of the sexiest men I've ever seen, and one of the biggest woman-haters." She shook her head. "Aren't you lucky that you're first cousins? He likes relatives."

"He hated my mother," Mina pointed out. "Actually, so did his mother," she added. "They were sisters, but they never spoke. Aunt Sallie died of cancer years ago, and Uncle Fred followed her the next year when he got kicked in the head by a horse he was trying to treat. I'm the only relative Rogan has left."

"It's like that with my family, too," Sassy confided. "It's just my mom and me and Selene."

"Does she still want to be a fighter pilot when she grows up?" Mina asked with a gentle smile.

"Yes. She's been studying every book she can find on Raptors. F–22s," she added when Mina gave her a blank look. "She knows all about them."

"She'll be an amazing pilot."

"Oh yes."

Mina looked in the mirror again. "How did you do that?" she asked, fascinated.

"I'll show you another time. You'd better get started over or you'll be late. I have to go by the house and get John."

"So I'll see you there."

Sassy nodded. "And don't be nervous. Most of these people have lived here all their lives, just like you."

"I never traveled in those circles, though," Mina said. "High society, I mean. I'm just a cowgirl."

"You're a famous writer, Willow Shane," she teased, "growing more famous by the day. And *SPECTRE* is going right to the top, you mark my words. I love your books, but this latest one is astonishing!"

"Thanks. You can have as many as you want," Mina laughed. "I get boxes of free copies."

"You're sweet, but you need to let me buy my own so you get royalties," she teased.

Mina just shook her head. "Money never has mattered to me, except that time my mother forced me to work as a waitress so she and Henry had money for groceries. If it hadn't been for Cousin Rogan, the whole ranch would have gone on the auction block. He loved my father. It broke his heart when Dad left my mother for another woman."

"Do you ever hear from him?" Sassy asked.

"No." Mina drew in a breath. "Mama said she wrote and told him that I never wanted to see him again or talk to him, that I hated him." She looked down at her hands. "I did say it. He left me at her mercy and never looked back. I understood why he didn't stay. But he threw me to the lions. I couldn't forgive him for it." Her face tautened. "She hated me my whole life. I still don't know why."

"It's never wise to look too closely into the past," Sassy advised. "You're going to be fabulously wealthy and well-known, and I can say I knew you when you were a skinny kid in third grade!"

Mina laughed. "So you can! I hope you're right, about that prediction. I don't really want to be fabulously wealthy, but I'd love it if the book topped the *New York Times* list, just for the guys. They've been so good to me."

"You and those commandos," she laughed, shaking her head. "I can't imagine running through the jungle in camo carrying an automatic rifle."

"Actually, it's a .45 auto," Mina corrected. "Took me forever to learn how to use it, but the guys were persistent. I spent hours and hours on the gun range."

"You're lucky you don't get shot on those missions."

"I did, but only once, and it healed nicely," Mina replied with a smile.

Sassy rolled her eyes. "Just remember, you'll be more famous alive than dead."

"I'll tell the guys." She sighed. "I really would love to see *SPECTRE* get to the top," she added. "I dedicated it to my team, you know. Well, just their first names. They still go incognito in a lot of places, so I had to limit what I said about them."

"They sound like a good bunch of guys."

"They are. The very best."

"Okay, there you go," Sassy said as she finished with the brush. "And don't you touch your hair when I walk out the door. You leave it down, just like it is."

Mina made a face. "It looks, well, wanton...doesn't it?"

"You have beautiful hair. There's nothing vulgar about it. Or about your very conservative dress. Stop worrying! You're Cinderella, and tonight is the big ball!"

Mina smiled blandly. "With my luck, the big ball will roll right over my foot and break it."

Sassy just made a face and left her there.

The mansion where the party was being held was ablaze with light. It was in the rich part of Catelow, where the wealthiest citizens lived. A huge, two-story building with a flat face sitting on about two acres of land with lodgepole pines framing it against the distant mountains, it was the sort of house Mina's characters would have lived in.

She gave the keys of her little VW to the valet, grimacing as she noted the new Jaguar XJL that stopped just behind it. Well, she wasn't rich. She wasn't sorry, either. Her little car might look out of place here. But then, so did she.

In her black dress, a nicely marked-down sale item from a clothing store, she was hardly going to raise any eyebrows. This crowd would wear couture, and the women she met as she walked in the door certainly didn't buy their dresses off-the-rack.

She'd never seen such beautiful dresses. She felt dowdy by comparison. But then, she saw a few other women who were dressed much like she was. How obliging of the leading citizens to invite the working poor, she thought wickedly, and smiled as she went down the receiving line. She didn't know a single face, but a tall, handsomely dressed woman came to speak to her.

"You're Willow Shane," the woman said gently, using Mina's pen name. "I'm Pam Simpson, your hostess. I've read that copy of *SPECTRE* that you gave Bart three times already! He was such a doll to loan it to me. It's going all the way to the top of the *New York Times* list, I just know it! I've bought copies for all my friends!"

Mina flushed. "Thanks so much. I'm glad you liked it."

"The realism. Wow! You actually go out with commando groups to do the research?"

"I actually do," Mina confessed. "It's an ongoing adventure."

"Well, I love the way you write. And I'm so very proud that you came! You must have invitations from everyone, but you chose to come here."

Mina laughed. She was still getting used to her pen name. Few people knew it, even around Catelow. "Thank you so much for giving this party for me."

"It's my pleasure. I wanted to show you off," Pam confessed, and laughed. "Your books are so full of humor and adventure. I adore them. You're so talented! This new book is the best of the bunch. You wait—it will be the one that catapults you to the top of the national bestseller lists!"

"You'll inflate my head to a shocking size," Mina cautioned, flushing. "And my ego as well. You mustn't do that. I'll become haughty and unmanageable."

Pam laughed with pure delight. "Never! Come, and let me introduce you to some people. A lot of us read you, including at least one of the husbands. He hunts in the fall. He takes your books with him to read while he's waiting lonely hours for deer or elk to show up!"

"How very flattering," Mina said, and meant it.

"And I shouldn't say," Pam added, lowering her voice, "but at least one husband used your latest book to compromise his wife. He bought it in a bookstore and brought it home. She said she'd have done anything to get it." She laughed. "And just between us, I believe she did!"

"Oh my." Mina burst out laughing.

"And there's my friend Mary," she indicated a brunette standing just apart from the others near the drinks table. "She's dying to meet you…!"

Mina had been introduced to so many people, her head was spinning with names. But she and Sassy and John, Sassy's husband, moved to a corner to talk cattle after the first fervor of Mina's presence was past with her hostess and guests. They didn't drink, which set them apart from some of the other guests, who were going through their hosts' stock of liquor like water.

"I'm giving Bill my oldest bull," Mina told them. "It got through the fence and damaged a young bull, again. It hurt another so badly that he had to be put down. It was either give him away or sell him for beef, and I think poor Bill would have worn black for a year. He loves that old bull."

"Nice solution," John Callister chuckled. "A bull who hates the competition that much is dangerous to have around," he added more somberly.

"Yes, which is why Bill's getting him."

Sassy had gone to the drinks table to get ginger ale for herself and her husband, after Mina had declined. She looked out of sorts.

"What's ailing you?" John drawled with a tender smile.

"That Merridan woman," Sassy said curtly, glaring toward a brunette with sleek, short black hair wearing a dress that showed most of what she had. "She's gone through two husbands and now she's flirting with Daisy Harrington's husband. He's just eating it up and Daisy went toward the restroom with tears running down her cheeks."

"Every apple barrel has a rotten apple somewhere in it," John said. "But in case you wondered, I'm immune," he added with a rakish grin and bent to brush his lips over Sassy's pert nose.

She wrinkled her nose at him and laughed. "I knew that."

To Mina, who knew women like Ida Merridan very well, that kittenish, come-hither attitude was disgusting. That it worked on men so well was unfathomable. Couldn't they see that it was just an act? Her mother had been exactly the same, promising paradise, but for a price. Ida was dripping diamonds and rubies, and Mina would have bet that she hadn't paid for a single one of them herself.

She was working on an older man, who was dressed in what looked like a designer suit. Her long red nails teased at his chest, like blood against the blinding white of his shirt. He was flushed and laughing, obviously flattered by the attentions of a woman half his age, more beautiful than any other woman in the room.

She really was gorgeous, Mina was thinking. Ida had jet-black hair, cut short, like a pixie cap around her delicate features. She had blue eyes and a pretty, pouting mouth. Her figure was perfect, displayed in a dress that probably cost more than Mina's whole net worth—a black sheath with crystal accents that hugged every curve, cut low in front, but just low enough to still be decent in company.

Obviously, she thought, that woman had never been hunted by men when she was in her early teens. Just thinking about how her mother's endless parade of men had approached her made her sick. One or two had been actually kind. The rest...

She sipped her soft drink and sighed. She wished she could find an excuse to go home. She felt as out of place as a cotton handkerchief at a silk bazaar.

"Hey, Miss Mina," Bill called from behind her.

She turned, brightening. "Hi," she returned. "Get the fence sorted out?"

"I did," he said. He looked around at the glittering array of guests and winced. "Didn't realize there were going to be so many fancy people," he said in a low voice.

"Never you mind," she returned. "Fine feathers make exotic birds, but it's the drab little birds that excel."

"Now that makes me feel better," he said with a grin. He glanced at the dance floor, where people were shuffling around to the melody the live band was playing. "That's a two-step. Only dance I know how to do," he added with a meaningful look at Mina. "You did promise," he reminded her.

"So I did. We mustn't be wallflowers," she teased. She put down her soft drink. "I hope I can remember how to do a two-step. I watched a dance competition once."

He led her onto the dance floor. "Didn't you go to dances at school?"

She shook her head. "I was much too shy. I never even looked at boys." She grimaced, remembering why.

He danced well. "Your mother was a piece of work," he murmured.

"She was that. But lots of people have bad childhoods and survive them." She grinned. "I got a career as a writer for my own reward. It was worth it. Well, almost."

"Hard times make tough people," he agreed. "It's no sort of world for cream puffs these days."

"My thoughts, exactly." She sighed. "What did the vet say about our injured young bull?"

"He said he'll mend. Made me feel better that he wasn't going to have to be euthanized, like the other one was."

"Me, too," she said, and smiled.

"There's Bart," he said, looking over her shoulder. He sighed. "He's got that pretty feller with him."

Her heart jumped. She hated it when it did that. Her brown eyes turned toward the newcomers. Bart looked nice in a suit. His cousin, however, was absolutely devastating. He knew it, too. That insolent, arrogant smile said everything. His pale brown eyes slid around the room until they lit on Mina. One eyebrow went up.

"I've surprised him," she told Bill as they danced.

"Excuse me?"

"Bart's venomous houseguest. He's staring at me."

"No surprise there, Miss Mina. You look real pretty."

"I'd rather have a copperhead find me pretty," she muttered under her breath as Bart and his cousin Cort came onto the dance floor toward Mina and Bill.

"So you did make it," Bart said with a big grin. "You look gorgeous, Mina," he added gently.

She smiled. "Thanks. I had a little free time, so I took down the curtains in the living room and made this cool ensemble."

Cort's pale brown eyes swept over her. "Not bad, for a home-made dress," he said indifferently.

She flushed. He made her feel poor and cheap. The dress was off-the-rack, but he made it sound as if she'd sewn it by hand, and badly.

"It was a joke. I don't sew," she said icily.

"No. You knit. Don't you?" His smile was arrogant and cold.

She couldn't kick him. She really wanted to.

"How about giving me a turn, Bill?" Bart asked when the music stopped.

"Sure thing, Mr. Riddle," the older man returned with a grin. "Thanks, Miss Mina," he added, making her a half bow before he melted into the crowd.

"I haven't ever danced much, you know, Bart," she faltered.

"We'll struggle along together."

"And I thought this party was going to be dull," Cort mused. His eyes were focused on the refreshment table. Or, rather, what was standing beside it. Ida Merridan was giving Cort the eye, smiling like a tiger looking over a piece of juicy meat. "Who's the gorgeous lady?" he asked Bart, with a smug, dismissive glance at Mina before his eyes went back to the brunette.

"That's Ida Merridan," Bart told him. "She's divorced from her second husband."

He pursed his sensuous lips. "What sort of fool divorces a woman who looks like that?" Cort wondered.

"Men who can see beyond makeup," Mina quipped. "But then, it takes a discerning man to manage that." She smiled demurely.

Cort glared at her. "At least she doesn't dress like a woman from the Third Crusade," he said in a soft, cutting tone, his eyes disparaging Mina's very conventional dress.

She just looked at him and smiled, her heart breaking at the sarcasm that came so easily to him. "Oh, I don't have a good divorce lawyer, much less a rich ex-husband, so I can hardly aspire to her wardrobe."

"You could hardly aspire to a man, full stop," he retorted, turning to go.

"Cort, for God's sake," Bart began.

Mina put a hand on his arm. "Your cousin is entitled to his opinion," she said. "He likes sausage grinders."

Cort stared at her, confused.

"You'll understand after Mrs. Merridan feeds you through one. Do have fun."

She turned back to Bart, pointedly ignoring Cort. "I need to ask you something about my taxes," she began.

Cort cursed under his breath and went across the room to the divorcée. He didn't even look back.

"He's more abrasive than he used to be," he told Mina. "I'm sorry. I wouldn't have brought him to the party if I'd realized how he was going to behave toward you. I don't want your special evening ruined."

"As if he could," she said, pretending for all she was worth. She smiled. "I'm having a good time."

"Well." He drew in a long breath and glanced over at Cort, who was just drawing the divorcée onto the dance floor. "I'm glad."

They were playing some Latin tune now. Bart stopped and led Mina off the floor. Neither of them could do those dances. Cort, apparently, could. He drew Ida along with him to the rhythm and sighs went up from the female guests as he danced a samba with his partner. He was good. He laughed as he moved to the rhythm. The divorcée laughed, too. She had stars in her eyes. *Or diamonds, more likely*, Mina thought wickedly. She was going to be so disappointed when she discovered that her partner was just a working cowboy. It made Mina feel better. Well, a little better, at least.

"What about your taxes?" Bart asked as they sat down in the living room among several other guests.

"It wasn't really that. I'm just not sure I did the right thing about my bull."

He frowned. "What bull?"

"Old Charlie. He attacked another of my young bulls and did so much damage that the younger one had to be put down. I gave Charlie to Bill. I was afraid to sell him, in case he did the same thing to another rancher's bulls. He's aggressive."

"Bill loves the old animal. And he's only got a handful of female cows. It should be all right. Charlie doesn't attack people. Well, not often—just when he's moved off the cows in late summer. And Bill can handle him. He's worked cattle for years."

She looked up at him. "Anybody can get gored. I'd feel responsible if anything happened to Bill."

He patted her hand. "Don't you worry about him. Everything will be fine. That was a generous thing to do. Charlie would have sold for a good bit of money."

She made a face. "I'm signing a new contract next month. It will be for ten times what I could have sold Charlie for."

He laughed. "Congratulations! I told you that talent would make you rich one day."

"Not rich. Not just yet. But much better off than I've ever been. Cousin Rogan says I need to buy at least two new bulls and some open heifers at the Production Sale the Terrances are having next month." She glanced at him. "Want to go with me? I could use some advice."

He chuckled. "I'd love to. Just let me know when."

She glanced toward the dance floor. A bluesy tune was playing now, and Cort Grier had Ida wrapped around him like ivy. The way he was holding her made Mina uncomfortable. Even a novice could see experience in the way he looked at the woman in his arms, in the way his body melded itself to hers.

"How long is your cousin staying?" she asked stiffly.

He sighed. "Not for long. Maybe."

That was less than encouraging. She changed the subject.

A few minutes later, while Mina was saying her goodbyes and getting her coat, Cort paused at Bart's side.

"Do you mind if I bring Ida back to the ranch with me?" he asked lazily.

Bart stiffened and glared at his cousin. "Yes, I do. That woman has the morals of an alley cat. I don't want her seen on my place."

Cort's eyebrows arched up. "I beg your pardon?"

"You tomcat around all you like, cousin. Do whatever you please, as long as you don't involve me. I don't approve of that sort of behavior and I won't condone it. Least of all on my own property."

Cort stared at his cousin as if he'd gone insane. "Everybody does it," he began hesitantly.

"I don't." Bart looked absolutely intimidating. "A lot of people around here don't. We're a churchgoing community, for the most part."

"Isn't that just a little backward?" Cort chided softly.

"Pardon me for being out of step with the anything-goes society you're used to. I don't deal in used women."

It took Cort a minute to get that. He had to stifle the laughter that welled up in him. "Used women."

"Damned well used, from appearances," Bart said. He glared at Cort. "There are three motels in town. Be my guest."

Cort sighed, shrugged and went back to the divorcée.

Mina came back with her coat draped around her, having thanked Pam for the party and said goodbye to a couple of readers. She was surprised at Bart's indignant look. "Everything okay?" she asked hesitantly.

He shook himself mentally and forced a smile. "Of course it is. I'll follow you home, just in case."

She laid a small hand on his sleeve. "You don't have to do that."

He just smiled at her. "You're my best friend," he said softly. "Of course I have to do that."

She smiled back.

Cort glared at the two of them. So much for Bart's assurances that the plain woman standing with him was just a friend. That looked a lot more than friendly.

"Wasn't this party supposed to be in honor of some author Pam Simpson knows?" Ida asked as they moved toward the front door. "Willow Shane, who wrote that new book *SPECTRE*?"

"Beats me," Cort said.

They moved just ahead of Bart and Mina in the small group headed out the front door.

"The dancing was fun, anyway," Ida said, almost purring. "Coming home with me?" she added to Cort.

"You bet," he drawled, making sure that his uptight cousin and that vicious woman beside him heard every word.

He took Ida's hand in his as they went out the door. He didn't look back.

"He wanted to bring her home to the ranch," Bart said when they reached her car. "I told him no."

She looked up at Bart. "The world moves on, but we don't, do we?"

He smiled. "I guess not. Cort isn't like us. He's more…well, more worldly."

"I guess cowboys do get around," she replied. "We had one who had a girl in every rodeo town," she chuckled.

Cort was no cowboy, but Bart didn't want to blow his cover. After all, Cort had come up here to get away from his life. Not that it seemed like it tonight. He was a rounder, and he'd scored at the first gathering he attended. Maybe he was used to doing things casually. Bart wasn't.

"I'll see you soon," she told Bart. "It was a nice party. I met a hunter who reads my books in the woods," she added on a laugh.

"I imagine it helps pass the time while he's waiting for a nice, big buck," he teased. "You drive carefully."

"I will. Thanks for seeing me home," she added, trying not to picture Cort alone with that beautiful, clinging woman. It bothered her, and she didn't know why. She didn't want to be bothered by it.

"You're more than welcome."

She got into her car and drove away, with Bart right behind her.

CHAPTER THREE

Cort had a nightcap with the merry divorcée, but he made no attempt at seduction once they were alone. He didn't know why, which irritated him. Women were a permissible pleasure and he'd never refused the offer of a passionate night.

This woman was overly seductive, but there was a coldness in the eyes above that sweet smile that made him hesitate. It was like looking into his own eyes. He had a fine contempt for most women. They were willing to do almost anything for the perks he could provide. He was jaded. She seemed very much the same.

"I hear that you've divorced two husbands," he said after a minute.

She shrugged, sliding into a chair near his with a snifter of brandy in her hands. She'd already given him one. "Yes. The first was gay, but I didn't know it. He wanted to look conventional for the sake of his corporate image. The second was a closet sadist who made me believe I was the most beloved woman on earth. I married him and came face-to-face with horror when he got me alone. He crippled me emotionally and physically. I ran from him and had him arrested for assault and battery, and then divorced him. There was almost a third…" She smiled sadly. She took a drink from the snifter. "He was a journalist who liked dangerous places and risk." She looked down at her shoes. "He was kind and considerate and I think I could have loved him. But I couldn't live with the terror, so I never let him get close. I was a coward."

He cocked an eyebrow. "You loved him."

"I could have, I think." She looked up into pale brown eyes in a hard, uncompromising face. "But you've never loved anyone," she said, reading him with textbook accuracy. "You love women, plural. You love the taste and feel and exhilaration of conquest. But the next day, you can walk away without being tempted to look behind you."

Both eyebrows arched. "Damn," he said softly.

She smiled knowingly, her pale eyes intent on his face. "You're a sad, lonely, lost person." She sighed. "Like me."

What began as a potential one-night stand was quickly turning into something else, something totally unexpected.

"You see deep," he replied after a minute, and with reserve.

She nodded. "I've been through a lot in my life. It's taught me to live for the moment. I don't look ahead, ever."

He sipped brandy. He was the same. After his stint in the Middle East, after what he'd been through, he'd lived only in the present. He was damaged. Broken. He would never again be the idealistic, patriotic young man who donned a military uniform and went overseas into combat. His worldview had changed.

"You don't even remember what they look like, do you?" she asked, bringing him out of his memories.

"What who look like?" he asked blankly.

"The women you've had," she said simply. "They all blend together."

He frowned. "Is it like that for you?"

She shook her head. "I don't sleep around."

His eyes widened. "Then what the hell am I doing here?"

She smiled. "Keeping up appearances. Living down to your

cousin's image of you. Discouraging that young woman in the plain dress."

He pursed his lips and let out a whistle.

"I dress like a woman on the prowl for a man. I flirt. I seduce. They all think that I'm hot stuff, that I've seduced a dozen men for what they have." She laughed. "I inherited from my first husband. He had millions and millions of dollars and no heir."

"The one who was gay," he recalled.

She nodded, her eyes sad. "His lover threw him over for a younger, more adventurous man. He went to see his attorney, made out a will that left me as sole beneficiary, made sure his employees were taken care of. A week later, he went up to the top floor of his corporation's headquarters building in New York City and stepped out into space." She drew in a long breath. "I didn't know about the lover. He was quite discreet. Actually, I thought there was something very wrong with me, because he never wanted to touch me." She laughed. "He left me a long letter, thanking me for marrying him, for being kind to him. He told me about the lover." She pursed her lips. "After he died, the lover filed a lawsuit and tried to get 'compensation' for my husband's attentions."

His eyes twinkled. "What did you do?"

"I set our corporate attorneys on him. It was brutal. He ended up with what he deserved—nothing. And besides that, he even had to pay court costs." Her eyes darkened. "I hear he went down to Acapulco to ply his trade and fell victim to a gangster. Poor little man."

"You were fond of your husband."

She nodded. "He was a good person." She looked up at him. "People are what they are," she said with a sad smile. "I don't think we have the right to tell anyone how to live."

"Amen," he agreed, and raised his glass. She raised hers as well.

He set the glass down and chuckled. "Well, as one survivor to another, it's been a nice evening."

"For me as well." She got up and smiled at him. "Sorry if I messed up your plans."

He shrugged. "I suppose I'm getting old. I don't really mind."

"Don't give me away, please," she said. "I like being the resident seductive witch. Most men run like hell from the image I present." She laughed. "They're afraid they won't measure up and I'll talk about them to other people!"

He laughed, too. "No problem. Just don't talk about me."

"Oh, I'll laud you to the skies. The most incredible lover of all time, a monument to mankind, men everywhere should be jealous!"

"Don't do that," he chuckled. "I'd never live up to that image."

"I'll modify it, just a little."

"Thanks for the brandy. And the company."

"I enjoyed it, too." She studied him quietly. "You're one of the Griers from over near El Paso, in Texas. You run purebred Santa Gertrudis cattle."

He nodded.

"But you're playing at being a cowboy."

He shrugged. "I got tired of being a walking bankbook."

"I know that feeling as well. If you get bored, come on over. I play a mean game of chess."

His pale brown eyes brightened. "So do I."

She stopped to jot down her number on a piece of paper. "It's unlisted."

He gave her his cell phone number. "I'll be in touch."

She smiled. "But just friends."

"Just friends," he promised.

Bart was still awake when Cort drove up to the front door and cut off the engine. He felt a little ashamed of what he'd asked his cousin, about bringing Ida home with him. Bart wasn't a rounder and he didn't move with the times. Cort never should have made him uncomfortable about his beliefs.

He was hesitant when he got into the living room. It was un-characteristic. "Listen," he told Bart. "I'm sorry. About what I asked you."

Bart didn't hold grudges. He just shrugged. "Different strokes for different folks," he said, quoting his late father. "Your private life is none of my business. As long as you don't try to bring it here," he added with a grin.

"Fair enough." He sat down heavily. "I guess I really am get-ting old. Women don't hold any mystery for me these days."

"Even the happy divorcée?" Bart asked with a chuckle.

He shook his head. "She isn't what she seems."

"There's a lot of that going around," Bart replied, thinking of his friend Mina.

His face tautened. "That 'friend' of yours is a walking irri-tant," he muttered. "What the hell was she doing at a high so-ciety party in the first place? I'd bet real money that her dress came off the sale rack at some bargain basement clothing store."

Bart almost told him. Almost. But it was fun watching his cousin make assumptions. When it came, the end result was going to be hilarious. "Oh, they invited the whole commu-nity," he said instead.

"It was supposed to be for some up-and-coming author, they said," Cort returned, "but I never got introduced."

"Too many people," Bart said easily. "I just stood in a corner with the Callisters and Mina." His mouth pulled down at one side. "None of us drink."

"Your loss," Cort chuckled. "They had some fine liquors."

"I like my brain functional."

"So do I, but the occasional drink helps to give it a brief va-cation," his cousin quipped.

Bart chuckled. He got to his feet. "Well, I'm off to bed. I'm not much for parties, and I've got a man coming over in the morning to look over my yearling bulls to see if he feels like spending some money."

"Your stock is outstanding," Cort said. "I like your breeding program."

"Well, it's not quite up to Grier standards," Bart said with a grin, "but I make enough to keep the ranch going, even if I do run Black Angus instead of Santa Gerts."

"All you need is a wife, and a few kids to inherit the place when you're gone."

"Chance would be a fine thing," he said, sighing.

"That 'friend' of yours seems to like you enough," he returned with a scowl.

"I told you, there's no spark," Bart returned with a sad smile. "It's like dancing with a sister. Nothing like I felt with the woman who married and moved away. I have the damnedest bad luck with women." He shook his head. "I guess some of us just aren't destined to help populate the planet. Maybe that's not a bad thing. See you in the morning."

"Yeah. See you."

Cort went into the guest room and stripped down to his shorts. He wasn't sleepy. In fact, he hated sleeping, because the dreams came. Every time, he was back in the war, back in the horror, the blood, the carnage. He pulled up the covers and rolled over. Maybe, just maybe, tonight he could manage to sleep without dreaming at all.

Mina stood quietly by while the local veterinarian, Ted Bailey, checked the stitches he'd put in her young bull.

He stood up and smiled. "He'll do, Miss Michaels," he said after a minute. "No evidence of infection and he seems to be healing well. But I'd keep him up for a few days, just the same."

"I'll do that. Thanks, Dr. Bailey."

"No problem." He shook her hand and went to his truck. She followed him outside after another glance at her young bull. She was grateful that Old Charlie hadn't done any worse damage to him.

Bill McAllister had just loaded Charlie onto his horse trailer, with a little help from her other part-time cowboys and a few false starts. The old bull hated trailers. He fought the ropes and the cowboys, but they managed to get him into the trailer without anyone being injured.

"Well, that was an experience," Bill chuckled.

"I noticed," Mina said with a grin. "Thanks for the help, guys," she told the part-timers, who nodded and went back to work.

"I'll get Charlie home and into the pasture, then I'll be back. Thanks again, Miss Mina."

"Oh, you're welcome," she told him with a warm smile. "I'm just happy we don't have to put him down. He's been around here for a while. Since I graduated from high school, in fact." Her face tautened at that memory of what had come before her graduation.

"You've got a good bull crop, and more expected," Bill said at once, hoping to wipe the frown off her face. He smiled. "You'll have ranchers milling around here like cattle, hoping to buy them on sale day."

She grimaced. "My operation isn't big enough for sale days, I'm afraid," she said. "Bart and I are going to go in together and do it at his place. He's going to get Dan Carruthers out of retirement to cook steaks for it. Dan's got that secret spice recipe," she added with a grin. "I've been after it for years."

"It will be buried with him," Bill predicted. There was a loud clang from the horse trailer. "I'd better get going. Be back soon."

"So long," she said.

She watched him drive off. She'd just finished a chapter of her new book that morning and she needed some fresh air. She saddled Sand and climbed into the saddle, dressed in jeans and boots and a red plaid wool shirt under a leather jacket, with a cowboy hat on her loosened hair. She'd meant to put it up, but Bill's arrival with the horse trailer had interrupted her. It didn't matter anyway, she considered, because nobody would see her except her part-timers, and even then from a distance.

She rode along the fence line, through the lodgepole pines, toward the boundary she shared with Bart Riddle's ranch. They ran the same breed of cattle, Black Angus, so there was no worry of crossbreeding if a bull wandered through a downed fence. Besides that, it was the wrong season for breeding. Her cows, and Bart's, would be dropping calves soon, just in time for spring grazing. While she rode, she looked for breaks and posts that needed replacing. She noted them on her iPhone with GPS, so that she could tell her part-timers where to find them.

Cousin Rogan had said that she needed at least one full-time man on the ranch, and she agreed that she did. But it would be expensive to hire somebody, and she wasn't about to trust her purebred bulls to just some person she knew from a newspaper or trade advertisement. Still, she could afford it now, with the money from the new contract and what she'd get, hopefully, from her yearling bull crop.

Maybe Bart knew of somebody local who'd be a good hire. She wanted somebody trustworthy.

It was a beautiful day, if cold. Mid-March, and her cows would be calving soon, to take advantage of the spring grass, which would hopefully come after the ankle-deep snow melted. The weather was getting warmer. She could see snow melting where the sun hit it, although it was still covering the ground in the shade. Snow in Wyoming was nothing unusual, even up until April or May. But it had been a rather warm winter, all the same.

She came to a gate that sat on the boundary between her land and Bart's. She dismounted to open it, led Sand through and closed it back. People who left gates open were severely punished in ranch country. Straying cattle could get expensive, especially if they spilled out onto a highway and caused accidents.

She looked around for her cousin. He was supposed to be

showing a visiting rancher around, hoping to sell some young bulls. She didn't want to interrupt him, but it was late morning and he'd probably gotten through his business already. She was going to invite him for lunch. She'd made a tuna salad and put it in the fridge. She could offer him sandwiches and coffee.

Then she remembered his houseguest. Well, the awful man had gone home with the happy divorcée the night before. He might have stayed for lunch. Odd, how it stung to think of him with the glitzy woman. He was jaded and sarcastic and unpleasant, so why should she care if he slept around?

She turned Sand in the general direction of Bart's house. On the way, she came across a lone calf, lying in the snow.

She climbed down and left Sand's reins trailing while she went to check the little creature for injuries. There were wolves in the territory who sometimes preyed on lone calves. The result could be horrible, because sometimes the calves were left alive after such an attack.

As she bent down, she heard hooves hitting ground and other hooves, galloping. She ignored both as her practiced, gloved hands slid over the little creature, looking for injuries. It stirred and looked up at her just as a charging cow with horns was diverted by a man on horseback.

"Get the hell away from it!" he shouted.

Shocked at his tone and his skill with the cutting horse, she backed away, toward Sand. The calf got to its feet and ran, bleating, to the cow, obviously its mother. She gave the humans a huffy snort and trotted off, after a feint that the horseman parried neatly.

She was still getting her breath when the horseman abruptly dismounted and stalked toward her.

"What the hell were you thinking?" he raged, raising his voice angrily. "The cow was charging, you damned fool!"

She shivered and backed away from him, keeping her white

face lowered. The man was Bart's horrible houseguest, his cousin from Texas.

She backed even more. Her eyes were wide with fear, but she wasn't seeing Cort Grier. She was seeing Henry, hearing Henry, waiting for his fist to connect with her, for the belt to come down. She was feeling the pain already, because shouting always brought back the horrible memories of her childhood, of the men her mother brought home…

Cort stopped short when he realized how frightened she was. He scowled. He'd never seen a woman react like that. He wondered who she was. With her head lowered to her chest, her arms crossed over her face, he hadn't recognized her. Who was she and what was she doing on his cousin's ranch?

"It's all right," he said, his voice dropping to a softness she'd never heard in it. He moved toward her slowly. "I've never hit a woman in my life," he added gently.

She took a deep breath, then another. Her arms came down. She bit her lower lip, still nervous of him and unable to hide it.

"There's nothing to be afraid of," he said quietly.

She looked up at him from under the brim of her hat, her face still pale, her big brown eyes wide with leftover fear.

He frowned as he suddenly recognized her. This was Bart's friend, the woman from town who'd stomped on his foot, the woman dressed in a sale rack dress from the party last night. She was wearing boots and riding a horse, the beautiful palomino that was obviously hers.

"You're Bart's friend," he said, not moving any closer. She still looked intimidated by him.

She nodded. She swallowed, hard. Her weakness showed, to her worst enemy. She was ashamed and embarrassed. She swallowed again.

He studied her quietly, his horse's reins held lightly in one hand. "What were you doing here?" he asked belatedly.

She had to try twice to get her choked voice to work. "I saw the calf down," she managed. "I was checking it for injuries. We have wolf packs around here. Sometimes they prey on our herds when they can't find anything else to hunt."

"The calf was separated from its mother because we were checking the herd and it scattered," he explained.

She looked up at him, still pale but faintly defiant. "And now I know that, don't I?" she asked.

He moved a step closer. She didn't back away, but she looked nervous. She looked fragile, vulnerable, with her long, blond-streaked brown hair loose around her shoulders under the cowboy hat. It was a worn hat, like her stained, warped boots.

"You know about cattle," he said after a minute.

She nodded. "I own the ranch next door," she said. "I have purebred bulls, just like Bart does. We have production sales jointly. I was coming over to talk to him about it."

He was still shocked by her unexpected behavior when he'd shouted at her. He felt guilty. Something had happened to her, something bad. She was afraid not only of loud voices, but she seemed to expect violence to accompany them.

"You didn't see the cow that was charging you," he said after a minute. "I wasn't sure I could cut her off in time. I lost my temper. I'm sorry."

She didn't expect the apology. It changed the stubborn, hard set of her face into something less antagonistic. She shifted from one foot to the other. "I didn't even see her. I should have realized that the calf was just separated from her. I thought it was hurt."

He smiled. It was a genuine smile, not the sarcastic one of their first meeting. "So you knit and run cattle."

She glowered at him. "And wear cut-rate dresses. Yes. I don't like dressing up."

He shrugged. "Neither do I, honestly," he said. "I'm more at home with cattle than people."

She smiled shyly. "Me, too. Cattle are usually nicer than people."

He chuckled. "Is that a dig at me?"

She flushed. "Not really. I was thinking about…other people."

He tilted her hat up just a little so that her whole face was on view. "Someone yelled at you and hit you," he said abruptly, and saw her wince and bite her lower lip. "A man."

She backed away a step. "It's ancient history. I need to talk to Bart."

He wanted to pursue the conversation. She troubled him. "Okay," he said instead.

She turned and went back to Sand, patting his neck gently as she took the reins and jumped up into the saddle with an ease that wasn't lost on her companion.

"He's beautiful," he said, indicating her mount.

She smiled. "His owner died and he was mourning. They had him at the sale barn. He saw me and trotted right over to the barrier and lowered his head against mine. I knew he belonged to me. My cousin gave him to me as a birthday present."

"Your cousin?"

She nodded. "Rogan Michaels. He owns a cattle station in Australia with Jake McGuire, who has a ranch outside Catelow, too." She laughed softly. "Their ranches make mine and Bart's look like hobby farms."

He knew Rogan Michaels. They both owned shares in an oil venture in Oklahoma. "Is he around?" he asked idly.

"No. Cousin Rogan has itchy feet," she said on a sigh. "He's back in Australia. He hates snow. His cattle station—well, his and Mr. McGuire's—borders on desert. No snow."

"I like snow," he commented, his eyes sliding over the white pastures. "Where I live, it's like desert most of the year. We get snow occasionally. Never enough to bother us."

"Do you work on a ranch there?" she asked.

He nodded, his Stetson slanted over one eye. "I work with purebred Santa Gertrudis cattle on a ranch in West Texas."

She glanced at him. "Bart has another cousin who's sheriff of our county," she said.

"That would be Cody Banks," he said. "He has a cousin down in San Antonio who's a Texas Ranger."

"My great-grandfather was a deputy U.S. Marshal," she said. "And my father used to be a policeman in Catelow, when I was a little girl." Her face tautened.

He frowned. "Is he still alive?"

She laughed shortly. "Who knows? I haven't seen him since I was nine. He ran off with another woman. I'm not sure my mother even noticed that he was gone."

She was as tense as a taut rope. "You don't like your mother," he commented.

"My mother died the year I graduated from high school." It was a flat statement.

"Of some illness?"

"You might call it that," she said quietly. "Her boyfriend was drunk. He ran them into a telephone pole. They died instantly."

Boyfriend. He was getting a cold feeling about her life, her past. *Drunk.* Did the boyfriend drink? Was he violent when he drank? It might explain her behavior earlier. He felt guilty that he'd brought it up.

"My father married a model," he said as they rode toward Bart's house. "She only wanted what he had—well, it was a small ranch," he lied, "and she thought he was rich. She managed to alienate his eldest son, my brother, and we didn't speak for years. In the meantime, Dad found her out and divorced her." He laughed. "He played the field. We had women all over the place."

That explained his cavalier attitude toward women, which reminded her of the happy divorcée he'd gone home with the night before. She felt less comfortable with him.

"He's married now," he added. "A former newspaper reporter tripped over him and he fell head over heels in love. He moved to Vermont with her, to be near her family. Her brother recently died of terminal cancer and she wanted to be near her relatives while they got over the grief."

"That's sad," she said. "Nobody in my family ever had cancer. My grandfather died in the rodeo arena, gored by a bull. My other grandfather bought and sold livestock and died of old age. You just never know."

"True."

They were at the gate that led to Bart's house, and as they reached it, they saw Bart coming toward it on foot, smiling.

"I know that smile," Cort chuckled. "Sold a bull, did you?"

"Sold two," Bart replied with a grin. "I can afford to pay taxes!"

"Me, too," Mina said, smiling. "Well, if we can do a production sale together the end of the month," she added as Bart opened the gate and she and Cort rode through. "I can't afford to do it by myself. Besides," she added with a sigh, "I'm too shy of people to actually invite anybody out to look at the calves."

"Speaking of which," Cort interrupted, "she almost got gored out in the pasture by an angry mama when she bent over to check a downed calf."

"Oh good Lord," Bart burst out. "Are you okay?" he asked quickly, his eyes scanning her.

"I'm fine. Your cousin really knows how to ride a cutting horse," she added with grudging praise. "He saved me. I thought the calf was injured and I stopped to check him."

"Thanks, but don't risk your life," he added. "You know I don't run polled cattle here."

She grimaced. "I knew that. I just wasn't thinking. We'd just loaded up Old Charlie for Bill to take to his place. He was a terror of a bull, but I already miss him."

"You can always go over to Bill's and visit when you want to," Bart said.

She nodded.

"Old Charlie?" Cort asked.

They dismounted. "He's my oldest bull," she told him. "He injured one of my young bulls so badly that he had to be put down. He just got another one—with lesser injuries that will heal. I couldn't keep him and I didn't want to sell him to somebody who might have the same bad luck. Bill didn't have a bull. So I gave him Charlie."

He was watching her with real interest. She improved on closer acquaintance. He smiled slowly. A woman who knew cattle, who could ride a horse. He'd never expected this feisty little woman to do more than knit.

Bart intercepted that look and ground his teeth together. Cort was a rounder. Mina was a recluse, with good reason not to trust men. It was an accident looking for a place to happen, but he didn't know how to stop it. Mina didn't like Cort, but she'd admired the way he cut off the mother cow before it could gore her.

Something had happened besides that. He knew it from the way they both looked. He'd get it out of Cort later, he decided.

"Want to come in and have lunch with us?" Bart asked.

She forgot all about the tuna salad invitation, because she really didn't want to sit and try to eat with Cort, and she'd have to invite him as well, out of politeness. "Thanks," she said, "but I've got things to do at the house. I just wanted to ask you about the production sale."

"I'll get something together and text it to you later. That okay?"

She nodded. "I'll have four yearlings out of Michaels' Red Diamond," she said, "and six out of Michaels' Charles Rex."

"Charlie's calves?" Bart asked.

She smiled. "Four of them are Charlie's. Now that Bill has

a few purebred Black Angus, he can sell calves along with us next year, maybe."

He chuckled. "Knowing Bill, he'll probably give them all names and put collars on them and buy them toys. I doubt he'll sell a single one."

She laughed. "Probably."

"Would that be Bill McAllister, who works for you?" Cort asked his cousin.

"Yes, it would. Mina and I share him, part-time. Neither of us can really afford full-time help."

"Cousin Rogan says I have to have a full-time ranch hand," Mina replied with resignation. "So I need you to recommend somebody. I'm not having some strange man on my place," she added firmly.

"I know that," Bart said gently. "I'll find you somebody. If I can't, I'll ask Jake McGuire or John Callister for a recommendation."

"That would be kind of you. I know how to do most everything on a ranch, but I don't have time to do it every day." She glowered. "I hate having to have somebody hanging around all day."

"I'll make sure it's somebody who won't interrupt you." He pursed his lips. "As you'll recall, I almost got hit face-first with a boot when I did it that time." He remembered having interrupted her in the middle of a scene she was writing.

"I didn't know it was you," she said, defending herself. "I thought it was Kit, and he knows how to duck." She shook her head. "He's like a force of nature. You can't make him understand that he has to be quiet—he just keeps right on talking until you answer him."

Cort didn't understand anything he was hearing. What would somebody interrupt that caused the woman to throw boots at him?

"I'll get home," she said with a smile. "But I think I'll take the front road home, just in case your mama cow's still around in the pasture."

He laughed. "Okay. I'll get the gate for you."

Cort studied her quietly while she mounted. "Be careful. We have horses that bolt when cars go by them on the highway."

"Sand isn't bothered by anything," she assured him, smiling as she patted the gelding's neck. "He's always calm."

"Sand?" he asked.

"Well, he's yellow, isn't he?" she asked. "Like desert sand."

Desert. Sand. His face hardened. Thirteen years and it was still yesterday. "Like desert sand," he said, and turned away.

Her eyes followed him, curious about his abrupt change of expression, but Bart called to her. She turned Sand and rode toward the gate.

"I'll text you," he repeated.

She grinned. "I'll be waiting. Thanks, Bart. I really appreciate it."

"No problem. We have to stick together or we'll both go broke."

"And isn't that the truth?" she chuckled. "See you!"

CHAPTER FOUR

Bart had sent one of his part-timers into Catelow to pick up a bucket of chicken and biscuits. He could cook, but it had been a long day and he wanted something he didn't have to produce. He and Cort sat at the table and ate it.

"What happened out in the pasture?" Bart asked as he sipped coffee.

Cort finished the last of his chicken and picked up his coffee cup. "She was inspecting the calf when its mother charged her. She didn't hear it or see it. God, I never thought I'd get to her in time! I barely made it at all. I cut off the mother cow and yelled at her." He grimaced. "I've never seen a woman react like that to a loud voice."

"You don't know about Mina's past," Bart said quietly. "Her mother loved men. Plural. She was a rich man's mistress for a time. She blackmailed him, threatened to tell his wife. Well, his wife found out and she had all the money. So after that, Mina's mother took up with any man who was willing to pay the bills. They came and went, and there were a lot of them."

Cort sipped coffee, his face solemn. "I gather that one of them hit her."

Bart nodded. "Yes. She doesn't talk about it much, but I think more than one of them did. Another one wanted to do a three-some with her mother, and she hid in the woods all night."

Cort winced. "My little mother was a saint," he said softly. "I barely remember her, but Dad talked about her a lot. She loved him so much. There was never another man."

"Mina's mother wasn't like that. The last man she lived with was Henry. He was an alcoholic and when he got drunk enough, he was violent. He beat Mina up, really badly. She called the sheriff, but when the deputy came, her mother lied and said Mina fell down the steps and blamed poor Henry, who'd never lifted a finger to her. The deputy went away without arresting him. Cody Banks, our cousin who's the sheriff, didn't believe her mother and he tried to catch Henry in the act. He never did. When Mina was eighteen, Henry and her mother were killed on their way to a bar, in a car wreck. She inherited the ranch, but the memories are pretty bad. She doesn't date."

"Now I understand why," he said. "She's afraid that a man she got involved with might turn out to be just like her moth-er's drunk boyfriend."

"That's why."

Cort was remembering the dream he'd had, of the shadowy woman crying, frightened, saying she'd never trust a man. *How odd*, he thought. It was almost as though he had some sort of mental link to a woman he didn't even know.

"All of us around Catelow know about Mina. Her mother was notorious." He glowered. "There was one boy, when Mina was sixteen. She was crazy about him. He liked her, too. He asked her out and went to the house to pick her up. Her mother was all over him. The next day, she lured the boy to her car after school and seduced him."

"Oh good God!" Cort said angrily.

"He was too ashamed to face Mina. It got around school,

too. So there went her only real taste of romance." He shook his head. "She's had a hell of a life."

"Her mother should have been prosecuted for child abuse. Seducing a teenage boy!" he scoffed.

"She should have been prosecuted for what she did to Mina," he agreed. "She hated her only child. I never understood why. Neither did Mina. She suffered after her father took off. Years and years of pure hell until her mother finally died."

"And I thought I had it bad, with my dad's model."

Bart's eyebrows went up. "How so?"

"She hated me. Well, she hated all of us kids. There were four of us. She played up to us, pretended she was crazy about us, until she got Dad to load her up with diamonds and stocks and bonds and marry her. Then the claws came out." He sighed, re-membering. "Cash hated her from the beginning. He saw right through her act. We didn't, and it alienated him from the fam-ily. Cash got the worst of it because he was Dad's favorite. Ac-tually, I think Cash was supposed to inherit the ranch, but after all the drama and alienation, Cash said he'd never come back to West Texas, even after Dad saw what she really was and di-vorced her. Garon joined the FBI and lived all over the coun-try. Parker's up in Montana, with their State Game and Fish. That left me, to inherit Latigo. Dad said that if I didn't learn to ranch, the whole place would go on the auction block. So I learned how to ranch."

Bart was surprised. "You didn't want to?"

Cort's smile was world-weary. "I wanted to be a mercenary, like Cash. He lived a life more exciting than anyone else I knew. It sounded romantic. You know, a hired gun, like in the old cowboy movies." His smile faded. "Only it's not like that. I joined the Army because I felt patriotic. It sounded noble, you know—defend the country, go overseas to Iraq, fight insur-gents." He leaned back in his chair. "I learned what Cash already knew. That taking a life isn't as simple as it looks on film. That seeing your friends, who've been with you since basic, blown into bits by an IED, having one die in midsentence right beside you from a sniper attack, those things are really sanitized even in the most realistic movies. In real life," he added coldly, "they're not romantic. When I got out of the service, I came home and threw myself into ranching heart and soul. I understood why Cash was so alone, why he never mixed with us, with anybody. When Garon opened doors for us with him, I went to Jacobsville to visit. We talked, a lot." He sipped more coffee. "I understood him then. So did Garon, who'd spent years with the FBI's Hostage Rescue Team. All of us had killed and very nearly been killed. It's a very exclusive club. Not one any sane person would want to belong to," he added.

Bart nodded. "I was in Afghanistan," he said after a minute. "I spent my whole tour of duty sleeping on the ground with a rock for a pillow, dodging snipers, hiding out from insurgents who were stalking us. When I first got home, I was so nervous that I'd jump out of my skin if a car backfired."

Cort cocked his head. "I didn't know you'd gone overseas."

"We didn't talk much until the past two years," he reminded his cousin.

"That's true. Imagine running into each other at a cattle convention and realizing we were related," Cort chuckled. "That was one for the books. We were like brothers by the time we went home. Think of all the years we missed being friends, because we never knew one another."

"You came up to see Cody a time or two, but that was while I was overseas," Bart said.

"Yes, it was. Poor Cody," he added quietly. "He's still not over his wife dying."

"She was a good doctor, they say," Bart replied. "I guess he'll mourn her for the rest of his life. He doesn't date anybody. Lives with that dog she gave him the year she died."

"Well, being alone isn't so bad," Cort replied. "I've got the ranch all to myself except for rare visits from my brothers. Even Dad was usually away in pursuit of some woman most of the time. It was just me and the cattle."

"That's how it is here. Just me and the cattle." Bart grinned. "You're right. It's not so bad. They never complain. They never want me to buy them things. They don't even pout when I ignore them for a whole day."

Cort threw back his head and roared with laughter. "I never thought of it like that," he confessed.

"Now you have," Bart returned.

That night, Mina had dreams. Nightmares. They came back with a vengeance, probably because of what had happened in her friend's pasture with the calf. She got up at three in the morning and made coffee.

The house was lonely. She had cats who lived in the barn to keep away rats, but she didn't have a pet indoors. She thought about getting a dog, but they required a lot of attention and she was having to travel on occasion to promote books. It would mean boarding a pet for long periods of time. So she went out to pet the barn cats when she was particularly lonely. Just not at three in the morning, in the dark.

She sat down at the kitchen table and sipped coffee. That man, Cort, had yelled at her and brought back terrible memories. He'd been sorry afterward. It finally dawned on her that he'd been afraid that he couldn't save her from the charging mama cow. *Imagine that*, she thought to herself with a faint smile. He'd actually been afraid for her, after all the insults they'd traded back and forth.

She couldn't go soft on him, however. That way lay disaster. Just because he'd saved her from a goring didn't make him an object of romantic dreams. He was just a cowboy, and she knew from experience that many of the single ones were drifters, who never stayed put. They liked variety not just in work, but in women as well. Cort had a very sensual way of looking at a woman, and it didn't take much guesswork to know that he was experienced. He'd spent the night with the happy divorcée, which tainted him in her eyes. Everybody knew the woman's reputation. She was a man killer. Well, Cort was a lady-killer, from what his cousin said. Maybe they were a match made in heaven, the jaded man and the promiscuous woman.

It wounded her. It shouldn't have. She had nothing invested in the cowboy who worked for Bart. She had to stop thinking about him. There was one way, at least. She carried her hot coffee to her desk in the living room and turned on her computer. When the world was sitting on her shoulders, writing was her salvation. She'd lived in her fantasy world for years, escaping her mother and the drunken boyfriends her mother brought home. It was a bright and beautiful place, where her heroes and heroines lived, and no ugliness was allowed there.

She smiled as she pulled up the chapter she was working on and began to type. She often wondered where the words came from. She had no idea what the characters were going to do until she started writing, and then they told their own story. It was a fascinating, delicious process that never failed to intrigue her. She didn't try to understand it. She simply accepted it.

She was invited over to the Simpsons' house later in the week by Pam Simpson, who'd had the party for her.

"You simply have to come," she told Mina excitedly. "One of your biggest fans is just home from Australia and he wants to meet you. He reads your books while he's watching over first-time mama cows until they give birth! He says he'll be doing it at the Catelow ranch for a while. Well, you know that your cousin Rogan is partners with him, and Rogan's still in Australia managing the station there."

"Yes, I knew. Is it Mr. McGuire?" she wondered aloud. "I think I met him once a long time ago. When my mother was alive," she added quietly. She didn't tell Pam that her mother had made a play for McGuire, who was years her junior, and he'd turned her down. His name was never mentioned at home after that.

"It is," Pam said. "Jake McGuire. He's really nice. I've had the cook prepare a special meal, just in his honor. Well, in yours, too. So you have to come for lunch."

Mina laughed. "Okay, then. It will save me from having to cook. Not that I don't love it, but there are a lot of leftovers when you're just cooking for one person."

"I can imagine. So then, we'll expect you."

"What time?"

"Eleven sharp."

"I'll be there."

Mina hadn't seen Jake McGuire in a very long time. She was a little intimidated by him. After all, he was a millionaire many times over and she was just beginning to make her mark as an author.

He'd be used to women who were sophisticated and wore haute couture. All Mina had were clothes off-the-rack. But she was going to wear the best she had. She put on her prettiest spring dress, a pastel floral concoction with a V-neckline and wide sleeves, belted at the waist and midcalf length. She'd left her hair long and experimented, lightly, with the makeup Sassy Callister had given her. She didn't look half-bad, she thought.

Jake obviously thought she looked very nice, because he just stared at her, smiling, when Pam introduced them.

He was good-looking. Very good-looking. Tall and tanned, with dark hair and light silver eyes, and a physique that would have done a rodeo rider proud. How odd that a man who looked like that, and was rich, wasn't married. Maybe he was a romantic and wanted that fairy-tale romance that both men and women dreamed of.

"We met a long time ago," Mina began hesitantly.

"No, we didn't. We're just meeting now," he said gently, and smiled. "Those long-ago, terrible days are done."

She let out a breath. "Yes, thank God," she replied, grateful that Pam had gone into the kitchen to check on the progress of lunch. "My mother was my worst enemy, most of my life."

"I know that. But she's gone. You're safe, now."

The way he said it made her feel warm and comforted. She smiled at him. "Thanks. For not blaming me, for what she did," she added.

"How could anyone blame you?" he asked. His face tautened. "We all knew what she was. Rogan was furious when he realized what she'd tried to do to you, what she'd let her drunken boyfriend do. Australia is a long way away. We didn't get any news from back home at all!"

"Cousin Rogan kept the ranch solvent, at least," she told him. "I don't know what I'd have done if he hadn't. He bought me a computer and kept the bills paid until I learned how to buy and sell cattle, and especially until I started selling books. He was my biggest fan. He always believed I could get published."

"So did I," he returned. "Your cousin told me about *SPEC-TRE*. I bought a copy and I was hooked! I couldn't imagine how a woman could write in almost a man's style about mercs and cops and soldiers. You even know about weapons."

She grinned. "I have a commando group that adopted me years ago," she confessed. "They take me out on missions occasionally, so that I get a real feel for what I'm writing about. That's how I came up with the idea for *SPECTRE*. I dedicated it to the guys."

"I did wonder about the dedication," he teased.

She laughed. "I also pumped Bart's cousin Cody for information. He's been sheriff of Carne County for years and years."

"He has, indeed. He's a good man. Shame about his wife."

"Yes, it was. He tried to help me, before my mother died. He just couldn't ever get anything on Henry that he could use to put him away." Her face hardened. "Henry was a bottom-feeder."

"I could think of some better adjectives." He smiled at her. "You came through it, though. What doesn't kill us…"

"…makes us stronger," she finished, and laughed. "Cousin Rogan's favorite slogan," she recalled.

"And a true one."

"Cook has lunch ready," Pam called from the dining room. "Come and get it!"

Lunch was delicious. The cook had made a bacon and egg quiche with fresh fruit and a poppy seed dressing, followed by Cherries Jubilee for dessert.

"I can't remember when I've had better food," Jake said as he worked on his last cup of coffee.

"Neither can I," Mina added, smiling at Pam. "It was delicious!"

"I'm glad you liked it," Pam said. She wiggled her eyebrows. "Was it delicious enough for you to tell me what the new book you're working on is going to be about?"

"You wish," Mina chuckled. "You know I never talk about them when I'm writing them. I'm afraid it will jinx them!"

Pam sighed. "I knew you'd say that."

"I can tell you that the hero is a mercenary, and it's set in Texas," Mina volunteered.

"Wow!" Pam frowned. "Why not in Wyoming?"

"Well, I'm from here," Mina said. "And Texas is one of my favorite states." She sighed. "Zane Grey wrote about Texas, you know. I think I have all of his books."

"So do I," Jake said. "I grew up on cowboys. I guess it's why I was so happy to inherit my dad's ranch."

"Your dad's ranch was a mess," Pam said with a twinkle in her eyes. "Dead broke and almost done for. You turned it into a going proposition and made a fortune with it."

"With oil and minerals, mostly," he confessed on a laugh. "I love cattle, but the by-products under the land made me rich."

"I need to have an oilman look under my husband's old classic car," Pam said with a straight face. "I'll bet he could find the mother lode."

They all laughed.

Jake walked out with Mina after they'd said goodbye to their hostess. Mina compared her little economy car with Jake's big, new Mercedes and grimaced inwardly. It certainly denoted the difference in their economic status.

"That's one of the new Mercedes," she noted. "I've seen them on the internet."

He chuckled. "What I really wanted was the one that lights up inside. The Maybach. But I needed a car right then and they said it would be a couple of months before I could get the Maybach. So I bought the best Mercedes they had on the lot instead. It's not bad. A real champ on the roads... When the state police aren't looking," he added with a grin.

"It goes fast, then?" she teased, and her big brown eyes sparkled.

He looked down into them with real interest. "It does."

She smiled. She liked him.

Unfortunately, it wasn't the sort of liking he wanted, and he realized it very quickly. She was pretty and sweet and he could do worse. But she wasn't feeling the things he was. He pursed his lips and considered that. Then he discounted it. He knew she wasn't seeing anyone locally. That meant he had a chance with her. He wasn't wasting it.

"How about a nice steak a week from this Friday?" he asked.

She hesitated, but only briefly. "That would be nice. There's a good restaurant in town..."

"Not here. In Billings."

She blinked. "Montana?"

He nodded. "Best steak in the northwest," he added with a grin.

"But it's a long drive," she began. "We're over a hundred and fifty miles south of Billings!"

"I have my own baby jet," he said easily. "We can land on the Rimrocks at the Billings Airport and I'll have a limo waiting to take us to the restaurant."

Her lips parted on a shocked gasp. The expense would be monstrous. She said so.

"I'm rich," he reminded her with a wicked smile. "There's no sense in being rich if I can't enjoy it while I'm still alive. I like a good steak. Best one in the whole territory is in Billings. I'll have you home by midnight," he added. "I promise."

She let out the breath she'd taken. "Well!"

"Come on. Say yes. I'm tired of my own company."

She searched his eyes. "You could get anybody, any woman, you wanted..."

"I don't have a lot of friends," he said, emphasizing the last word to put her at ease. It did, too. He saw her relax, saw the worried look on her face eclipse into a smile.

"Well, okay, then," she said finally.

His heart jumped. He laughed. "Okay." It was something that she'd even agree to be friends with him. He could hope for more, later.

"So I'll pick you up about five. That okay?"

She smiled. "Okay. What do I wear?"

"Jeans and a shirt. And a jacket. It gets chilly at night."

Her eyebrows arched. "It isn't dressy...?"

"Not really, and I hate suits," he murmured, although he was wearing one. A nice one, she observed.

"I wanted to impress you with my trendy wardrobe," he said outrageously, and smiled when she started laughing.

"I'm impressed," she said when she was able to contain the humor.

"Good. I'll keep that in mind for future outings," he said.

He frowned slightly. "Don't you have a signing coming up in Manhattan?" he wondered.

She grimaced. "Yes, I do. It's such a long way to New York," she began.

"I'll fly you up there, anytime you want to go," he said at once. "Sure beats trying to go on a commercial flight, packed in like sardines, eating peanuts instead of a nice meal."

"I'm convinced. If it wouldn't inconvenience you," she added quickly.

He waved a hand. "I have business interests in New York," he said easily. "I need to make a trip up to talk to one of my investment counselors. I can combine business with pleasure. What sort of entertainment do you like? Theater, opera, symphony concerts, ballet...?"

Her eyes lit up. "Ballet?"

He chuckled. "I'll see what's playing while we're in town. Just give me a week's notice."

"I'll certainly do that, and thank you very much for the offer of a ride." She made a face. "I hate flying."

"You'll love it in the jet," he promised. "I'll see you next Friday."

She smiled warmly. "Yes."

She climbed into her little car, waved and drove off.

"I hear you're going off to eat with that McGuire feller," Bill teased as they watched one of Mina's part-timers work a filly in the corral.

She gaped at him. "I just talked to him yesterday, and I didn't tell anybody."

"It's Catelow," he told her. "Small town, big ears. And your hostess can't keep her mouth shut, either," he added with a chuckle. "Made her feel good, playing matchmaker, I hear."

"It's not like that," she said softly. "Jake's a terrific person, but I don't feel that way about him."

"Shame," he said with a sigh. "He's got all the money in the world."

"Money is how we keep score when we're doing a job we love," she said lazily. "I don't care what I've got, as long as I can pay the bills. We're doing great here," she added with pride. "Cousin Rogan won't have to supplement us in a few months."

"No, he won't, the way your book is selling," Bill said with quiet pride. "You're on your way to fame."

She wrinkled her nose. "As long as it's distant fame, I don't mind. I'd hate to be one of those people who's on magazine covers and tabloid covers all the time, so they're recognized everywhere they go. It would be like living outdoors in the city, with people watching everything you do. I'd go nuts. I love it here." She looked around at the towering distant mountains with their snow-covered peaks, the buttes closer to the ranch that curved gracefully on the horizon. "This has to be the most beautiful place on Earth."

"I'd agree," he said. He frowned. "Jake McGuire's a great catch," he began.

"Money isn't enough. I'm holding out for a man I can love."

"Yes, Miss Mina, but you don't date anybody," he returned gently. "Never going to find a husband that way."

"Not sure I want one."

He turned his attention back to the corral. "Had a call from your cousin Rogan earlier today."

"Was he looking for me? I had my phone cut off while I was at the Simpsons'…"

"Sort of."

"Sort of?"

"He's heard from your father," he said.

Her face tautened. Once, when her mother was alive and she was younger, she'd wanted badly to keep in touch with her parent. But her mother had told her father that Mina hated him for leaving and never wanted to talk to him again. As the years passed, however, and she suffered her mother's incessant lovers, the lie had become truth. Her father had deserted her, left her to the torment her mother had given her. She blamed him, because his desertion had caused most of her pain.

"I don't want to hear from him," she said flatly. "Not ever again."

He hesitated for just a minute. "You sure? It's been fifteen years, you know."

She bit her lower lip.

"There's something he wants to tell you," he said finally.

"He can write me a letter."

He shook his head. "He wants to see you. He's in Billings."

Her heart jumped.

"You should think about it," Bill said gently. "When he's gone, there's nobody else who knows anything about your background. About your extended family. I know your mother never talked about her parents or their parents. History is important."

She knew that. Still she hesitated. She hated even the memory of the past few years, hated the anguish her mother had caused her.

"It might be your last chance, to find out why your mama was so mean to you," he finished. "He's the only person alive who would know."

She drew in a breath. "Okay, I'll think about it."

He smiled. "I'll tell your cousin."

She slept on the request. But after a sleepless night, reliving old nightmares, she decided that Bill was wrong. She didn't need to see her father. It was tempting, to tell him what he'd subjected her to by running off with another woman. That alone might help her to let go of the past. But she couldn't bring herself to do it. The pain went too deep, even after fifteen years. She could hardly even remember what her father looked like. His job as a police officer had kept him away most of the time, and there were hard memories in the way after he left. She wasn't sure she'd recognize him if she saw him on the street. But then, she didn't want to, either.

So she called Cousin Rogan and told him about her decision.

"I understand how you feel," he said, his deep voice soft and calming. "But people aren't just good or bad, honey," he added softly. "They make bad decisions and act on them. That's what your father did. His fancy woman dropped him flat the second month he was with her. He tried to get custody of you, but your mother got a lawyer and threatened him with lies that made him into a monster. He could have gone to jail if he'd persisted. He deserted your mother. He never deserted you."

She was quiet. She didn't answer him.

He sighed. "Okay, honey. It's your decision." Rogan had always liked him, but he didn't press it. "How are things going with you?"

"Jake McGuire is flying me up to Billings next Friday for a steak dinner," she said.

"Well, how about that?" he asked, chuckling. "I wondered if he might try to see you. He loves your books. He's got all three, and he was sure the newest one would be a bestseller. He's your biggest fan."

She laughed. "He's a very nice man."

"Oh dear."

"I don't like men. Well, most men," she amended. "I like you and Jake and Bart." Her voice cooled. "I don't like Bart's cousin."

"What cousin?"

"Some cowboy from Texas," she said. "He's about the worst enemy I've ever had. He's icy and hot-tempered and…impossible!"

Rogan was biting his tongue trying not to say what he thought. He'd never known mild-mannered Mina to get her dander up at any man.

"A cowboy?" he asked instead.

"A pain in the… Yes, a cowboy." She hesitated. "He loves animals, at least."

"That's something."

"But I don't like him. Not at all. Maybe he'll go home soon. Bart and I are going to have a joint production sale. We've got a really good calf crop. You should come and see it."

"When the snow leaves," he said shortly. "I hate snow. Australia is really nice. Hot and dry. Just like I like weather to be."

She sighed. "I love snow."

"You're welcome to my share of it. You take care of yourself."

"I will."

"You're still my favorite cousin," he teased.

"And you're still mine," she said, and meant it.

She went riding fence the next afternoon, and there was Bart's houseguest, bending over a cow that looked as if it had been dead for some time. He had a small calf in his arms. She pulled up her horse and sat, watching.

He cuddled the little thing in his arms and smiled. "You'll be okay, little fellow," he said softly. "We'll put you in the barn and give you bottles until you're ready to face the world."

He turned and saw Mina. She couldn't tell what his expression was, because the wide hat shaded the sun from his face.

"You going toward Bart's?" he asked.

"I can, if I need to," she replied.

"Okay. Can you take this little one with you? This may not be the only cow who was attacked. I need to track the killer."

"Of course I can take him back for you." She was worried. "Could it be a wolf?" she worried.

"It could. Or a coyote. Or even some fool shooting where he shouldn't. I took a rifle away from one of my…our own men back home at the ranch where I work," he said, correcting the slip so smoothly that she didn't catch it. "He was shooting at a target that he'd put facing the house. He didn't even know that a rifle bullet can travel for a mile before it hits something."

"I've seen one or two people like that, myself. Here, hand him up." She held out her arms and he put the little creature into them. The calf bawled for a minute, but then he relaxed in Mina's warm arms and settled against her. She smoothed his little head and muzzle and smiled at him tenderly.

Cort felt his heart skip a beat as he looked up at her. She could have been a hundred years out of time, holding a calf on a horse, just as some pioneer woman might have done in the distant past.

He smiled. "You look right at home on a horse," he said quietly.

She laughed. "I've been riding one since I was a child. But Sand—" she patted her palomino mount's neck "—is my favorite, of all the horses I've ever had."

"I have a coal-black Arabian that I ride," he said. "I call him Valeroso."

"Gallant," she translated absently. "You speak Spanish?"

He nodded. "We have a lot of cowboys who come from Mexico or down in the Yucatán. Many are Mayan, but they also speak Spanish." He chuckled. "Most of us have enough trouble trying to speak one language, but they come here speaking two already. English is their third."

"Intelligent people," she said, smiling.

"Indeed they are."

The calf was getting restless on her lap. "I'd better get him to the barn. Can you tell what killed his mother by the way she died?"

"Not so much," he replied. "It could have been a wolf or a big dog—maybe a pack of stray dogs. I don't think it was a person. The flesh was torn, not cut."

She nodded. She cocked her head. "Can you track?"

He chuckled. "I can track. I hunt deer every fall. I love venison stew."

"Me, too. I go with Cousin Rogan, when he's home. He's a good tracker himself."

His sensual lips pursed. There was an odd glint in his pale brown eyes. "Does McGuire hunt?" he asked abruptly.

CHAPTER FIVE

Mina was taken by surprise. The question, out of the blue, was unexpected. She colored just slightly. Obviously he'd heard that she and McGuire had eaten at the Simpsons' place.

"I, well, I don't know if he hunts," she stammered. "A lot of ranchers do."

He nodded. "He's a millionaire," he said. His eyes narrowed. "Is that the draw?" he added in a soft, but icy cold, tone. "Your ranch needs a lot of work and you're operating in the red. McGuire could fix that, couldn't he?"

"You're insinuating something very insulting, to both of us," she said shortly. "And in case you've forgotten, my cousin Rogan is rich, too!"

"Not as rich as McGuire, from what I hear," he returned, unruffled. "Cousin Rogan doesn't own a private jet."

Her face went red with mingled embarrassment and anger. "Lots of rich men do."

"And you'd know that, how?" he wondered aloud.

She gave him a cold going-over with her eyes, noting his worn chaps and dirty boots, his battered hat. "How would you know what rich men do, either?" she asked sarcastically. "You don't look as if you travel with the jet set."

Oddly, he wasn't insulted. He just smiled. She had no way of knowing that he had, when he was younger, traveled with the jet set. He was well-known among cattlemen. He had one of the biggest ranches in West Texas. Latigo was known far and wide, not only for Cort's innovative breeding strategy, and its prize bulls, but also for its history. It was founded by the Culhanes, a father and three sons, who passed it down to their children and their grandchildren. The grandchildren fought so hard over ownership that they lost it, running up litigation fees that finally led to the ranch being sold for money they no longer had.

Cort's father, Vince Grier, had bought the property and moved in with his own family, his wife and four sons. Little by little, he'd built Latigo into the property it was today. Not only did the Griers have cattle, they had real estate holdings all over the world, and gas and oil stocks that were worth even more than the ranch. Cort often thought that the Culhanes would be proud to see that their legacy hadn't been lost. Even if it continued under another family's name.

"I travel the rodeo circuit from time to time," he said. It wasn't quite a lie. He'd done a lot of rodeo when he was in his teens, before he joined the Army and went to war. "Lots of rich ranchers come to watch."

She could hardly argue that. She knew that Cousin Rogan loved rodeo and hardly ever missed one. Catelow had a weekly rodeo in the summer. Lots of other towns and cities hosted them as well.

"I guess so," she replied. She wasn't eager to go, despite the calf's infrequent movements as he rested between her flat belly and the pommel. She patted the calf absently.

"You should go," he said, because he wanted her to stay, too, and it was unwise. He was flying false colors. He didn't want

her to know the truth about his status. Not yet. Let her think
he was a roaming cowboy.

"I should." She gave him a last, wistful smile and rode on
toward Bart's barn. He watched her until she was out of sight.
He wished he knew why.

Bart came down to the barn and took the calf from her arms.
He carried it into a clean stall and placed it gently on the hay.
There was feed and water already in place. Ranchers expected
to find a few deserted calves during calving season. "What happened?" he called back to her.

"You'll have to ask your guest," she said as she dismounted
and followed him into the huge barn. "He found the little thing.
Its mother was dead. He thinks it might have been a wolf or a
pack of dogs. He's tracking them."

He chuckled. "He can track like a champion," he told her.
"Once, he caught a rustler by following a track with a break
in the horseshoe. Tracked the men all the way to their transfer
truck, pulled his .45 Ruger Vaquero and shot out their tires."
He shook his head. "Shot the head rustler as well."

Her eyes were like saucers. "He shot someone!"

"Well, the man shot at him first," he said defensively.

Her heart almost stopped. The thought of Cort being shot
down made her feel sick at her stomach. She couldn't understand
why. She hardly even knew him. She didn't want to know him.
He made her knees weak.

"He and the sheriff in his county back home in Texas are good
friends," he told her. "And he's well thought of by the Special
Rangers—those are the Texas Rangers assigned to investigate
livestock and ranch-and farm-related cases of cattle theft. The
man Cort shot got thirty years in prison for stealing sixty head
of cattle."

"Thirty years?" she exclaimed.

He nodded. "Texas is hard on cattle thieves. Here in Wyoming, it's ten years, tops. But in Texas, it's a third-degree felony, punishable by ten years in prison for stealing ten head of cattle. Sixty head, sixty years, it should have been—but the guy had a good lawyer so he only got thirty years."

"I will never steal even one head of cattle in Texas as long as I live," she said, putting her hand over her heart. "I swear!"

He laughed. "Me, too."

"I guess I'd better get back home. I'm stuck in the middle of a chapter on the next book, I thought getting out in the clean air might help me think. It sure did."

"You going to get serious about Jake?" he asked conversationally, and his eyes twinkled as he glanced at her. "You could do worse."

"He's really nice," she began.

He grimaced. "Ouch. Nice!"

"Well, he is."

He shook his head. "He's got all his own teeth, mostly, and he owns a private jet. He's filthy rich, got ranch holdings everywhere, and he's good-looking to boot!"

"And he's nice."

He just shook his head.

She glanced at him as they left the barn. "Are you sure your cousin isn't on some Wanted list somewhere?" she wondered.

"Not that I know of," he promised, and burst out laughing. "He's a good man. Temperamental, hot tempered, and he can be arrogant. But he's steady and strong."

"And if you're offering him to me—no, thank you," she said firmly.

"Could I ask why not?"

She turned and looked at him. "Because he's a cowboy, Bart," she replied. "I know about cowboys. I've been around them all my life. They carouse when they've got free time. They've got a girl in every little town who thinks she's the only girl. A lot of them move from ranch to ranch because they get the wanderlust.

They don't settle down and they never love just one woman."
She looked out over the pasture to the snowcapped mountains
beyond. "A man who works the land enjoys his own company,"
she said after a minute. "He's a loner. Men like that…" She
smiled sadly. "Well, they don't settle. Do they?"

He was caught between a rock and a hard place. What could
he say that wouldn't blow Cort's cover?

"Some of them do," he replied. "What about Joe Stamper?
He was a rounder, and he settled down with Martha. They have
three sons. He's the foreman over at the McGuire Ranch."

"I'd forgotten Joe."

"I could name you two or three others who got married and
made good husbands and fathers," he added.

She sighed. "I guess so. But marriage isn't something I want,
Bart," she said sadly. "I guess I've had a close look at the worst of
it, and it warped something inside me. I don't believe in happy
endings anymore. Life," she added, "is not a fairy tale."

"That depends," he said.

"On what?"

He looked beyond her to the mountains she'd been watching. "It depends on the people involved," he replied. "Life is
what you make of it."

"I stand corrected." She grinned at him. "But you're not
married."

"She ran off with another man," he reminded her.

"There was Sally…" she began.

"Married a Norwegian tourist and went home with him."

She furrowed her brow. "Agatha."

"Moved to California and said we'd see her on television one
day." His eyes twinkled. "And we did, I guess, when she got
mixed up with that married actor who went on the news and
said it was Agatha's fault, that she seduced him against his will.
I laughed so hard I almost busted a rib."

"Poor Agatha," she agreed. "No film studio would touch her after that."

"She went to New York and got a job modeling," he recalled.

"She was in a magazine I thumbed through just the other day at the drugstore. She looks very pretty. She wasn't, you know," she reminded him. "She was just average looking. It's amazing what they can do with makeup."

"Tell me about it."

"She might come back here one day," she said.

He sighed. "She might. But she said she didn't want to spend her life on a ranch, smelling cow poop and alfalfa from dawn to dusk." He glanced at her. "I like the smell of alfalfa."

"Me, too, Bart." She patted him on the shoulder. "Maybe we should form a club. And only people with lost loves could join."

"Lost loves, huh?" he mused. "And where's yours?"

She frowned. "That's right. I don't have one."

"Yet," he said, just as Cort Grier came riding up on the bay horse he'd appropriated for the length of his visit with his cousin.

"Did you find what killed the cow?" Bart asked.

Cort nodded, leaning forward with his hands crossed over the pommel, holding the reins. "A wolf."

"We need to track it…"

"No, we don't." Cort dismounted gracefully and joined them, with the reins threaded through his fingers. "The wolf was dead as well."

Bart and Mina both stared at him.

"What?" He read the expressions well. "No, I didn't do it," he said. "Somebody with a high-powered rifle took him out. The shot blew out part of his rib cage. Had to be a hollow point, to do that much damage."

"Who?" Bart wondered.

Cort shook his head. "No idea."

"You're sure it was the wolf that killed Bart's cow?" she asked.

He nodded. "Still had blood on his muzzle. Probably separated from his pack, and too old and disabled to hunt anything that could run fast. He had a bad belly wound, almost as long as he was, and not healed. He was probably in terrible pain. The cow had just given birth and she was weak."

Mina sighed. "Nature is cruel," she said. "But that's the way of things around a ranch. Some animals kill, some die." She looked up. "God's will."

Cort chuckled.

"What's funny?" she asked.

"I had a college professor in history who used to say that all the time. He'd been lecturing about deism in the past. He tried to put up a map on the blackboard to point out where deism had its beginnings. It kept falling down. Finally, the last time, it hit him right on the head. He turned to the class and said, 'God's will,' with the straightest face you've ever seen. We all roared."

She cocked her head, curious about him. "You went to college?"

"Just a couple of courses, when I was out of high school," he lied. "I used to love history."

She smiled. "Me, too. Napoleon. Scipio Africanus. Hannibal. Alexander."

He frowned. "Conquerors," he said. "Military history."

"Oh yes. I take courses online. Those are my favorites. They were innovators as well as warriors. They used brilliant strategy and tactics to win battles."

Cort chuckled. "Of all the coincidences," he murmured.

"What do you mean?" she asked.

He couldn't tell her that and maintain his masquerade. His minor was military history. "I like Patton and Rommel," he said instead.

"World War II, African theater of war," she said, nodding.

"You know about that, too?"

"It was a gentleman's war, in North Africa," she said. "One of

my great-great-uncles died there, fighting with Patton's Third
Army."

"One of mine as well," Cort said.

They were staring at each other without realizing it. Mina's
heart rate shot up and her breath caught in her throat. Cort was
feeling something similar and fighting it tooth and nail. This
sweet little country kid would never fit into his lifestyle, even
if he let himself care about her. He had to remember that. Yes,
he wanted to get married. But he was realistic enough to know
that he had to have a partner with a similar background. In his
case, it would have to be a wealthy background.

So he dragged his eyes away from Mina's face and turned to
his cousin. "I'm going to ride over and help your men fix that
broken fence near the highway, if that's okay with you?" he
added, living up to his cowboy image.

"Sure. I've got a few calls to make, then I'll ride over and
help."

Cort chuckled. "We'll be done by then."

"Son of a gun," Bart mused. "I'll miss all that fun work. I do
love digging postholes and stretching fencing wire."

"Liar," Mina said in a loud whisper.

He just laughed. Cort smiled, but not at Mina, and rode off
without another look in her direction. She pretended not to
notice, of course.

Bart had meant to tell Cort that Mina was his novelist friend.
But the longer he waited to do it, the less he wanted to. Cort
was a rounder. He loved women, plural, and he was still seeing Ida Merridan, the divorcée he'd met at the Simpsons' party.
Mina was naive and it was obvious to Bart that she was attracted
to Cort.

Right now, Cort thought Mina was just a country girl with
a small ranch. He'd mentioned to Bart that she'd never be able
to hold her own in high social circles. He wasn't sure she'd even

know which utensils to use in a fancy restaurant. Obviously, he'd added, she wasn't the sort of woman he could consider settling down with. He did want to get married and have a family, he murmured. He was just less certain now that he was ready for that responsibility. He was free to date any woman he liked, he had no restrictions on his travel, he wasn't tied down to the ranch unless he wanted to be. He had all the advantages and none of the disadvantages. In short, he didn't want to give up his freedom for a marriage that might not even work.

"I thought you were all gung-ho on getting married and having kids," Bart teased as they sat around in the living room after supper drinking second cups of coffee.

"I was," he replied somberly. "Then I started looking for the perfect woman and I discovered that they were all looking for the richest man." He gave Bart a droll look. "A woman who puts money before anything else isn't going to want to settle down with a husband and babies who need changing."

"Good point."

Cort's eyes were wistful. "My illusions left jet trails taking off," he said. "I was sure it would be easy to find a nice woman who wanted a family. The problem was that every woman I dated saw me as a walking checkbook."

"You're rich."

"I noticed," Cort said, glowering at his cousin.

Bart grinned. "That's my great advantage. I'm not rich. Any woman who wanted to settle down with me would know she wasn't looking at diamonds and Ferraris."

Cort nodded. "Believe me, that's a real advantage."

"A week from Friday night, there's a square dance in town at the civic center. You going?" he asked.

Cort stuck his hands in his pockets. "I might take Ida."

Bart felt a sense of relief, although it was going to mark his cousin as a man with few morals in a town the size of Catelow. Everybody knew about Ida.

Cort noticed his companion's expression. "She isn't quite what she seems," he said.

Bart just smiled. "It isn't what people really are in small towns, Cort. It's what people think they are. Ida has a scarlet reputation."

"Don't worry," Cort chuckled. "Nobody's going to say bad things about you because I date her."

"I know that."

He cocked his head and his eyes narrowed. "Your neighbor. She has a real issue with men."

Bart nodded. "She's had a hard life. At least her cousin kept the ranch going. Her mother tried several times to sell it for ready cash. Rogan stopped her."

"What was her mother like?" he asked.

He smiled. "Like Ida, except that she didn't have Ida's looks."

He scowled. "She was divorced?"

"Her husband never divorced her. He just left. A visiting socialite fell in love with his uniform and seduced him into leaving Anthea. So Anthea took it out on Mina. We all lost count of how many men moved in with them. Mina used to hide out in the woods…well, that's all in the past."

"She's afraid of men."

"Yes."

"No hot dates?" Cort asked with a faint smile.

"No dates. Ever."

He scowled. "Ever?"

"She doesn't want to take the risk," Bart told him. "She said some of her mother's boyfriends seemed nice until the doors were closed."

He was recalling that Ida had said that about her second husband. Cort had never raised his hand to a woman. Neither had his father or any of his brothers. But there had been such a man, a neighbor, whose wife had run screaming into the road, bleeding and horrified. A passing motorist had stopped and given her a ride into town, to the sheriff's office. The husband had been arrested and charged, and ended up in jail.

"I guess some people are harder to know than others," he conceded. "But I don't need to hit a woman to feel like a man. And I have a very low opinion of men who do."

"So does our cousin Cody," Bart chuckled. "He took a domestic call one Saturday night when all his deputies were tied up. A three-year-old boy had bruises all over him. His mother was bleeding and crying and her husband was drunk and aggressive and tried to fight Cody."

"That would have been interesting to see," Cort mused.

"It truly was. Cody made the man walk every step of the way to town and threw every charge he could think of at him. There was this really avid public defender who thought he could come in here to circuit court and throw his weight around." He whistled.

"He learned some things, including some brand-new words that Cody taught him after the man's client was sent to jail for five years."

"Hardly sounds like enough," Cort murmured.

"I'm not finished. He got five years on two of the felony counts. But it seems that he was on parole for an assault that he served time for. After he serves the five years here, he goes to Montana to serve the parole violation. Cody made sure he would."

Cort chuckled. "Our cousin is a bad man to rile."

"Yes, he is." He cocked his head and smiled at Cort. "He's not the only one."

Cort just shook his head. He looked at Bart curiously. "How old is Mina?"

"Twenty-four," he said. "But she looks younger, doesn't she?"

"A lot younger." He was surprised at her age. Bart seemed to think that she had no interest in men, but he couldn't believe that a woman could be innocent at the age of twenty-four.

Surely she'd had some experiences that Bart didn't know about. He laughed to himself. Mina Michaels was probably as experienced and jaded as he was and didn't like men because she'd had her fill of them. Innocence in this day and age was a joke, he was absolutely sure of it. And Mina, whatever else she was, was no innocent.

Mina was interviewing men for the full-time position on her ranch. She wasn't happy about having to do it, or about the applicants themselves. She had an attorney's investigator running background checks on the men. Two had been fired for stealing from their employers, although the ranchers hadn't been able to prove it. Another was wanted for child custody payments that he'd been dodging.

Out of the five contenders, only one stood out. He was an older man with thinning gray hair and dark brown eyes. He looked as if he'd never smiled in his life. He wasn't wearing expensive clothing, but he was nicely dressed and very clean. He had a soft voice and a pleasant personality. He came with several job references from ranchers who had employed him. None were unfavorable. It was the oddest thing; there was something familiar about him, as if she'd seen him somewhere. But he was from Arizona, he said, and she'd never been there.

She drew in a long breath as she studied his job application. She looked up suddenly and surprised an odd, watchful look in his eyes. "Why do you want this job?" she asked with her accustomed bluntness.

He smiled sadly. "Nobody else had one," he said simply. "Early spring's a bad time to be out of work, because most ranchers have already hired on any extra hands they need for calving. And this isn't Arizona. I wanted a place that wasn't so hot." Arizona was where his references were from.

She looked back down at the paper. "What sort of salary would you expect?" she asked, and lifted her eyes to his.

He spread his hands. "Whatever the going rate is up here in Wyoming," he said simply. "I don't have a family to support and I don't drink or smoke or gamble. I just mainly need a place to stay and food." He smiled. "I'd work hard. I've always worked hard. I think a man should earn his keep."

She smiled at that, noting the curious look on his face. "Well, I can pay you the going rate," she said after a minute. "It's not a fancy operation, just a beef enterprise. I have two part-time cowboys and a part-time foreman, Bill…"

"…McAllister," he finished for her, and smiled. "I met him in town Sunday. We're both Methodist. He's the one who told me about this job."

"Well." If Bill had pointed him in Mina's direction, he must have seen something good in the man. She clasped her hands on the desk in front of her. "Suppose we give it a try for a month and see if we suit each other?" she asked. "And I have to tell you that I won't be here for a good bit of the year. I write books. I'm already fairly successful so my publisher is sending me on tour, all over the country, to sign books, in a few weeks. Before that, I have a research trip planned. You'll mostly be working for Bill until I get home. And he won't be here all the time," she added.

He shrugged. "I'm a self-starter," he said. "I'll see what needs done, and I'll do it." He hesitated. "There's just one thing. Do you mind dogs?"

Her brows drew together. She'd only ever had one, when her father was still at home. It had been a German shepherd, a huge, beautiful red-and-black one named Duke. The dog had gone with her father, all those years ago.

"I guess not," she said finally. "As long as he doesn't eat calves."

He chuckled. "He's a sweet boy. He never bothers other animals. In fact, he has an actual distaste for raw meat. He likes his cooked."

"My goodness," she laughed. "What breed is he?"

He shrugged. "Sort of Heinz 57, if you get my meaning. There's husky in him, and some border collie, too, I think. His name's Sagebrush."

She sensed a story there. "Sagebrush?"

He smiled. "I found him in a clump of sagebrush, half-starved, barely weaned. I never knew what happened to his mother or other pups, if there were any. I took him home, cleaned him up, took him by the vet for shots. He's been with me ever since."

She was intrigued. "I'd really like to meet him."

"Sure. Come on out. I left him in the truck, just in case you said no."

She paused at the door. "And what would you have done if I did say no?"

He sighed. "I'd still be looking for a job."

She smiled. That told her worlds about the man. She opened the door.

Sagebrush was big. He had to weigh at least eighty pounds. But he was friendly and sweet and seemed as if he'd never met a stranger. He had a big head and fur like a husky, and even big blue eyes. The rest of him had black-and-white mixed fur. He had huge paws.

"I've had calves smaller than him," Mina laughed.

"Me, too," he confessed. "I didn't expect him to grow so much."

"He looks very healthy. And he isn't overweight," she added, studying the dog.

"The vet said that his size predisposed him to hip dysplasia. I didn't want to take any chances, so I make sure he has enough to eat, but not too much."

A man who was that good to a stray dog would be equally good to people. Bill McAllister had made a good decision, sending him on to Mina. She'd have to remember to thank him.

A truck drove up before she could tell her applicant what

he needed to do. It was Bill McAllister. He climbed down and joined them, grinning.

"I see you found it," he told the younger man.

He chuckled. "I found it. Thanks a million. She just hired me," he added, nodding toward Mina. "I'll work hard."

"I know you will."

"Okay, then, Bill, if you'll take Mr...." She stopped, blinked, flushed. She hadn't even asked the man's name and she hadn't looked at that part of the job application.

"Jerry Fender," he said, holding his hand out. He was certain she wouldn't recognize the last name. It was his legal one now. It had been for years and years.

"Mina Michaels," she replied, shaking his hand. "I hope you'll like it here. Bill, can you get him settled? And Sagebrush there can sleep in the bunkhouse with him." She glanced at Jerry and grinned. "You'll have the bunkhouse to yourself," she added. "My other guys, including Bill, are part-timers."

He cocked his head. "Sagebrush won't mind sleeping outside..."

She waved away the suggestion. "He's a good dog," she said. "You know, it will be nice having one on the place. We haven't had a dog since..." She broke off, remembering. The look on her face was painful. The new man grimaced and turned away.

"Okay, then," he said, interrupting her. "If you're sure you don't mind, I'll clean him up."

She laughed. "That's a deal. He sure does have a lot of fur."

"That's the husky in him," Jerry said, bending down to ruffle the dog's fur.

Funny, Mina was thinking, how that simple act prodded memories of a time long past when her father had loved Duke so much. She turned back toward the house. The new man was oddly familiar to her, but she was sure she'd never met him before. It didn't matter, anyway, as long as he did a good job.

★ ★ ★

"She's nice," Jerry told Bill as he moved into the bunkhouse with his dog.

"She is. One day, she'll be at the top of the *New York Times* bestseller list," Bill predicted. "She can really write. They've had parties for her all month, introducing her to the best families."

"The ones with money, I presume?" Jerry replied, and not with much enthusiasm.

"Mostly. She's got a beau. Jake McGuire. He owns one of the biggest ranches around and he likes Mina. But she's not much on men." He shook his head. "What she went through at home," he added, wincing. "Her mother's lovers came and went. One beat Mina up, another had her hiding out in the woods all night. She's had a hell of a life."

The other man swallowed, hard. "She seems to have managed pretty well."

"She did. She's strong and tough." He laughed. "You should read her latest book, *SPECTRE*. She went crawling on her belly through jungles with an AK-47 with this merc commando group that adopted her to research the damned thing. She loves mercs and cops." He shook his head. "It's a runaway bestseller."

"Good Lord," he exclaimed, and laughed. "I'll have to give it a look."

"You won't be able to put it down," the older man promised. Jerry just smiled.

Mina had lunch with Bart in the local restaurant a few days later.

"How's your new hired man working out?" he asked.

She laughed. "Now how did you know that?"

"Bill," he returned. "He says you've got a real winner there."

"I heard that he goes to church with Bill."

Bart studied her. "You haven't set foot in a church in years."

Her face closed up.

He sighed. "Okay. Don't talk to me."

"I hear your houseguest is squiring the happy divorcée around," she said after a minute. "Is he bringing her to the dance Thursday night?"

"He hasn't said. Are you going?" he added.

She smiled. "I don't know. Probably not. Next Friday, Jake's taking me to Billings for what he says is the best steak west of the Mississippi River. If I go to the dance, I'll be too worn-out the next day to go off with Jake."

"Jake's a cool guy. You could do a lot worse."

"I guess I could," she said with a sigh. "But I don't feel that way about him." She glanced at Bart. "Is it getting serious, between your cousin and Ida?"

"No idea. He says she has hidden qualities."

She looked up and pursed her lips. "Oh, I'll just bet she does."

The way she said it had Bart doubled over with laughter. Just as he started to answer her, Cort walked in the door with Ida.

CHAPTER SIX

Mina's heart ran wild. She put both hands around her cup of black coffee and held on tight. She didn't care if Cort dated that wild woman. He didn't belong to her. He was arrogant and domineering and she wouldn't have wanted him even if he'd been interested in her.

But her eyes went involuntarily to the woman, who was gorgeous in just an ordinary checked blouse and blue jeans. Mina would have given a lot to be that pretty. But the woman had the morals of a cat, she reminded herself. Just like Mina's mother.

Cort spotted Bart and his friend at the back table and made a beeline for them with Ida at his side.

Mina's teeth clenched so hard that she worried she might have broken one.

"Mind if we join you?" Cort asked easily. "We're on our way to the hardware. I need a new pair of gloves."

"But I'm starving, so he offered to feed me," Ida added with an affectionate glance at Cort, who returned it with interest.

"Sure," Bart said, and didn't look at Mina because he knew what her expression would be. "Have a seat. We've just finished, but tables are at a premium right now," he added with a grin, noting that they were all full. "Looks like everybody in Wyoming knows where the best food is."

"No joke," Cort said, pulling out a chair for Ida before he sat down. "This place has a great cook."

"So does the Sheraton in Billings," Bart noted with a grin at Mina. "Jake McGuire's taking her up there for a steak Saturday."

"That's a long drive," Ida noted.

"Oh, he's got a private jet," Bart said easily. "It's no distance when you're flying."

That was something Cort already knew. His own ranch had a jet, along with two prop planes they used for roundup, and pilots who flew the family anywhere they needed to go on business. Or pleasure.

"That must be nice," Ida said with a shy glance at Mina. "Everyone says Mr. McGuire has a good heart."

"He does," Mina said tautly. She didn't say another word. Ida grimaced and Cort glared.

Bart, sensing disaster pending, looked pointedly at his watch. "We have to go. I've got a man coming over to look at one of my young bulls." Actually he didn't, but he was going to call somebody to do that, so Cort wouldn't catch him in a fib. He stood up and waited for Mina to join him.

"I'll see you back at the house," Bart told Cort.

Cort stared at Ida and smiled. "Okay. But don't wait up," he added, his voice deep and sensuous as he looked at Ida.

"I won't," Bart said. He took Mina's arm and almost herded her out of the restaurant.

"Okay, what was that all about?" Ida asked when the others had gone.

He chuckled. "Just heading off trouble."

"Mina's not forward," she said, her eyes curious. "She'd never chase you."

"I'm making sure. Do you mind?" he added.

She smiled sadly. "No, of course not."

"Why do you think she's going places with McGuire?" he asked shortly.

She blinked. "Well, because she likes him, I suppose."

"He's filthy rich," he returned. "Even richer than her cousin Rogan."

"Both of them put together wouldn't equal half your net worth," she pointed out, keeping her voice low so that she wasn't overheard.

"Nobody around here knows that," he replied. His face tautened. "I've been hunted like an elk by women for years. I got jaded, I guess. I don't mind paying my way, but there's a limit. I wanted to be liked for myself, not my wallet."

"I've had the same problem," she confessed on a sigh. "So I developed this scandalous reputation that puts most men off. With an exception here and there," she mused, eyeing him.

He chuckled. "Well, I did take the reputation at face value, just at first."

"I noticed."

He cocked his head and studied her. "You really are beautiful," he remarked quietly.

She smiled. "Thanks."

"You could marry me, you know," he said. "At least I'd be sure it wasn't for what I had."

She slid her hand over his on the table. "That's very flattering and I appreciate the offer. But I'm done with marriage." She pulled her hand back. "Never again." Her eyebrows rose. "And you've been looking for a wife in all the worst places," she added. "Models and actresses and debutantes aren't looking for a man who digs postholes and babies calves."

He chuckled. "I suppose not." He had a sudden picture of Mina on her horse, holding the orphaned calf in front of her on the saddle. It made a warm place inside him. "But most women in that category aren't rich. Some of them are predators and they can put on a good act. I've been with women who swore they were virgins." He gave her a droll look. "And they never were."

"I was, when I first married," she said. "My husband never touched me. I felt absolutely worthless as a woman. After he died and I was rich with what he left me, I was infatuated with a man who seemed like the toughest, manliest man alive. So I married him." She shivered. "I'd never really believed all those stories I heard about brutal men. I do now," she said coldly. "I believe every word."

He shook his head. "What a hell of a shame they don't still have public stocks for men like that."

"Jail is much better. My ex-husband is residing in a state prison for assault and battery. He killed another inmate five months into his sentence, so he'll never get out now." She smiled, a smile that was icy and never reached her eyes. "I like to think of him being some other inmate's significant other."

"Wicked woman," he teased.

She shrugged. "I didn't start out that way." She smiled at him. "How long are you going to visit with your cousin?"

"I don't know. A few weeks, maybe. My foreman is almost as good as I am about ranch management and he calls me if there are any problems he can't handle. There won't be. My dad is coming down with his new wife so she can experience ranch life. He always managed the ranch while I was off marketing cattle and talking business. I don't expect his new wife will last long if she comes with him. None of his women ever took to cattle and dust."

She drew in a long breath and waited until the waitress took their orders before she spoke. "Your father's lifestyle affected you, I'll bet. You didn't grow up in a stable home with two parents who loved each other."

"I did, actually. My mother was a little saint. After she died, Dad seemed to lose his mind. He stayed with the model for a few years, but after that, he set new records for promiscuity. I guess maybe it did affect me."

"My parents married just out of high school," she recalled with a smile. "They loved each other, and me, so much. He had a heart attack at the age of thirty-five and died in the doctor's office. It was so massive that nothing would have saved him. My mother grieved and grieved. She kept going for me, but her heart was in the grave with my father. When I was twenty-one she went on a cruise and fell overboard. They never found the body."

He winced. "That must have been traumatic."

She nodded. "It's so much worse when people die like that. You never really give up hope that maybe somebody fished them out, they lost their memory, things like that." She looked up. "I know that she drowned. I just couldn't accept it, for a long time. Finally, I bought one of those urns for people who are cremated. I put her favorite jewelry and some hairs from her hairbrush, a ring she liked, a Christmas ornament, and sealed it up. It sits on my mantel. So I have something of her near me."

"That's a special kind of memorial," he said. "I never would have thought of it."

"An innovation," she said. She smiled. "It helped me adjust to life without her."

"We buried my mother in the cemetery at our local Methodist church. I put flowers on her grave on holidays and her birthday, for me and my brothers."

"I do that for my father."

The waitress came back with their order.

"Are we going to the dance Thursday night?" he asked.

She smiled. "We'll be gossiped about."

"Good," he said.

She just laughed.

Jake McGuire was right on time to pick Mina up for their date on Friday. As he'd said, they didn't dress up. But he was wearing designer jeans and boots, with a Western-cut blue plaid shirt under a black leather coat, with a top-of-the-line cream Stetson on his dark hair. He could have modeled for a couture house. But Mina was too shy to mention that.

She was wearing slacks and a simple white camisole under a long sweater that came to her ankles. It wasn't expensive, but it was a trendy outfit. She added cultured pearls to it, around her neck and in her earlobes. They were a graduation present from her cousin Rogan.

"You look very nice," Jake said, sighing as he looked down at her. "I like it that you didn't screw your hair up into that bun."

She laughed self-consciously. "I'll probably be eating it, too. It flies up into my mouth constantly when I leave it down."

He bent and smoothed the honey-brown strands behind her small ears. "There," he said huskily.

She smiled at him, but she didn't feel anything at all, and he knew it. He moved back. He forced a return smile. "Ready to go?" he asked.

She nodded. "Oh yes. I've never been in a jet."

"Never?" he asked.

"Well, not a small one," she qualified. "I had to fly to New York to talk to my agent and my publisher. But I flew tourist."

He chuckled. "This will be much better than tourist," he promised.

And it was. The baby jet had fantastic seats and tables. There was a small bedroom and a bathroom, and even television.

"This is incredible," she exclaimed as she buckled herself into her seat for takeoff. "Did you steal this from an alien?" she wondered with an impish grin.

He laughed. "Not quite."

"It's got everything!"

"Well, everything except a flight attendant," he amended. He leaned toward her. "Which means we'll have self-serve packets of peanuts in flight."

She burst out laughing. He smiled to himself. At least she liked him, he thought. He could build on that.

Billings was a sprawling big city with a small-town atmosphere. The people in the restaurant were friendly and outgoing, and the food was unbelievably good.

"This is awesome," Mina exclaimed as she savored the steak she'd ordered. "I've never tasted beef this good! Not even my own."

"They have a reputation for it locally," he told her. "I love to eat here. Hey," he added with a grin, "we could fly down to Galveston for seafood one weekend."

She hesitated and just a hint of color touched her cheeks. She didn't want to offend him, but she couldn't go off with a man for a weekend.

"Oh. I see," he mused. He smiled gently. "It would be a day trip. Just down and back. Honest."

She let out the breath she'd been holding. "Sorry," she said. "I'm not modern."

"Honey, I don't mind that at all," he said softly. "Neither am I."

She smiled back. He really was a good person. And it was nice to have a man be friendly. Nothing like that animal of a cowboy who worked for Bart and did his best to put her back up at every opportunity. Even now, he was squiring the promiscuous merry divorcée all over Catelow. He'd taken her to the dance last night and people were already talking about them. Bart had mentioned it when he phoned her early this morning to get some stats on her calves. Presumably the divorcée was good in bed, Mina thought darkly. Everybody said so.

"What's wrong?" Jake asked, concerned by her expression.

She flushed. "Oh. I was thinking about Charlie," she lied. "I do sort of miss him."

He blinked. "Charlie?"

"My bull. Well, the bull I had to give away."

"Why did you have to get rid of him?"

She told him, relaxing more as she related the sad tale. At least she'd covered her bases by not mentioning Cort. And why she should be thinking about him and Ida was a puzzle. She didn't even like him!

Jake flew her back home. It was late when the limousine he'd hired dropped her off at her front door.

"I had a very good time," she said, clutching her purse in front of her. "Thanks."

"I enjoyed it as well." He slid his hands into his pockets and smiled down at her. "Galveston, next weekend?"

She laughed. "Well…okay."

His heart lifted. He grinned from ear to ear. "That's a date, then. I'll pick you up about nine in the morning next Saturday."

"I'll look forward to it."

"When do you have to go back to New York?"

She told him. "In four weeks, I think, unless they change it. It's to sign a new four-book contract," she said, "and do a few local signings. And a satellite media tour."

"A what?" he asked.

"Satellite media tour," she said. "They have a makeup artist come in and work on me, then I sit in the room with a sound guy and a cameraman, and the guy in the booth makes the connections to television stations around the country. The hosts ask me questions and I try to answer them. It takes a long time."

"I've never heard of such a thing."

She smiled. "I hadn't either, until I did the first one. But now I don't mind so much. And I can pump the people at the television station we broadcast from. I learn all sorts of things from stories they tell me about other people they've worked with."

"Sounds fascinating."

"It certainly is, to a small-town girl who's never been anywhere." She laughed. "I keep thinking that one day I'll wake up and all this will have been just a dream."

"It's no dream. Honest." He checked his Rolex and grimaced. "I hate to run, but I've got a conference call incoming."

"At this hour?" she asked, surprised.

"I do business all over the world. In some areas it's morning."

"I didn't realize."

"Life is a learning process," he teased.

She grinned up at him. "I'll say!"

"When you get ready to go to New York, I'll fly you up," he said.

She beamed. "That would be really nice of you."

"I have ulterior motives," he teased. "I know where all the good restaurants are in Manhattan."

She laughed. "Okay."

He laughed softly, too, and bent to touch his mouth to hers in a gentle, respectful kiss. "Good night, sweet woman."

She flushed. "Good night."

He sighed. She wasn't going to love him, but she liked him. It was a foundation, of sorts, that he could build on. "See you next Saturday," he said.

She nodded. "Next Saturday."

He gave her a long, soulful look and went back to the limousine. She went inside. He was infatuated with her. She could tell. But she couldn't really feel that way about him. She didn't understand why. He was pleasant, handsome, brilliant, rich—but there was no spark, no leaping pulse, when he touched her.

Involuntarily her mind went to Cort Grier and how she had felt when he looked up at her as she held the calf in front of her on the pommel. His pale brown eyes were steady and curious. Her heart jumped. She ground her teeth together. She couldn't afford to get mixed up with a stray cowboy who probably wouldn't stay at Bart's ranch more than a few weeks. She wasn't going to, either.

★ ★ ★

She was making a pie Monday morning when she heard someone at the front door. Irritated, because her hands were full of
flour from making the crust, she went to answer it, wiping her
hands on a kitchen cloth at the same time and muttering.

She opened the door and Cort Grier was standing there, with
a basket of apples.

She just stared at him. He'd been with that beautiful divorcée in town Friday. What was he doing here?

"Bart sent these over," he said curtly. "He said you liked to
make fresh apple pies with them."

"And he was hoping for one, I'll bet."

He shrugged. "He says you're the best cook in two coun-
ties." His practiced eyes went all over her, narrowed and curious. "Can I put these down?" he asked.

"Oh!" She opened the door to let him in with the heavy basket. "Just bring them into the kitchen, if you don't mind. I've
been doing piecrusts…"

He put the apples on the floor and looked at the fancy fluting
around the edge of the dough in the pie plates. "That's pretty,"
he said involuntarily.

She smiled. "I learned by watching videos on YouTube," she
confessed. "It's much better than cookbooks because you can
see every step of the process and follow along. I don't remember
much of what I read, and I can't follow directions." She made
a face. "It's why I mostly make hats and scarves when I knit. I
tried to make a pair of socks once from a pattern." She sighed.
"Bart saw them and asked if they were antenna covers."

He chuckled. "He would."

"I love to knit and crochet," she said, "while I'm watching
television."

"I don't have much time for TV," he replied.

"I can imagine. Especially during roundup. There's so much
work."

He nodded. He wasn't going to tell her that a great deal of his work was administrative. He did help his men during roundup, but it wasn't really required.

"Bart said you hired a full-time man."

She smiled. "I did. He's experienced in working with cattle and he came with great references. I like him. He's an older man, settled, with no obvious dependents."

"Do you trust him?" he asked quietly, and seemed really concerned. "When the part timers go home, you're here alone with him."

"He doesn't sleep in the house," she protested.

"That's not what I mean. Did you do a background check?"

She put her hands on her hips and stared up at him. "I'll get my attorneys right on it, after they settle the claim for damages to my new yacht."

He thought for a minute and then he chuckled. "You're unpredictable," he said. "Just when I think I've got you pegged, you do something out of character."

"It's part of my deadly charm," she said without smiling.

He cocked his head and looked down at her. "Speaking of deadly charm," he said with a bite in his deep voice," how did the date with McGuire go?"

"How did yours with the widow go?" she shot right back.

He lifted an eyebrow. He smiled, very slowly. "How do you think it went?" he asked in a slow drawl with a world of sensual knowledge in his pale brown eyes.

Mina's high cheekbones colored, and she dragged her gaze down to his chest. Another mistake, because it was broad and masculine and there was thick, dark hair peeking out of the top of his shirt, where it was unbuttoned down to his collarbone.

He frowned. She was so unlike women he'd known. She kept to herself. Bart had mentioned that she really didn't date anybody. She stayed home. He recalled what he knew of her childhood, her trauma with her mother's lovers. Intimacy would be difficult for a woman who'd been through what she had. An indifferent or selfish partner would destroy what little self-esteem she had left.

An innocent, he thought, his mind whirling with odd, unacceptable ideas. She wasn't beautiful. But that hair, that exquisite hair hanging like a brownish-blond flag at her back, those pert little breasts that were visible under the sweater she wore, her sweetly curving hips. He felt his body responding to those images and he fought to keep it under control.

"Where did you get apples in March?" she asked when the silence became too full of tension.

"There's a whole food market that just opened in Catelow," he said, his voice sounding oddly strained. "Bart went shopping. He likes organic."

"Me, too." She'd heard about the market. She'd have to check it out. She turned and looked at the pretty red apples in their small barrel. "These are nice," she said.

He came up behind her. Close. Too close. She could feel the heat of his tall body, smell the faint cologne that clung to him.

She was breathing oddly. Her heart began to race. She was nervous and couldn't hide it. She'd never had such a reaction to a man. He was a rounder, they said. Would he know?

Of course he knew. He could almost feel her heart beat. She smelled of wildflowers and flour. Without realizing why, his big, lean hands slid around her waist and pulled her back into his body.

"How long does it take, to make a piecrust like those?" he asked, for something to say.

"Not…not a long time." Her small hands went to push his away, but they lingered as his fingers spread to her waist and moved to hold her there. Involuntarily, her hands slid over his. Her heart was almost shaking her.

His mouth went to her neck. His lips smoothed over it,

through the soft strands of her long hair. Odd, how hungry he was for her. He'd never toyed with innocents, not ever. He confined his pursuit to women who were in his own class, models and debutantes, movie stars, even sports stars. This was a tragedy in the making, and he knew it. But she was so damned sweet. She made him ache for things he'd never wanted.

"Mr... Mr..." She swallowed hard. "I can't remember your last name."

"My name is Cort," he whispered at her ear. His big hands contracted, warm and strong around her waist, and pulled her closer. "Say it."

"Cort," she whispered shakily. This was wrong. She had to stop it, now while she could. She turned in his grasp.

But before she could protest or say a word, his pale brown eyes caught hers and held them. His hands went to her back and pulled, ever so gently, until she was almost completely plastered to his long, muscular body.

"I... I can't..." She tried to speak.

"Yes, you can, Mina," he whispered as his head bent. "Easy," he murmured as his mouth smoothed tenderly over hers and she jerked in his arms. "Slow and easy. It's like...dancing."

She wanted to push him away. She really did. But her body ached from the contact with his. She felt safe. Restless. Hungry. Shaky. And his mouth was doing something unfamiliar to hers. It wasn't like with Jake. This was arousing, the soft, slow brushing, the faint nip of his teeth, the harsh sound of his breath as the contact worked on him.

Over the years, there had been just a few kisses, most recently Jake's. But this was totally out of her experience. He made her want something more, harder, deeper, and she found herself going on her tiptoes to try and coax his teasing mouth to do what she wanted it to do.

He smiled against her lips. He knew how women reacted. He knew all too well. He was practiced in this ancient art. His lips

coaxed hers apart and his hands half lifted her into a more intimate contact with him. And then the teasing stopped.

His mouth ground into hers, hard and hungry, his arms en-
closing her, possessing her, as the kiss grew more intimate by
the second.

She felt his powerful body shudder. He groaned against her
lips. She was lost, floating, starving to death for something she
didn't understand.

One big hand went to the base of her spine and pushed her
hips into his. He shivered, letting her feel the sudden, growing
hunger of his body as it began to swell.

She wasn't so innocent that she didn't realize what was happening to him. She was almost drugged by the pleasure his
mouth was giving her, but the abrupt change of his body brought
her back to reality. He was a cowboy. He'd had plenty of women.
She knew by the way he was with her. She could recognize experience, even though she had very little. She eased her mouth
from under the crush of his and tried to move back.

He was aching all over. He'd gone in headfirst, so used to
women who followed him helplessly into the bedroom that he
had no practice at stopping short of intimacy. She was pulling
away. His slow brain finally realized that she was protesting the
hold he had on her.

He lifted his head. He felt it spinning like a top. She was po-
tent, this sweet, fragrant little virgin.

"I'm…sorry," she whispered. "But…"

He let her ease away from his hips, but he didn't let go. His
pale eyes, darkened with passion, searched hers. The soft swell
of her mouth, the quick little breaths that he could feel against
his lips, the faint trembling of her body told him things she
wouldn't.

He shuddered faintly, helpless in his hunger as he fought for
control.

She watched him, fascinated, embarrassed, a little shamed. "I'm sorry," she whispered again, grimacing.

So she knew it hurt men when they couldn't go past petting, he thought absently. Was she an innocent? "How do you know that?" he asked in a strained tone.

"Know what?" she asked.

"That it hurts a man to have to come to a sudden stop."

She bit her lower lip and looked away.

He trowned. That didn't look like any experienced woman he'd ever known. "Tell me," he said quietly.

She pressed her small hands into the softness of his shirt, feeling thick hair and muscle under it. "Mama's boyfriend. Henry. He tried to…" She bit back tears. "I was asleep. I had the door locked, but they all opened with one of those funny-looking long keys and he had one. I woke up with him on me. I pushed him away and he groaned and said it hurt him to stop and why wouldn't I let him do what he wanted to? After all, my mother did…"

He wrapped her up in his arms and just held her, rocking her. "How old were you?"

She choked back a sob. "Fifteen."

"That wasn't the only time, was it?" he asked, his voice deep and cutting. Angry.

"No. But I learned to push heavy furniture against the door. That made him mad. It was just after that when he came after me with the belt and beat me bloody."

"Dear God," he whispered.

"I called the sheriff and they sent a deputy, but my mother said I hated Henry and made up stories about him. She wouldn't let the deputy see me. I was covered with bruises all over my back." She choked back another sob. "The only good thing," she said in a miserable undertone, "was that Mama kept him away from me, after that. Well, after he got even for me calling the police. I was really bruised then. I missed two days of school."

His big hand smoothed her long hair. "You poor kid," he
ground out, pressing his mouth to her forehead. "What a hell
of a life you've had."

"They say what doesn't kill us makes us stronger," she said,
her voice wobbly. "I guess it does."

"No kid should have to go through that." He eased back
from her and looked down into her wet eyes. He bent and softly
kissed away the tears. Which only brought more. Nobody had
ever been comforting to her. Not even Bart, who knew that she
disliked being touched, even if they were friends.

"I never had anybody to run to," she whispered, leaning her
head against him. "Cousin Rogan lived mostly in Australia. Bart
was my friend, but much later." She sighed and laid her cheek
against his broad chest. "I've never had anyone to talk to, about
what happened."

His arms tightened. She felt his lips in her hair.

"I went to Iraq to save the world," he whispered. "But combat isn't like that. It's bloody and cruel and you lose buddies who
die right beside you." His eyes closed. He'd never talked about
it, either, except to his brothers. "It does something to you, inside, to go through an experience like that."

She pulled back and looked up into his eyes. "You have nightmares, don't you?" she asked, as if she knew.

He hesitated. Then he nodded. His face was hard and cold
and taut with remembered pain.

She reached up a small hand and smoothed back a strand of
cool, dark hair that had fallen onto his broad forehead. "I have
nightmares, too."

He smiled tenderly. "Life is hard."

She smiled back. "'The night is dark and full of terrors,'" she
quoted from her favorite television series.

He chuckled. "So it is. Wolf or lion?" he added.

"Wolf. Definitely wolf. I love Ghost," she said, referring to the direwolf who was the companion of one of the main characters of the show. She cocked her head. "And you?"

He shrugged. "Bear."

Her eyes widened. There was only one faction that had a bear as its sigil, and it was headed by a little girl with a brave heart and a bad attitude. "You're kidding!"

He smiled. "She's the underdog. She doesn't even have a hundred fighting men. Besides," he added with a chuckle, "she's got more guts than some of the soldiers."

She beamed. "Yes, she does."

He framed her face in his big hands and slid them back into her long, soft hair. He sighed. "I loved what we did," he said after a minute. "But I'm not prepared."

She flushed. "Excuse me?"

He grinned wickedly. "I'm all out of prophylactics," he said bluntly, and laughed when she flushed even more. "And you probably wear a metal studded chastity belt."

"It has spikes, actually," she chided.

He laughed. "Just as well. I'm terrified of virgins."

"Are you really?" she asked and seemed curious about the answer.

He drew in a long breath. "How much do you know about your own body?"

She cleared her throat. "I know enough. Health class was very specific."

"You learned about...barriers?"

She flamed. "Well..."

He bent and brushed his mouth over hers. "That's what terrifies me," he concluded. "Just so you know." He lifted his head, but his eyes were solemn. "I get hot when I touch you. Really hot. I almost lost control, before you pulled away." His big hands rested on her shoulders, and he looked ages older than she was. "It's been a while since I've indulged my base urges. So we need to cool it."

She lowered her eyes to his shirt. "I didn't start it."

"You didn't have to." He tilted her chin up and studied her. "Did McGuire get what you gave me?"

Her mouth fell open. Her eyes were like saucers.

He thought about McGuire and his wealth, and a nagging thought came into his mind and refused to be banished. He didn't like her around the other man. He wondered what she saw in him. If she wasn't indulging her hunger with McGuire, why wasn't she? Was she stringing the man along, for some ulterior motive? Making him hungry so that he'd give her anything she wanted? The thought wouldn't go away. He knew about mercenary women. They came in all shapes and sizes, and some of them were really good actresses. They could fake innocence. He didn't trust women. Not even this one, who appealed to his senses in an uncommon way.

His pale eyes darkened. "McGuire could buy and sell most men around here. And you've got a tiny little ranch. Compared to some others."

She drew back and her dark eyes started to glitter.

CHAPTER SEVEN

"That's a nasty insinuation," she said shortly.

He pursed his sensual, slightly swollen lips as he studied her. "It is, isn't it? He's rich and you're not. And you're dating him."

She bit her lower lip, almost drawing blood. She looked up at him with pain in her eyes. How could be believe that she was that mercenary?

The answer was that he'd seen it firsthand. He was richer than McGuire, but she didn't know. She felt and tasted innocent. But he'd been fooled before. Maybe she knew about him, knew the truth, and she was just playing a game.

His pale brown eyes narrowed. "You were dirt-poor growing up, weren't you?" he asked suddenly.

She swallowed, hard, and pulled away from him. "Yes."

He studied her, taking in her soft mouth, her hostile eyes, her rigid posture. He was confused. It had been a long time since he'd wanted a woman so much. What if he leveled with her; told her who he really was, offered her pretty things?

She drew in a breath, turned and went back to her piecrusts. "In case you were wondering," she said in a voice that was just a little shaky with anger, "I won't do anything for money. That was my mother. Not me."

Why he should feel guilty was a puzzle. But he did. She couldn't be making it up. He'd heard the truth about her past from Bart already. She'd been victimized in a terrible way by her mother's boyfriend. So why was he accusing her of being mercenary? Perhaps because he'd had experience with women who'd had nothing and wanted everything.

He didn't want to be taken in again. He had to keep his hands off her and put some distance between them. She was sweet and responsive and he was hungry. Very hungry. It had been a long time. Well, it had been a long time for him, he amended. And if there was even a chance that she really was a virgin…

His pulse jumped, just thinking about it. He'd never had an innocent. She made him ache. It was uncomfortable.

"Was there anything else?" she asked tersely.

He moved to the table and leaned his hip against it while he watched her hands work. His own hands were deep in the pockets of his jeans, to keep them honest. Her face was averted, but he could see the pain in it. Would a mercenary woman really look like that?

"I don't trust women," he said bluntly. "I don't like them much, either."

She glanced at him, surprised at the honesty. She swallowed. "I don't like men much," she replied. She grimaced. "There's all this hoopla about how women can do anything. But when Henry took that belt to me, all I could think about was how big he was. I was afraid to fight him, because he was drunk and I thought it would just make him use the belt even harder."

"There are a lot of things women can do," he said quietly. "But some they can't. Basically, a woman can't match a man's upper body strength. That puts her at a disadvantage if things get physical. Well, if she hasn't had training in martial arts or hand-to-hand combat," he amended.

"I would have liked a few lessons in martial arts," she said. "But I never had the money. All I had coming in was what I made as a waitress, and my mother got that."

He scowled. "Why didn't you run away?"

She turned and looked up at him. "Where would I have gone?" she asked solemnly. "Mama convinced people around here that I was a liar. Nobody would have believed me about Henry."

"Bart would have."

She smiled sadly. "Henry was dangerous when he drank, and he kept a loaded pistol in the house. I wasn't willing to risk Bart's life, even to save myself."

He drew in a long breath. She seemed genuine. It would have been hard to make up so many lies about her past.

"I was never around drunks," he said. "Well, not until I went overseas." He sighed. "A lot of men drink after they've had a taste of combat."

"Including you?" she asked, as if she knew.

He averted his eyes. "For a time," he confessed. "I had a pal that I went all the way through basic training with. He was a great kid. Grew up in Dade County, Florida, and his dad was a detective there." His face tautened. "We'd just been deployed in Iraq. It was our first day there. A sniper took him out. He was standing next to me one minute and dead the next, with part of his head missing. I'd never seen anybody killed before," he added very quietly.

She was listening. Just listening. Her dark eyes were steady on his face, soft with sympathy.

"There was a lot more than that, too, wasn't there?" she asked.

His teeth ground together. "A lot more."

"My father was in the military, in combat," she said, turning her attention back to the flour. "I heard him talk about it to my mother, just once. He said it was like being sentenced to hell."

"That's not a bad analogy." He sighed. "You never heard from your father, after he left?"

She shook her head. "I don't want to hear from him. He walked out without a word to me, deserted me, for a woman he barely knew. My mother had a lot of lovers before she ended up with Henry," she added bitterly. "I wouldn't wish my childhood on my worst enemy."

"You're just like me," he said absently. "Living in the past and can't move forward."

She grimaced. "Maybe so."

"Are you in love with McGuire?" he shot at her.

She caught her breath, her eyes huge as they met his. "I hardly… I hardly even know him," she stammered.

"He's a rounder," he said shortly. He knew that, because McGuire ran in the same social circles that he frequented himself. He'd heard stories about the rancher, even though they were only distant acquaintances.

"Well, look who's talking," she retorted, glancing at him as she went back to work, her hands covered in dough. "I've never met a cowboy who didn't have a girl in every rodeo town!"

He bit his lower lip to keep the words back. He wasn't just a cowboy, but the rounder part was true. He was a pot, calling the kettle black.

"Women are a permissible pleasure," he said lazily. "I have no plans to marry and settle down and start changing diapers," he added. It was a lie, but he wasn't about to encourage Little Miss Muffet, here. He had to marry a woman from his own class, not some rustic cowgirl who wouldn't know a dessert fork from a butter knife. Why did that bother him? She wasn't even his type. Ida was.

"I don't want to get married, either," she confessed quietly.

He frowned. "Why not?" he asked. "Don't you want kids?"

She felt hot all over, just thinking about them when he was

standing so close to her. The way she'd felt in his arms was scary. She wanted him. She hadn't known she was vulnerable.

He watched her cheeks color with fascination. If she was really experienced, that flush wasn't something she could fake.

"Kids are nice, I guess," she said after a minute. "I've never been around them much."

"Two of my brothers have toddlers," he said quietly. He smiled, reminiscing. "I don't live close enough to visit often, but I like my niece and my nephews."

"How many brothers do you have?" she asked.

"Three. And they're all in law enforcement."

She smiled. "Are they older than you?"

"All of them are. You don't have siblings, do you?"

"None at all. It was a lonely life, even when my father was still at home. He wasn't, much. Law enforcement takes you out at all hours."

He recalled that her father had been a policeman. "You'd know, I guess."

She nodded.

"You like to cook, don't you?" he remarked as she finished the piecrusts and covered them with clear wrap.

"Very much."

"Knitting and crocheting, romance novels and cooking," he mused. "Do you know what century this is?"

She turned with floury hands to glare up at him. "It's my life and I live it as I please. I don't make snide remarks about you, do I? I mean, you walk around in cow manure all day and muck out stables. How is that better than knitting? At least yarn doesn't stink!"

He burst out laughing.

She glared at him. "Thank Bart for the apples, please, and tell him I'll bring him a nice apple pie tomorrow."

"He'll be thrilled. He's partial to apple pie."

"I know."

He scowled. "Why don't you have anything going with him? He's got a ranch of his own and he's a good man, steady and law-abiding."

"He's my friend," she said. "I don't feel that way about him."

"And he's hardly in the same league as McGuire, right?" he persisted. "If you get involved with McGuire, you've got a steep learning curve ahead of you. It's not like this." He looked around the house. "You'd have to entertain his guests, know how to organize parties, wear the right clothes, use the right utensils at table."

"Do you think I'm stupid?" she asked, aghast, because she was well on her way to the sort of life McGuire lived. Not that she was going to tell this cowboy anything!

He shrugged. "I guess you can learn. But if you don't grow up in those circles, it's not so easy to fit in," he added with faint hauteur.

Her full lips flattened as she glared up at him. She knew how to wear the right clothes—she'd learned how from a kind makeup artist at the studio where she'd done her very first satellite media tour. It had led her to a high-ticket department store and clothes that suited her slender body. She'd learned how to use utensils in a fancy restaurant simply by observing her editor when they went out to eat. Organizing parties? She hadn't done it yet, but that was something Pam Simpson could certainly teach her.

"Yes, I can learn," she said shortly. But she wasn't thinking of Jake McGuire and fitting into his life. She was thinking of her career, the one she had that this cowboy didn't even know about.

He looked odd as he studied her in silence for a long moment. She wasn't really a pretty woman. She had a nice figure and a pretty mouth and that glorious honey-streaked brown hair. It was what was inside her that made her look beautiful. She had a kind heart. He barely remembered his mother, but that was what people always said about her, people who knew her when she was still alive; that she was kindhearted.

"Anyway, my future doesn't concern you," she said shortly, turning away. "If you're like most cowboys around here, you'll be moving on to greener pastures in a few months. Bill McAllister is the only cowboy I've ever known who stayed put."

"He never married?"

She sighed. "Yes, he did, years and years ago. She died of pneumonia. He never got over it."

He laughed shortly. "The world is full of women," he said. "Surely he could find somebody else."

She turned, frowning. "Haven't you ever been in love?" she asked, stunned.

"Not really," he said, searching her eyes. "I've had my share of lovers, I guess."

"It isn't the same thing," she returned.

"And how would you know that?" he asked sarcastically.

She averted her eyes. "I was in love once, when I was sixteen," she said quietly. "I would have died for him." She wrapped another piecrust in plastic wrap. "My mother noticed how crazy I was about him and she seduced him. Then she came home and told me about it, and she laughed. He was so ashamed that he couldn't even talk to me anymore."

Anger flashed in his pale brown eyes. "What a hell of a thing to do."

"That was my mother," she said simply. "Anything I cared about was fair game. I wouldn't even pet a stray cat, because I knew if I did, she'd kill it or have one of her lovers carry it off."

He winced. "Why?" he asked.

She sighed. "I've been asking myself that for years and years," she confessed. "I don't know."

"Was she like that, before your father left?"

She thought back to her childhood. She remembered her mother hitting her, slapping her, when she was just starting in grammar school. She remembered being cursed and belittled, anytime she was alone with her mother.

"Yes," she said. "All my life."

He frowned. It didn't make sense that a parent would be that cruel to a helpless child. He wondered what she looked like when she was small. He could almost picture her in a frilly dress, with her long hair down around her shoulders and a bow holding it out of her eyes. She would have been a precious child. Odd, how that thought made him wish he had a little girl of his own...

"Your mother cared about you, didn't she?" she asked as she finished the last piecrust.

"She loved all of us," he said, remembering with sadness those last days she was in the hospital before she died. Cash had stayed with her. Cort had been too young. He sighed. "One of my older brothers was with her in the hospital. Dad couldn't stand to watch it. He'd gone off with the model he later married. It sounds heartless—maybe it was. But he loved our mother. I always thought it was a defensive thing, hiding his head in the sand with another woman to keep the pain from killing him."

"If I had a spouse that I loved in the hospital, that's where I'd be, right until the bitter end," she said, her dark eyes catching his.

"So would I," he said softly. "My father isn't like the rest of us. He doesn't feel things as deeply as we do." He sighed. "He was never around when we were kids." He stopped himself just in time from telling her about the yacht races his father loved, the sporting events he haunted, the jet-setting reputation his father had.

"I wish my mother had never been around," she said with a whimsical smile. "My life would have been easier if I'd been an orphan, I think."

"You love cattle, don't you?"

She smiled. "Yes, I do. Cattle and horses, dogs and cats. It's so nice, being able to have them and not worrying about something happening to them." She glanced at him. "Cousin Rogan told my mother that if any of the cattle or horses had 'accidents,' he'd make sure the proper authorities were contacted, and she'd read about herself in the tabloids. It was the only time I ever really saw her frightened."

"Your cousin is a card," he mused, and could have bitten his tongue for making that slip. He wasn't supposed to know the man.

But it went right by her. "He is," she agreed. "I wouldn't even have had the ranch if he hadn't intervened."

"He and McGuire are partners in that Australian cattle station, aren't they?"

She nodded. "Cousin Rogan hates snow. The station is near the desert, always hot," she said on a laugh.

"I like snow," he mused. "We don't get a lot back home in my part of Texas."

"I like it until I have to drive in it," she sighed. "I've been stuck in ditches too many times in my life because I never learned how to drive properly."

"Was there a reason for that?"

She nodded. "My mother couldn't drive at all, and I'd have walked two miles to town before I'd have asked any of her lovers to teach me—especially Henry."

"I thought they had classes in high school."

"Not here, they didn't. Budget issues," she added. She put the piecrusts aside and started to pick up the basket of apples.

"Here. Let me do that," he said softly. He lifted it up onto the table for her and set it down.

"Thanks," she said huskily. "I didn't realize how heavy it was."

He smiled. "It's only heavy to shrimps like you," he said on a grin.

She laughed. "I'm not a shrimp."

"Honey, compared to me, you're a shrimp." He moved closer,

catching her by the waist. He pulled her against him and bent to brush his hard mouth against hers almost tenderly. "You taste like those apples," he whispered into her lips. "Green. Very green."

She hated herself because she couldn't manage to pull back or protest. She looked up into his pale brown eyes helplessly as he teased her mouth.

"It's a learning curve," he whispered as his lean hands framed her face. "We all start out as beginners."

While he spoke, he began to fit his lips exactly to hers, coaxing them to part, brushing and stroking until she was rigid with unexpected hunger. Her hands, still floury, pressed into his blue flannel shirt, feeling muscle and soft, cushy hair under it while she stood, breathlessly fascinated, in his arms.

She felt his tongue easing under her top lip, smoothing against the warm, moist skin with a motion that was arousing. It made her hungry. She went on tiptoe to tempt him to do it harder, but he drew back a breath and started all over again.

His own breath was coming hard and fast. She was delicious. He'd never tasted a woman with such delicacy, such tenderness. He didn't understand why he wanted it like this. Perhaps because she was so green. *First times*, he thought, *should be tender*.

She let him kiss her. It was so sweet, to feel him close like this, to feel his mouth savoring hers like a particularly delicious pastry. She smiled under his lips.

He drew back a breath. "What's funny?" he whispered.

"I feel like a nice dessert," she whispered back, her dark eyes sparkling as they met his.

He smiled, too. "You do taste delicious, little virgin," he murmured as he brushed her mouth again. He drew in a deep breath and his lean hands caught her waist and moved her, reluctantly, away.

"I'm not used to sudden stops," he said. "I've spent too much of my life enjoying women I barely knew." He searched her eyes. "I'm not adding you to the notches on my bedpost."

She flushed and then laughed. "Okay." She peered up at him. "Thanks," she said with a faint grimace. "I don't know enough to cope with...with experienced men."

"I noticed." He was thinking how easy it would be to kiss her into fascinated submission and carry her to the nearest bed. Which was why he backed up a little. A lot of women pretended innocence with a flair. But this one was the genuine article. He'd have bet his life on it. "So we'll cool it."

She nodded. "Thanks."

"I'd prefer to toss you down on the nearest bed, of course," he confessed, grinning at her scarlet flush. "You are one delicious little pastry."

"I'd give you indigestion," she teased.

"I don't think so." His face tautened. "You watch McGuire," he added. "He's been around the world a few times. Sophisticated men are devious."

"He's not like that," she said. She put some apples into a bowl and found a paring knife before she sat down in a chair at the table with the bowl in her lap. "He really likes me." She made a face. "It's worrying."

He was puzzled. She didn't act like a mercenary woman. McGuire was rich. But she wasn't talking about his wealth. She was worried that he liked her.

"You don't like him."

She looked up. "Oh no. I like him very much." She bit her lower lip and tasted Cort there. Kissing him was addictive. She didn't look at him. "It's just that what he wants goes beyond liking."

"Easy fix. Don't go out with him."

"Well," she sighed, "I already promised to go to Galveston with him this weekend."

"For the weekend?" he asked, angry and frankly jealous.

She laughed. "No, no, no. I balked, and he said it would just be a day trip. He promised."

Something inside him relaxed, just a little. "Why Galveston?"

"Seafood," she replied. She laughed. "He seems to know all the best restaurants in the country. In fact, he knows them in Manhattan as well. He offered to fly me up there in four weeks. That one's a business trip, though."

He didn't like thinking of her with McGuire. It made him irritable that he was vulnerable. He'd had so many women. He couldn't understand why he felt differently about her.

"I see," he said after a minute.

She started to explain why it was a business trip. He didn't know about her career. Perhaps it was time that he did.

"About New York," she began.

He glanced at his watch and grimaced. "Bart's meeting with some advertising person about your production sale," he said abruptly. "He wants me to help come up with some ideas."

"Why you?" she asked, surprised.

Because he owned the biggest ranch in West Texas and had production sales of his own each year. He was experienced in advertising for them. In fact, the production sale at Latigo was why he couldn't stay more than another few weeks. Odd, how uncomfortable it made him feel to think about leaving. She was getting under his skin. He didn't like being vulnerable. He never had been before. Not with a woman.

It took him a minute to realize that he hadn't answered her. He shrugged. "Back home, boss always asked for my input on ads. I dated an executive from an ad agency for a few months," he added involuntarily.

She frowned.

He could have chewed his tongue through at that slip. How would a plain cowboy, which she thought he was, have anything to do with an executive of any sort? It was hardly a common match.

"She came to the ranch about a production sale. We started

talking and found a lot in common," he improvised. Actually, he'd met her in Manhattan, on a business trip, and they'd been an item for two or three months, until the passion wore out. Passion always wore out, he'd found. Women in his life lacked staying power. They came and went. Mostly they went.

"Oh," she said, having lacked any sort of sensible reply. She didn't like the jealous feelings he engendered in her. He went around with Ida, which wounded her, and now he was talking about yet another woman. Well, he was experienced, and it showed. Probably there had been a lot of women. She felt inadequate.

"Not to worry," he said softly. "I'm not in the market for a woman who reads romance novels."

Her eyebrows arched. She wouldn't ask, she wouldn't ask…!

"You have a rose-colored view of life, honey," he said gently, and made the endearment feel like a verbal caress. "Mine is raw and blunt. They won't mix."

She sighed. She nodded. "Like oil and water."

"Pretty much." He moved closer, bent and brushed his mouth softly against hers. "I'll see you around."

He left before she could recover from the endearment, the kiss and the insinuation that he wasn't coming here alone again. It should have made her happy. Instead, it was actually painful. He didn't want to get mixed up with an innocent. Jake did. Poor Jake, for whom she had no feelings. Jake, who wanted so desperately for her to love him.

Life was messy, she thought. Which was why she liked reading—and writing—romance novels. There were very few happy endings in life. There were, in her books. She felt that a romance should be uplifting, especially at the end. Even though there were some powerful dramatic moments in between the kisses. She wondered what that wild-eyed cowboy would think if he knew how she researched her novels. It made her laugh.

★ ★ ★

Bart was curious about the taut expression on his usually carefree cousin's face when he came back from delivering the apples to Mina.

"You look glum," he observed.

"She reads romance novels and she knows less about men than I know about theoretical physics," he murmured.

Bart's eyes widened. "Please tell me you're not trying to add my best friend to your list of permissible bedmates."

"Not a chance," he said curtly. "Virgins are right off my wanted list."

Bart let out the breath he'd been holding. "Sorry," he said, when Cort glared at him. "But I'm sort of protective about her."

"Are you in love with her?" Cort shot back.

Bart's eyebrows arched. "With Mina?" he asked, aghast.

Cort scowled. "Why the shocked expression?"

Bart laughed. "She and I have known each other for years. If we were going to get romantic, it would have happened a long time ago."

"I guess so."

Bart was puzzled by his cousin's attitude about Mina. How did Cort know she was innocent? He studied the other man covertly, noting his swollen lips, and came to an interesting conclusion.

"Did she mention how her date with Jake McGuire went?" Bart fished.

Cort glared at him. "He wants her."

"That was blunt."

"Well, he does. But not like I want women," he added quietly. He sighed. "I think he's in love with her. She says she doesn't feel like that about him."

Cort didn't comment on his own curiosity about her motives for seeing the wealthy rancher. He wasn't convinced that she wasn't resisting McGuire to keep him interested. He was rich and she wasn't. He couldn't get past that. She might be innocent. In fact, he was convinced that she was. Would she barter that innocence to McGuire to land him as a husband and acquire the wealth she lacked? The thought unsettled him.

"Love begins slowly and grows," Bart said, recalling his own broken heart. "I know how that feels. I lost the only woman I ever loved to another man."

Cort turned, surprised. "You never talk about it."

"Hurts too much," Bart replied with a sad smile. He cocked his head and studied the other man. "You don't even know what love is," he said gently. "You think it's two compatible bodies in bed."

Cort sighed. "Well, that's all I know about it," he confessed. "The type of women I attract aren't homebodies. They're models or actresses or debutantes." He glanced at Bart. "I had sort of a feeling for a debutante once, but her father broke it up before it began. I don't belong to the old money crowd, you see. They marry among themselves. No outsiders."

"I'd never be able to run in that sort of social circle," Bart chuckled.

"Neither would Mina," he said surprisingly. He turned to the window and rammed his hands into his pockets. "Even at Latigo, we have business dinners and parties. I travel all over the world on business, go to conferences, meet with legislators." He sighed. "She dresses like a cowgirl. I doubt she's ever organized even a small dinner party."

"A lot of woman never have. But they can learn."

He laughed coldly. "She said that." He turned back to Bart. "She couldn't cope with Latigo, or me. So I'm not going back over there. You'll have to carry your own apples next time."

"That's decent of you," Bart said.

"It's self-protection," came the dry reply. "Maybe even survival. I grew up rich. All the people I associate with are rich. I've never been poor. We come from different worlds. It's best to keep them separate."

"I guess so."

"Mina said she'd bring you an apple pie tomorrow," he added.

Bart laughed. "I was hoping she'd do that, when I sent the apples over. Nobody makes an apple pie like Mina!"

CHAPTER EIGHT

Cort slept late the next morning. Bart was just finishing bacon and eggs and biscuits provided by the bunkhouse cook, when his cousin dragged into the kitchen and poured himself a cup of black coffee.

"Have some eggs," Bart offered.

Cort made a face. "I don't usually eat breakfast. Where did you get all that?" he added, because Bart had been eating cereal in the mornings.

"Bunkhouse has a cook for a couple of weeks," he said. "Until the production sale. We have to feed people who come to buy our bulls."

"Nice. We do the same thing at Latigo," Cort replied. "Except we have a permanent cook and a full bunkhouse."

"Considering the size of Latigo, I'm not at all surprised," Bart chuckled. "You even trot out a chuck wagon during roundup, I hear."

"We have to," Cort explained "The damned ranch is so big that it would take half a day for the hands to go all the way back to the bunkhouse for every meal. We also have extra nighthawks

who have to watch over the herds when we have calves dropping, and they have to be fed at odd hours."

"I think I'm glad my ranch isn't that big." Bart grinned.

"You still have the problems I have," came the amused reply.
"Just on a smaller scale."

Bart studied him. "You're dragging this morning. Bad night?"

He hesitated. Then he nodded.

"Combat comes back to bite us in our dreams," he said quietly.

Cort couldn't tell him that his particular dream was of Mina
Michaels in his bed. He woke squeezing the hell out of a pillow,
so hot that he wondered if he'd burned the sheets. He couldn't
get the taste of her out of his memory. He'd as much as told her
he wasn't going to see her again. Now he was wondering how
he could find an excuse to go back. She haunted him.

She was so different from the women who passed through
his life. He was used to glitter, perfume, flashy couture clothing, nights on the town riding in stretch limos with some of
the most beautiful women on Earth. He'd been on the cover of
tabloids at least once when a movie star accused him of assault.
It went to court. She was lying and Cort produced witnesses to
prove that he wasn't. Instead of his good name being ruined, hers
was, and she faced not only jail time but a million-dollar lawsuit filed on Cort's behalf. It was still going through the courts,
and he didn't feel any sympathy for the star, who apologized on
live television, in tears, pleading for forgiveness. The tears were
crocodile ones, however, as one astute newscaster mentioned
during his broadcast. Cort wished he'd never met the woman.
Bedroom skills were hardly worth the misery she'd caused him.
Not because he missed her, though. Until she made the accusa-
tion, he'd even forgotten what she looked like.

The women in his past were a colorful blur of memory. They
were as far away from ranch life as it was possible to get.

"Deep thoughts?" Bart asked, interrupting his train of
thought.

Cort looked up. "I was thinking about Stella Hayes," he said.

"Oh. The woman who accused you of assault." He chuckled. "We heard about that even up here. She was so shallow that nobody believed her. Served her right to get caught in a lie and sued to the back teeth for lying."

"She's still pleading for me to drop the lawsuit." He shrugged. "I don't need the money. I just want to make sure her reputation gets the attention it deserves, to save some other poor fool from her lies."

"It's a sad thing she did," Bart agreed. "When women really get attacked—and far too many do—they have to face ridicule because of women like Stella, who lie to get attention. We live in a mad world."

"Mad and bad."

"And 'the night is dark and full of terrors,'" Bart said on a chuckle.

That made Cort smile. "I was talking to Mina about the series. She watches it, too." He frowned slightly. "It doesn't seem quite her type of show, does it? I mean, the language and nudity and the gore..."

Bart choked on his coffee. He recovered quickly and didn't let on how amused he was at Cort's impression of Mina. If he knew what that woman had done in the past few years to research books. He almost howled at the thought of Mina being shocked by a television show. He glanced at his cousin and thought again that he'd done the right thing, keeping Mina's profession a secret. One day Cort would find out what she did, and how. It was going to be a shock.

On the other hand, Mina had no idea that Cort was worth millions or that he owned the biggest ranch in West Texas.

"She's going to Galveston with Jake McGuire," Cort murmured. "Then he's flying her to New York City, to another restaurant. Or so he says," he added darkly. "I hope she's not being taken in by him. He likes women."

"So do you," Bart reminded him. "And he isn't being seen around town with the happy divorcée."

Cort made a face. "She's really not what people think she is," he said.

"There's a lot of that going around lately," Bart replied, and averted his eyes.

"No, I'm not kidding," Cort said. "Ida isn't a scarlet woman. It's a defense mechanism. If she flaunts her scandalous reputation, men leave her alone. They're afraid they won't measure up to her expectations. She avoids relationships like the plague."

"She goes out with you," he was reminded.

Cort smiled. "We're friends, and that isn't a euphemism. I like her. I don't like most women."

"Do you like Mina?"

Cort looked worried. He shifted in his chair and refreshed his coffee from the pot sitting on the table. He sipped it before he answered. "She's an odd mixture," he said. "She's nervous around men. I can understand why she's that way. Her mother should have been in federal prison."

"A lot of us around here felt that way," he replied. "Cody tried so damned hard to get anything on her that would get Mina out of her life. He never could."

"Her father was a piece of work, too," he murmured. "He could have tried to keep in touch with his daughter. We have all sorts of ways to do that, even snail mail if it came right down to it."

"If he'd tried, Anthea would have burned any letters he sent while Mina was out of the house."

"Damn!"

"I understand that he did try to get custody of her, but Anthea made up some false charge—sort of like your starlet did—and threatened him with prison if he tried to take Mina away."

"She didn't want the child," Cort said, frowning.

"No. But she didn't want her husband to have her, either."

"I've never understood how women like that get away with so much."

"Me, neither."

Cort looked up at him. "What do you think of Mina's new hire? The full-time man. I can't remember his name."

"His name is Jerry Fender," Bart said, frowning. "McAllister and he go to the same church. He told Fender the job was available, so Fender applied."

"Does McAllister know if he's trustworthy?" Cort wondered. "Mina's over there with him alone at night," he reminded Bart.

"If Bill McAllister says he's okay, he is," Bart replied, surprised at his cousin's concern for a woman he wasn't overly fond of.

Cort sighed. "I hope so. She's…innocent," he said finally, and the way he said it was almost a caress. "That's why I don't like her going around with McGuire. He's too experienced for a young woman."

Bart burst out laughing. "Do you know what century this is? Most women Mina's age have been in at least one serious relationship, sometimes many more. Women are street-smart, and sassy, and many of them don't like men at all."

"Sad news for the future generations we won't have," Cort replied on a laugh.

"Oh no, we'll have kids," Bart assured him. "Women will keep men in cages for breeding purposes."

"Not on my ranch," Cort chuckled.

"Nor mine." He sighed. "City fellers aren't like us, though. They eat tofu and quiche and talk about stock options and the latest physical fitness craze." He sipped coffee. "You and I are throwbacks to another whole generation." He leaned forward. "We're victims of toxic masculinity!" He waved both hands in the air and made a face.

Cort burst out laughing.

Bart just smiled.

★ ★ ★

Mina was having problems. She'd never had a boyfriend. Well, except for the high school boy her mother had seduced. But now she seemed to have two. Jake McGuire wanted to take her to exotic places. Cort wanted her in his arms, but not for keeps.

Every time she remembered the feel of his hard mouth on her lips, she went weak at the knees. It was a memory that burned in her mind like a beautiful candle, lighting her up, making the world joyful.

She knew that Cort didn't have staying power. He wasn't going to settle down in Catelow, Wyoming, and work for Bart and marry her. He was a cowboy. Roaming was in his very nature. He didn't have any money. He'd never have it. He'd be poor all his life. But he'd be doing what he wanted to. He'd have a sort of freedom that most men never knew, living on the land. She couldn't afford to let herself be drawn to him too closely. Her body wanted him. That way lay disaster. She knew nothing about birth control past what she'd learned in health classes in high school. And she was far too intense for an affair. Cort could sleep with her and walk away. His sort of woman was Ida Merridan, who was as much a rounder as he was. But Mina would never get over being intimate with him. It would destroy her life.

So it was better for both of them if she stepped back and treated Cort like a distant relation. She could have fun with Jake McGuire as long as he kept it low-key. She knew he had feelings for her. It made her sad, because if they dated for a hundred years, she'd never be able to feel that way about him. She was sorry. He was a good man.

But as long as he knew she was only looking for friendship, they could have fun going places together. She enjoyed his company very much. Just as long as he didn't try to get serious, she'd be okay.

★ ★ ★

Jake picked her up early Saturday and they flew to Galveston. He apologized, but he had a business meeting early the next morning and he had to be back in time for it. She offered to postpone the trip, but he wouldn't hear of it. He just smiled. It flattered her that he put her above business.

He was courteous and the soul of respect.

He'd found a little seafood restaurant in a town on the coast. It was constructed so that boats could sail right up to the landing and come ashore to eat. Mina was fascinated with it.

"How did you find it?" she asked when they were eating delicately breaded oysters with cocktail sauce and homemade French fries. "These oysters are delicious!"

He chuckled. "A friend of mine pointed me in this direction. I love food."

She smiled at him. It didn't show, that he loved food. He was streamlined. No fat, anywhere.

He caught that searching scrutiny and grinned. "I work it all off," he said, anticipating the question. "I'm not the type to sit at a desk and let my men do the hard stuff."

She laughed. "I didn't think you were."

"How do you manage a ranch and what you do for a living, as well?" he wanted to know.

Her dark brown eyes twinkled. "I wasn't doing so good at that," she said. "Cousin Rogan insisted that I needed a full-time hire, so I got one; a guy named Jerry Fender. He came with good references. Plus, he goes to the same church that Bill McAllister and I do. Bill likes him."

He sighed. "Mina, Bill likes everybody."

"True. But he really is a decent judge of character. Besides," she added, "Fender's got this great horse of a dog and he said that if I didn't want the dog in the bunkhouse, he'd pass on the job and go hunting for one someplace else."

That caught Jake's attention. His dark eyebrows rose. "What sort of dog is it?"

"Sort of a duke's mixture," she replied. "Big and sweet and cuddly."

"Honestly," he told her, "I'd take a dog's instincts about people more seriously than another human's. They can sense dishonesty. My German shepherd, Wolf, is my best personnel sniffer." He chuckled. "He growled at a man who applied to the ranch for work. I had a quick background check run on the man, who turned out to be an escaped felon. Dogs are smart."

"A German shepherd," she said, smiling gently. "People say they're very smart."

"Smart." He finished his fries and sipped black coffee. "He's too smart. He can open doors and cabinets and once he turned on the stove."

"Goodness!"

"I try to keep him out of the kitchen." He burst out laughing. "I missed my wallet one morning when I got up. I looked in the living room and Wolf had my wallet open and my credit cards spread out on the carpet. I wondered if he planned to go shopping while I was still asleep."

She laughed, too. "What a charming dog!"

He pursed his lips. "Want to meet him? You could come to the ranch one day for lunch."

Her eyes met his. She bit her lower lip.

He slid a big hand over hers. "I know. You don't feel what I do," he said quietly. "But at least you like me, so that's something. Maybe," he added slowly, "one day, you'll feel something more."

She drew in a long breath. "That won't happen. I'm really sorry, but it's best to be honest about these things. So, if you'd rather not fly me to New York, I'll understand."

Both eyebrows arched. "Oh no," he teased, "you don't get

rid of me that easily. I'll be your second-best friend after Bart, and I'll teach you about restaurants."

She laughed. He was incorrigible. "Okay," she said.

He relaxed. "Okay." He wasn't giving up. But he knew how to do a strategic retreat. "So, how about trying their house dessert? It's a waffle with strawberries and sour cream and syrup."

"It sounds wonderful," she said, relieved that he knew how things stood. "I'd love to try it."

"You won't be sorry," he replied, and signaled to a passing waitress to take their order.

After they finished eating, they sat out on the long patio that faced the Gulf of Mexico and stared out at the waves rolling lazily to shore, whitecaps breaking on sugar sand.

"It's beautiful here," she remarked.

"I love beaches," he replied. "I collect them. So far, my favorite one is down in Cancun, on the Mexican Caribbean. It's one of the most exquisite views I've ever seen. My second favorite is in Nassau, right on the beach, where you can watch little tugboats turn big ocean liners to head them back out of port when they're ready to leave." He smiled. "I've been everywhere."

"I'm just starting to go everywhere," she remarked.

He laughed heartily. "Your favorite places, as I recall, are in some of the most dangerous jungles on earth, carrying an AK."

She grinned. "Well, if you want to learn how commandos do stuff, you ask to do stuff with them."

"Commandos, mercs, U.S. Marshals, FBI agents, cops, Texas Rangers," he mused. "And once, I believe, an actual head man of the Outfit—a euphemism for the Mafia—in New Jersey." He shook his head. "You like to live on the edge, don't you?" he added seriously.

She nodded. "I've never lived a really safe life. It warps you. But honestly, what I write needs good research. I like to see what I'm writing about, in real life."

"As I recall, you took a bullet when an insurgent came a little too close to you in one of those incursions."

"Just nicked me," she said with magnificent disdain. "Hardly even bled." She grinned, because she liked having a battle wound. She pulled up her sleeve and showed it to him. There was a scar that was indented on her upper arm, evidence of a bullet wound.

"That looks a little more serious than a flesh wound," he replied. He knew, because he had wounds of his own from the war in the Middle East.

She shrugged. "Some minor surgery, a few days in the hospital and some physical therapy. But it wasn't as bad as it looks."

He chuckled. "Pull the other one, kid," he teased. "I've got wounds of my own. I know a bad one when I see it."

She grimaced. "Well, I couldn't show weakness around the guys, could I? Who wants to be thought of as a wimp?"

He grinned at her. She really was unique.

She noticed that rapt stare, but she smiled back. Plenty of time to convince him that she meant what she said about not wanting a serious relationship.

Jake was good company and she liked him. As he loosened up and stopped staring at her as if she were the Golden Fleece, she relaxed, too.

"You text me two days before you have to be in New York," he reminded her when he left her on her doorstep. "I want to be sure I'm not tied up when you want to go."

"I'll do that," she promised. She smiled at him. "I had fun. Thanks so much."

"Oh, I had fun, too," he said, grinning. He bent and kissed her cheek. "Good night, gorgeous."

"You flatterer, you," she teased. "Good night."

He waved as he went back to the waiting limousine.

She relaxed as it drove away. If he could be just a friend, she wouldn't mind going out with him anytime he liked.

She turned to go inside and found Jerry Fender coming up the steps on the other side of the porch.

"Good evening," he said pleasantly. "Just getting home, boss lady?"

She smiled, a little uneasily. "Jake flew me to Galveston for seafood. Anything wrong?"

"Nothing at all," he replied. He smiled as his dog came galloping up on the porch with him. "My buddy and I were just taking a last turn around the place to make sure everything was the way it should be."

She felt oddly safe at the way he said that. "Thanks," she told him.

He shrugged. "I take my responsibilities seriously. I'm just grateful to have a job. So is my furry friend, here. I've put him to work helping us herd cattle."

She laughed. "Well!"

"He's a natural," he said. "Well, good night, Miss Michaels," he said, and tipped his hat courteously. "We're going to turn in."

"Good night," she called after them.

He threw up a hand. Sagebrush wagged his tail.

She'd no sooner gotten inside the house than her cell phone rang. It took her a minute to wrestle it out of her big purse.

"Hello?" she said as she fumbled it to her ear.

"So you're finally home."

She frowned. "Who is this?"

"It's Cort." There was a pause, during which her heart skipped a beat. "I just wanted to make sure you got back okay. The weather's taken a turn for the worse. Flying can be dangerous when it's blowing snow."

She flushed because she hadn't even noticed the snow. "Oh." She hesitated. "I hadn't really noticed the snow."

There was another pause. "Haven't you?" he asked, and his voice was curt the point of rudeness.

"Honestly, first Mr. Fender and now you…!"

"Mr. Fender?"

She grimaced. "He was on the porch when we drove up. He said he and his dog were just checking to make sure everything was okay."

Mr. Fender took a step up in his estimation. "It's late."

"Well, yes. We sat on a bench outside the restaurant and watched the waves for a while. Galveston is really beautiful."

"Yes, it is," he agreed. "I like to go deep sea fishing when I'm down there."

She'd always thought that was a sport for rich men, but apparently even cowboys could afford it. She sat down in her armchair. "Did you catch anything you could eat?"

He chuckled. "I caught a record-breaking swordfish and threw it back in."

"You didn't have it mounted?"

"I don't need trophies to prove I'm a man," he said simply. "But there are plenty who do."

She smiled. "My dad used to hunt before he left us. He never had deer heads mounted, either."

"Do you remember him?"

She drew in a breath. "I was only nine years old when he went away. I remember the uniform more than I remember his face. I doubt I'd recognize him if I met him on the street. Not that I want to," she added harshly. "Cousin Rogan said he was in Billings and he wanted me to talk to him. I refused."

"You don't forgive."

"Not something as harsh as what he did, leaving me at my mother's mercy," she said shortly.

"I have a hard time letting go of things, too," he replied.

"When people hurt you, it's human nature to resent them."

"It is. What did you eat in Galveston?"

She laughed. "Oysters. I love them, fried."

"Me, too. I'd rather have them raw, though, with just a little Tabasco sauce."

"I expect we'll both die of mercury poisoning if we keep it up."

He burst out laughing. "Maybe so, but what a way to go!"

She grinned. "It really is."

"I'll let you go. I just wanted to know if you got home safely," he said in a soft, husky tone.

"I got home just fine." She paused. "Thanks. For checking."

He chuckled. "No problem. Bart was worried. See you around, cowgirl."

He hung up and she felt her heart sink to her feet. Bart was worried. What an idiot she was, to think Cort cared one way or another. She got up from the chair, turned out the lights and went to bed.

Cort cursed himself roundly for that lie. Bart was already asleep. Cort had paced the floor, but his cousin had assured him that Mina was in safe hands. McGuire would take good care of her, he affirmed.

But Cort had worried anyway. He knew about airplanes. He'd been flying around in private ones for years, and he knew what could go wrong at the drop of a hat. He'd been in planes that came near to crashing. He couldn't shake off the concern, although why he'd feel it for a woman he didn't care about was disturbing. They had nothing in common except anguish from the past. She was a small-town cowgirl who didn't know any-thing about the world he lived in. She'd never fit in his circles.

So why did he care?

He wished he knew. He turned out his bedside lamp and went to bed. But he didn't sleep.

In the distance were big guns firing. Closer, there was the sharp *ping* of bullets hitting nearby. His friend called a greeting to him just as another bullet sang and the man's head exploded in a spray of blood. Cort closed his eyes and shuddered. He wondered if he would ever be free of the war he fought in, so long ago.

Mina was planting flowers. She was also working on the next book, in her head. It was how she furthered plots, by doing mundane tasks that didn't require much brainwork while her mind grappled with complicated scenarios. Some fit, some didn't. By the time she started writing at the computer, it would all resolve into a comfortable scene.

She was still astonished at how quickly her novel, *SPECTRE*, was rising on the bestseller lists. Her agent had called the day before to tell her with unbridled excitement that *SPECTRE* was climbing the *New York Times* hardcover bestseller list and had already landed in the top ten on the *Publishers Weekly* list—one much harder to hit. It was a contemporary romance, but with so much drama that even men read it. The plot followed a group of commandos who were trying to liberate the wife of a well-known billionaire from a minor bunch of terrorists looking for a quick way to finance their objectives.

Few people who saw Mina in her garden would ever connect the shy Wyoming cowgirl with the sweeping, violent and passionate drama of her novel. Not that she used her own name. She wrote under the pseudonym Willow Shane, and only a handful of people knew.

Bart was one. Mrs. Simpson was another. There were people in Catelow who had known Mina all her life who had no idea what she really did for a living. She liked it that way. If fame came—and it seemed likely that it would, now—she didn't want her precious privacy invaded. The pen name, hopefully, would assure that.

She thought about Bart's cousin and laughed inwardly as she considered how he was going to feel when he found out what she did for a living. Eventually, she was sure, Bart would tell him. Right now, Bart was enjoying himself as he kept the secret. And so was Mina. That arrogant cowboy could use a little shock in his life, she thought, considering how disparaging he'd been about her knitting and her romance novels.

Well, technically they were romance novels. But they were filled with action and suspense, and *SPECTRE* had been marketed as a suspense novel, not a category one. It had made Mina so proud when she knew that. It still gave her a massive thrill to go to signings at bookstores and see her novels on the shelves. It never got old.

She finished planting the flower seeds and moved to another manicured plot to start planting herbs.

She loved to cook. She loved to have fresh herbs in what she cooked. So it was much better to grow her own than to buy them at the store and have no idea how fresh they actually were.

"Ma'am, I can do that for you, if you'd like," Fender said from behind her.

She half turned, her blue-jeaned knees in the grass that surrounded the fresh dirt. She laughed. "Thanks, but I love planting things."

"You aren't even wearing gloves," he chided.

"Oh, I like feeling the earth between my fingers," she said with a warm smile. "It gives me a sort of connection to the things I plant. I like to think it makes them grow better," she added on a laugh.

"Okay. I just came to ask you about those cattle you're planning to sell at the production sale," he replied. "Do we need to launder them and pretty them up for it?"

She burst out laughing, visions of calves dressed in frilly skirts filling her head. "Well, we could launder them, I guess," she said when she stopped laughing. "But no frilly dresses or short pants. Okay?"

He chuckled. "Okay."

"It's just as well that we're doing it soon," she added. "I'm going to be tied up in New York for a few days next month."

"New York?" he added.

She nodded. "Yes. I have a business meeting there. Mr. Mc-Guire is going to fly me up in his plane."

"Not my business, but is it something about the ranch?" he asked. "I mean, you aren't going to sell it or anything…?"

She smiled. "Of course not! It's my legacy. No, it's other business altogether. You won't lose your job anytime soon. I promise."

He let out a breath. "Okay. Thanks."

"Meanwhile, how about getting the part-timers on mucking out the stable? I know, they'd rather be shot. But somebody has to do it, and I don't have time."

"Not a problem, ma'am," he said, and tipped his hat. "I'll do it right now."

"Thanks," she said. She frowned. "Where's your fuzzy shadow?" she asked.

"Sagebrush is helping move one lot of steers into new pasture. He's handy as a cattle dog." He shook his head. "He loves to herd me, but I never realized how good he'd be with animals until I watched him work. Maybe he's part sheepdog," he chuckled.

"More like part border collie," she teased.

"Could be. I'll get back to work."

She just nodded and went back to her chore.

CHAPTER NINE

Cort had been mooning around the ranch for days. Bart couldn't figure out what was the matter with him. He wasn't eating the way he had when he first arrived, and he was restless. He went out with Ida a time or two, but he wasn't gone long even then.

"Is there something wrong?" Bart asked finally, and his concern showed.

Cort took a deep breath. "Your best friend is what's wrong."

Bart's eyebrows arched. "Did you two have a fight or something?"

Cort shook his head. "Nothing like that. She bothers me, that's all."

"Bothers you how?"

"She was riding a fence line all alone. She doesn't carry a gun and some animals could be on her so quickly that she wouldn't have time to pull out a cell phone to call for help."

Bart hid a smile. "Her ranch hands watch out for her."

"Not always," came the curt reply. "We had a wolf attack a calf, and then a cow giving birth, remember?"

"The wolf was shot, remember?" Bart replied. "I had to report that to the appropriate state agency, by the way, and they came out and took genetic samples from the carcass. Gray wolves are off the endangered list, but the state still wants to maintain a standard of breeding pairs."

"Any idea who shot that wolf?" Cort asked.

Bart shook his head. "I asked all my hands. Nobody, not even the part-timers, knew anything about it. I had Mina ask her cowboys. Same answer."

"Curious."

"Very."

"Just as well the wolf's gone, though. They can be dangerous," Cort said.

Bart just smiled. "People can, too. I like wolves. I've never had even one livestock attack until this calf was brought down. Wolves mostly prey on deer and elk and antelope. If we ever got an aggressive wolf, I'd call in the state wildlife people to have them trap it. I'd hate to kill something so majestic, even though I love my cattle."

"We don't have gray wolves on my ranch," Cort said. He grimaced. "But I've heard that the ones you get in Wyoming can weigh over 150 pounds, and that they can sprint up to thirty-five miles an hour. A lone woman couldn't outrun one, even on horseback." Cort grimaced. "Where there's one wolf, there are usually others. They run in packs, don't they?"

"Mostly, yes. The authorities still warn people to stay away from them in state parks, even where they're protected," Bart agreed. "A wild animal is called that because it's wild. Any of them will turn on a human for the right reason, and they're not predictable."

Cort leaned back in his chair. "Mina doesn't even carry a gun with her, I noticed."

"She doesn't like guns," Bart volunteered.

"Odd attitude, for a rancher."

"She was more or less forced into ranching because she had

to have a place to live and she didn't want to give up her legacy. That's not what she plans to do with her life."

"What does she plan to do?" Cort asked. "Spend her time knitting and reading romance novels?"

That attitude made Bart want to throw something at him. But it was Mina's secret, not his.

"Cooking and homemaking," Cort muttered. "Who the hell does that anymore? I've never dated a woman who wanted to spend any time in a kitchen."

"The women you date wouldn't know what a kitchen was," Bart teased. "They're more fit for bedrooms."

Cort chuckled. "I guess so. I've had my fill of them, though. After a while, they all taste alike, feel alike, sound alike." He sighed. "I guess I'm jaded."

"Too much success too soon in life," Bart said philosophically.

"You're probably right," Cort admitted. "I grew up rich. My dad taught me that women were a permissible pleasure and I never forgot it. He went through them like a knife through butter, even while our mother was still alive, from what my older brothers said. He went wild after he found our stepmother in bed with his best friend. He said modern women had no morals, no sense of justice, and they only had one use. He taught us what it was."

"That's a shame," Bart said. "There are some nice women in the world."

"Like your friend," he chided.

"She's very nice," Bart replied. "She isn't sophisticated or rich or spoiled. She's just like the girl next door."

"Deliver me from that sort," Cort chuckled. "I have no wish to be herded into marriage because a woman got careless in bed with me."

"Practical solution is to carry protection with you."

He shrugged. "I used to. But these days the majority of women are on the pill or the shot or whatever the hell they use these days. I never met a single one who wasn't a fanatic about birth control. They all had careers in mind, even the models."

"That was to your advantage."

"It was. No worries about unexpected surprises," he returned. He glanced at Bart. "You really are a Neanderthal, you know."

Bart laughed. "I guess so. I'd never fit in those exalted circles you swim in. And honestly, Cort, I wouldn't want to. I like small-town life. You don't. We're worlds apart."

"I'd still die for you, cousin," Cort said gently.

Bart smiled. "I'd die for you, too."

"So much for philosophy. How about a beer and a ball game?"

"Done!"

Bart and Cort were up very early the day of the production sale. So was Mina, nicely dressed in slacks and boots and a pearly gray sweater with buttons that ran from below her waist up to her throat. They were all buttoned and Cort kept getting uncomfortable urges to unbutton them. She had a nice figure and pert, firm little breasts that made him hungry. It bothered him that he was attracted to her. She was completely the wrong sort of woman for him, and he knew it, but he seemed to have no willpower at all. He couldn't get the taste of her out of his mind. And always, there was the threat of Jake McGuire. The man wasn't as rich as Cort, but Mina wouldn't know that.

He noticed that she was shy with the out-of-town buyers. Bart was staying close to her, but as more people came in for the sale, she found herself deserted, and with a cattleman she didn't know who had a roaming eye and, quite suddenly, a roaming hand as he slid his arm around her shoulders.

Mina had been trying to move away from the visiting cattleman in a nice way, without starting trouble. The man was big and overpowering, like Henry had been. He had the same coloring. She felt isolated and frightened. She should say something about that roaming hand. She already would have, to any other man. This one scared her. Even so, she was girding herself for a confrontation when help came from an unexpected quarter.

Cort noticed her hunted expression and the cattleman's unwanted familiarity, and he saw red. He walked up to the cattleman and removed the offending arm before Mina got her mouth open.

"We're selling cattle. Not women," Cort said. He smiled. But it wasn't a nice smile, and his pale brown eyes had sparks in them.

The man glared at him, "Isn't the young lady the one who should be speaking to me if I offended her?" he asked haughtily, his eyes on Cort's unimpressive cowboy duds.

Cort cocked his head. His chin lifted. The smile was replaced by a cold glare and glittering eyes. This time, the visiting cattleman got the message and moved off with a huffy sound. He went toward his car instead of the cattle.

"We've lost a sale," Mina said softly. But she wasn't complaining. She looked up at Cort with a smile. "Thanks. I was about to protest, but you beat me to it." She sighed. "He was a pain. But he might have bought one of our bulls."

Cort glanced toward the man's automobile. "Unlikely. He's driving a three-year-old Lincoln with a bald tire," he said. "He was wearing a suit off the sale rack at a men's store and boots he probably got from Walmart. He'd be lucky to afford a steak, much less prime beef like you're selling here."

She was surprised at the way he sized up the other man. She hadn't noticed those things. Well, she still didn't know much about fancy clothes or fancy cars.

"How did you know how old the car was?" she asked.

He chuckled. "Boss's foreman drives one just like it," he said.

"Oh!" She laughed. "Well, thanks for saving me."

"I beat you to it by a few seconds," he said easily, and he smiled down at her. "I could see the storm clouds gathering on your face."

She wrapped her arms around her. "I'm not sure about that,"

she confessed. "He looked a lot like Henry," she added, alluding to her mother's old boyfriend. "Same build, same coloring... I guess I got inhibited."

He felt protective. It wasn't a feeling he associated with women at all. Not the women in his life, at least.

"The past doesn't really die. Even when the main character in a movie advises the heroine to let it," he added facetiously.

Mina laughed. "*Star Wars*," she said at once.

He nodded. "I've seen both of the new ones. I'm looking forward to the next."

"So am I," she said.

"We seem to share a common taste for medieval television series and science fiction movies," he noted.

She grinned. "I love science fiction. I'm rather fond of war movies, too."

"War movies." He was surprised.

"But documentaries on the great battles are my favorites," she sighed. "I love anything on Alexander the Great and Hannibal."

He shook his head. "Knitting, romance novels and war. An odd combination of hobbies," he noted with a smile.

He didn't know the half of it. Her memory was full of first-person accounts of some of the bloodiest conflicts in modern knowledge, from men who fought them. And not only soldiers. Her collection of battles included those of men and women from various law enforcement careers.

"It fascinates me, the innovations men have found to win battles."

He nodded. "Me, too."

She recalled that he was a combat veteran with some horrible memories. "Sorry," she said belatedly. "I don't imagine it's a pleasant subject to you."

He cocked his head. "I don't like remembering the Middle East," he returned. "But I'm rather partial to military history."

She smiled. "So am I."

Bart had noticed the cattleman leaving in a hurry. He finished talking to a potential buyer and came to see what had happened.

"One of the customers got out of line with Mina," Cort said quietly. "I sent him on his way."

"Good for you," Bart replied. "That was Myron Settles," he added. "He's a second-rate buyer for a feedlot over in Oklahoma. Nobody likes him. Got fresh with Ned Taylor's wife, and Ned laid him out on the ground, over at the stockyards in Billings." He chuckled. "It was a sensation. Sadly, it doesn't seem to have made a lasting impression on him," he added, the smile fading. "Sorry about that, Mina."

"It's okay. We can't pick and choose buyers," she added.

"We'd better circulate. But if you have any more issues…" Bart began.

"I can handle most of them," she said with a shy glance at Cort. "This one looked a little too much like Henry. Thanks," she added, her voice soft as she spoke to Cort. She flushed and turned away before he could answer.

"Insolent polecat," Cort muttered after she left, looking toward the highway where the offending buyer had vanished. "He'd have to pay a woman to go to bed with him in the first place. I should have decked him. He frightened Mina."

Bart had to hide a smile. It amused him to see his worldly cousin defending the very woman he'd complained about for days on end when he'd first come to Catelow.

"She likes military history," Cort mused. "And science fiction movies. She's a conundrum."

"Lots of women like those things," Bart replied.

"Not in my world, they don't," Cort told him. He shook his head. "I don't think half the women I've dated would even know who Alexander was."

"That would be a good guess."

"Know any of these other buyers well?" Cort added, glancing around to make sure Mina wasn't getting hassled.

"Not all of them," Bart said.

"I'll stroll around and keep an eye on your friend over there. Just in case," Cort said, and sauntered away, with his hands in his jean pockets.

Bart just grinned to himself and went to speak to another buyer.

They sold all their combined bull calves. Some of them would be used for breeding. Others would be sent to a feedlot, under contract from a buyer who'd shown up late. Mina was all too aware of Cort's scrutiny, and grateful for it. He was close by when she spoke to prospective buyers, courteous and friendly, but watchful.

After the barbecue had been eaten, and the guests were filing out, she paused to thank him.

"I don't usually need looking after," she said, smiling, "but thanks for keeping an eye on me. It's hard being a woman rancher sometimes."

"It's hard being a male cowboy sometimes," he teased. "I get my share of propositions and 'feely' women."

Her lips fell apart. "Really?" she asked, and seemed genuinely curious.

He chuckled. "You aren't worldly, are you?" he asked softly.

A little color heightened her cheekbones. She shrugged self-consciously. "I grew up in Catelow. We've got, what, a thousand souls living here? It's like growing up in a goldfish bowl." She sighed. "Everybody knew my mother and what she was. But a few people believed the lies she told about me. It's been hard, from time to time, living down those lies."

"My dad's pretty much the same way," he said quietly. "He was running around on my mother when she was dying." His face hardened. "He's never really stayed with one woman for long."

"How old were you when your mother died?" she asked gently.

"I was five," he said. "Not really old enough to understand that death was permanent. They said Mom went to live with the angels, and I thought that meant she was coming back to visit."

She got a sad picture of his life. He hadn't really known his mother, but he'd ended up with a stepmother that apparently none of the sons liked, and a father who cheated even on her. "You haven't had it much better than I did," she said absently.

He almost said that wealth made up for some of it, but that would be a mistake. He liked having her think he was just a cowboy. She was the first woman who'd ever liked the man instead of the wallet.

She wasn't pretty, but there was a quality about her that drew him, like a moth to a flame. Ida was beautiful and fun and exciting. Mina was quiet and shy, but with hidden depths. He wanted to know what those depths were. She intrigued him.

"Since you have such a bad opinion of cowboys, I guess you wouldn't want to date one of us," he mused, watching the flush on her cheeks grow.

She drew in a breath. "You asking me out?" she said. It was pure bravado. She was going to cringe into a corner later.

He chuckled. "Yeah."

Her eyes widened. She looked up at him with absolute wonder. "Really?"

"Why are you so surprised?"

"Well, I'm not pretty," she said, stammering. "I'm not rich. I smell like cow manure a lot of the time..."

He laughed out loud. "You're describing me, too, except the pretty part," he returned.

She grinned. "In that case, yes. I'd go out with you."

His heart jumped. He didn't pause to consider the implications of that reaction. "Great. What do you want to do?"

"There's not a lot to do in Catelow," she began.

"There is in Lander," he mused. "There's a casino. It's on the Wind River Indian Reservation. Plenty to see and do there, including tours of the area round it. Arts and crafts. Walking trails…"

"It sounds lovely," she said. "I've never been inside a casino in my life. Although I'd really love to see the reservation."

"I read up on it," he said. And he had, during a business event nearby. "It's home to the Eastern Shoshone and Northern Arapaho tribes. Lots of history there."

"I suppose it's too early for any of the pow wows," she said wistfully.

"Afraid so. They come later in the year."

"When?" she asked huskily.

"Well, tomorrow's Easter," he began.

She nodded. "I go to church on Easter."

He didn't, but he wasn't going to make an issue of it. "How about next Saturday?" he asked. He hesitated and his face tautened. "If you don't have anything going with Jake McGuire that day."

"I don't," she said quickly. It was much later that Jake was flying her to New York, but she wasn't mentioning that. It was flattering to have Cort pay her any attention at all, especially since it was common knowledge that he was taking Ida Merridan around. "Ida won't mind…?" she blurted out.

He chuckled. "We're friends. Just friends. So. Next Saturday?"

She grinned. "Okay."

"I'll pick you up about nine in the morning and we'll make a day of it. How's that?"

She just nodded, her face almost glowing with delight. He couldn't take his eyes off her. No woman had ever looked at him in that particular way. It made him glow inside. He smiled and couldn't stop.

"Okay, then. It's a date."

★ ★ ★

"Well, you are beaming," Bart teased as she was getting ready to drive home.

"Your cousin is taking me over to the Wind River Reservation next Saturday," she said.

He frowned. "Mina, I don't want to interfere. But Cort, well, he's something of a rounder."

"I know," she said gently. She made an awkward gesture with her shoulder. "I know he is. But it's been so long since well, I've never had a real date."

"You went out with Jake McGuire," he reminded her with a smile. "Twice, in fact."

"Yes, but I don't... I'm not...he isn't..." She scrambled for words.

"But you aren't attracted to Jake, and you are to Cort," he translated.

She went scarlet, aware that Cort was glancing in their direction and smiling at her. She was visibly disconcerted.

"Just take it easy, okay?" he asked, and he smiled. "He's a good man. But he likes woman a tad too much."

She laughed. "I like him a lot. But I'm not blind."

He laughed, too, but without humor. He had to hide how worried he really was. Cort was dangerous to a green girl, and that's what Mina was. Well, if worse came to worst, at least he'd be there to pick up the pieces.

Mina went to church the next morning and sat next to Bill McAllister and her new full-time hire, Jerry Fender. They stood talking to the minister when she walked out, but they left him to join her as she went to her car.

"Bart says you're going to that casino with his cousin next Saturday," Bill began.

She flushed and glared at both of them. "I'm twenty-four years old. I've only ever really dated one man up until now. Cort isn't likely to put me out on the side of the road with a note in my mouth and leave me there."

Fender sighed. "It's your life, boss lady," he said gently. "But the man has a bad reputation locally. Sometimes people who get notorious like that can give you a bad one just by being seen with them."

"I don't believe you two," she said, exasperated.

"We worry," Bill said gently.

Fender just nodded.

She glowered. But after a minute, when she realized how genuinely concerned they were, she backed down.

"I'm not going into any dark rooms with him alone," she said in a stage whisper. "And I won't have a single drink in the bar. We're going to tour the reservation, not participate in any orgies."

They laughed. It was outrageous, the way she said it.

She grinned at them. "But thanks for the concern," she added, and meant it. "You guys are pretty cool."

They thanked her, tipped their hats and went off to Fender's truck, where his big dog, Sagebrush, was occupying the passenger seat. They spoke for a minute or two before Bill went to his own car. By the time Mina got into her little car, they were both long gone.

She debated for the rest of the week about her decision to go out with Cort. Yes, he was a rounder. Yes, he was dating a notorious local woman. Yes, it might damage her reputation to be seen with him.

But he'd been tender with her. Protective of her. She remembered helplessly that hard, beautiful mouth pressed so hungrily to her lips. She tingled all over at just the memory. She'd had so little joy in her life, outside her career. Was it too much to ask to spend an innocent evening with a man to whom she was violently attracted?

Bart was concerned. So were her part-time foreman and her newest hire. It made her feel good that they cared so much for her well-being. But in the end, it was up to her to make decisions that affected her life. And she'd rather have died than refused to go out with Cort.

The one burning issue she had at the moment was what to wear. She had a few nice dresses, a pretty pantsuit, some dress slacks and mix-and-match blouses that were trendy. What did a woman wear to a casino, an evening gown?

Then she remembered the one concert she'd gone to in New York with one of her editors. People had dressed in everything from velvet to denim. It seemed to be a matter of personal taste. So she picked out a long denim skirt that swirled around her ankles and paired it with a pretty blue-and-white cotton button-up blouse with pointed collars. She left her hair long, brushing it until it shone. She put in turquoise stud earrings and wore a turquoise bracelet that her grandmother had given her, so long ago. She looked in the mirror and smiled. Well, she was no great beauty, but she didn't look too bad, she thought.

While she was studying herself, there was a hard rap at the front door.

Her heart went wild as she almost ran to open it. And there he was, wearing denim jeans that outlined his long powerful legs, and a blue shirt that was almost the twin of her own. She caught her breath.

So did he. Then he laughed. "Well, people can't say that we don't match," he teased.

"No, they can't."

"Got everything you need?" he asked.

She patted her fanny pack. "Right here." She made a face. "I know they're out of style. I don't care. I got this one in Mexico years ago. It's soft leather and I love it. I hate purses," she added. "They just get in the way and you stuff things you don't even need in them."

He grinned. "That's why blue jeans have pockets," he re-marked, jingling his car keys and change.

She laughed.

"We'll have to go in Bart's best truck," he warned her. He'd thought about renting a limousine with a driver, but he didn't really want to give himself away so soon. He was enjoying being seen as just another cowboy. It was refreshing.

"I don't mind trucks," she said. "I ride around with Bill in his a lot. It's got springs sticking out of the seats and a dash that was broken in two when he wrecked it and a crack in the wind-shield. It still runs," she added, laughing.

What an attitude. Nothing seemed to faze her. He was more enchanted by the minute. She didn't know who he was, or what he had, and she was as honest a person as he'd ever met. She didn't mind beat-up trucks. What a change from women who complained that the gifts he gave them weren't enough, when he gave diamonds and furs and gold. If he was jaded, he had good reasons for being that way.

He drove well, she noticed. Not too fast, or too slow, and he kept his eyes on the road. Not that there was much traffic. There was still a little snow on the roads, and he was cautious. But it was daylight, and the only patches of it were in areas shaded by trees overhanging the road.

"You and Bart sold all your young bulls," he remarked with a smile. "Quite a feat."

"I know! We're both still reeling from it."

"You got good prices for them as well."

"It's sad, why," she murmured, her eyes on his strong, lean hands on the steering wheel.

"Sad?"

"Well, all the flooding in nearby states where cattle died by the thousands," she remarked. "Some of the people who bought our bulls came from there. A lot of places are still flooded."

"I know. They say that only thirty percent of the corn crop

is being planted this year." He glanced at her. "Food prices will go through the roof."

"Yes. And a lot of that corn was destined for fuel," she added. "How will they decide between cattle feed and gas?"

"It's going to be a long year for a lot of livestock producers and farmers," he predicted.

"I know. The weather is crazy."

"You said you'd never been in a casino. Didn't McGuire take you to one?"

She laughed. "No. We just went to restaurants. He really does know how to find the best food in the world."

"And you look like you never eat," he remarked, glancing at her trim figure.

She sighed. "I do eat, but I have to eat carefully. I tend to gain weight around Easter."

He frowned. "Why?"

She turned her head toward him. "Easter eggs? Chocolate Easter eggs? Chocolate bunnies?"

"Oh!" He burst out laughing. "I get it."

"Don't you like chocolate?"

He shook his head. "It's one of my triggers."

"Excuse me?"

"I get migraine headaches," he said. "Doctors say there's always more than one thing that sets them off, but chocolate and nuts and red wine will do it to me in a heartbeat. I avoid all three. And I love damned red wine," he added on a sigh.

"I get headaches, but not those." She winced. "My grandmother used to get them. She went to an herbalist who gave her valerian root for it."

"I tried the herbal methods. They didn't work."

"There are preventatives now, aren't there?"

He smiled sadly. "Yes, but I'm allergic to the oldest type, and I want to see some more tests on the new ones before I'll take them."

"You're very cautious."

"My grandmother died of a stroke," he said. "I'm cautious because migraines predispose you to strokes." He glanced at her obvious concern. "Not at my age," he said, and smiled at her blush. "But thanks for the concern."

"They can do all sorts of DNA tests now, to see what sort of ailments run in your genetic makeup. I've thought of doing one," she added. "I don't know anything about my father's health or about his family at all."

"Your cousin said you should talk to him when he was in Billings, didn't he?" he asked, because Rogan had told Bart, who told Cort.

She didn't wonder how he knew that. He was right, and the memory still bothered her. She turned her eyes to the passing landscape. "My father tossed me headfirst into hell and ran like a scalded dog. I don't want to talk to him."

Impulsively, his hand reached for hers and linked into it, comforting and strong. "Let the past die," he said in a mock *Star Wars* tone.

She burst out laughing, although she curled her fingers into his trustingly and felt her whole body glow. "Okay," she said. "But if you pull out a lightsaber, I'm jumping out the window."

"No chance of that," he said. He might have made a vulgar joke about the lightsaber with an experienced woman. But not with this one, who was like a daisy in a meadow, pretty and sweet and removed from the glitz and glitter of his world. He smiled at her and felt her small hand jump in his big one. He was going in headfirst, and he didn't care. It was addictive. He wasn't going to think past today.

Mina, beside him, was thinking the same thing. She'd worry about whether or not she'd made a good decision later. Despite the concern of her friends, she was happier than she'd been in her life right now, riding down the highway in a pickup truck with a man so handsome that her whole body felt as if it were glowing from the inside. He'd wanted to take her out, when he could attract women as beautiful as Ida Merridan. She still couldn't quite believe it.

"You said you've never been to a casino before," he said.

She laughed. "I haven't. Actually, I don't drive very much. And especially not in snow. I tend to land in ditches."

He chuckled. "I may have the same issue," he murmured. "I can drive on muddy roads, though, so maybe it's not so different."

"That's what they say."

"I didn't realize it would take so long to get here," he said when thirty minutes had passed and they were still a half hour away from the reservation. "We'll be late getting home."

"I'm not afraid of the dark," she teased.

"Oh yeah? But 'the night is dark and full of terrors,'" he intoned.

She made a face at him. "Only another month until the last season of that wonderful show." She sighed. "I guess it will be like a Shakespeare play. Everybody will die at the end."

"Maybe so. But it's been a great series to watch."

"Yes, it has." Her fingers curled closer into his.

His heart jumped. He smiled. No date he'd ever been on had been this much fun, and they were barely starting.

CHAPTER TEN

The Wind River Reservation was huge. There were plenty of tourists here, even in mid-March with snow still lingering on the sides of the roads. The hotel and casino drew people from all over this part of Wyoming, including tourists coming out of Yellowstone National Park.

Mina was fascinated with the crafts she saw. She started to buy a sterling necklace with a wolf's head, only to have Cort lift it gently from her fingers and pay for it himself.

She tried to protest but he took the necklace from its packaging, unhooked the catch and draped it around her neck. The pretty wolf's head, small but perfect, fit in the hollow of her throat. His hands lingered on her shoulders as he studied her, without smiling.

"You like wolves," he said quietly.

"Yes. There's a reason."

"Because of that television series we both watch, and you like the family from the north?"

She shook her head.

"Tell me."

She looked around uncomfortably.

He chuckled and caught her fingers in his. "I'll find a more private place."

He led her back to the casino and lifted her onto a high bar stool. He gave the bar man the order.

"Piña coladas?" she asked. "But listen, I've never had hard liquor…"

"I'm here to protect you," he said gently. "And one drink isn't going to affect you. Trust me."

"Didn't that snake in the *Jungle Book* movie say that?" she asked suspiciously, but with a smile.

He leaned toward her. "I'm much more dangerous than any snake," he whispered. He grinned. "But just for tonight, I'll make an exception and behave myself."

She grinned back. "Okay!" She fingered the cold silver of the necklace. "Thank you. For this. You shouldn't have."

He shrugged it off. "I like having something I gave you lying against your skin," he said, his voice deep and soft as velvet.

She flushed. No man had ever talked to her that way.

Their drinks came. She was surprised at the size of them. She looked at Cort worriedly.

"It's mostly pineapple juice and coconut milk. A little rum," he added with a smile. "Nothing to be concerned about. They don't put a lot of rum in them."

"Well…okay."

She sipped it and made a face. The tang of the liquor was uncomfortable, and she wondered if it was just that she wasn't used to liquor. It seemed very strong. But she took another sip, and another, and soon it didn't bother her at all.

Cort moved them to a table and they ordered shrimp cocktail and steaks and salad. While they waited for the order, Cort made slow circles around the back of one of her hands while he stared into her eyes.

"Why wolves?" he asked abruptly.

"My grandfather had Shoshone blood," she said. "He taught

me about totem animals. He said that mine was a wolf. That I'd always be protected by them if I ever chanced upon one."

"And you did?"

She nodded. "It was just before my mother and her boyfriend went driving and died in the wreck. Henry had made another really serious pass at me and I'd run into the woods to hide from him. I always seemed to be hiding," she added wearily, aware of the anger in his taut face. "I didn't mean to go so deep. There are rattlesnakes and bears and other predators, but I was heartsick and so afraid." She swallowed. "I walked into a clearing and there was this huge, and I mean huge, silver wolf. He was bigger than a Saint Bernard. I know he was well over a hundred pounds, maybe a hundred and fifty. I'd never seen such a large wolf. He didn't make a move toward me. He just stood there, looking at me."

"What did you do?" he prodded.

"I was afraid to run. If you show fear to most predators, they tend to attack. And a wolf can sprint to about thirty-five miles an hour. There was no way I could have outrun him. So I stood my ground, waiting to die."

She paused to take a sip of the drink. "He came right up to me, very slowly, as if he knew how frightened I was. Goodness, he was huge! His eyes were almost on a level with mine. He looked right into my eyes, as if he could see into my very soul. I waited with my heart beating me to death, to see if he was going to eat me. And then…" She swallowed hard, and looked around to make sure nobody was close enough to hear her. She leaned toward him. "Then he vanished. Like fog. Like smoke. He was there, and as real as you are. And then he was just…gone." She drew in a breath. "It shook me up. I had no idea what I'd seen, if I'd been hallucinating, if it was real. Or if I was losing my mind," she added on a faint laugh.

"Your totem animal," he mused quietly, but he wasn't making fun of her.

"I remembered, afterward, what my grandfather had told me. He said that a totem animal was a protection and a warning. The next day, Henry ran his car into a tree and killed himself and my mother."

He whistled softly. "That's heavy."

She nodded.

"Have you ever seen him again?"

"No." She made a face. "When we found the calves that had been attacked, the live one and the dead one, I was afraid that it was a wolf and that it would have to be hunted. I knew Bart would trap it. But we have other neighbors who aren't that charitable. And sure enough, somebody shot the old wolf."

He nodded. "You understand how it is with ranchers, though," he said softly. "Times are hard. Ranchers and farmers are going bust all over the country. You can stand a calf now and then, but it gets expensive."

"And you can't let wolves feed on your livestock. I know."

"Besides that, the old wolf would have died anyway, from that long, jagged wound that ran the length of his belly. It was infected."

"I guess the rifle shot was a mercy," she conceded.

"We don't have wolves," he mused. "But we have something worse. Rustlers."

"We've had some of those around Catelow, too," she said. She laughed. "Most recently, a security guy who works for Ren Colter nabbed a couple of them with a transfer truck. They said the rustlers were babbling their heads off to law enforcement the minute they arrived and even asked to be rushed to jail. Apparently J. C. Calhoun is as mean as gossip says he is. Not so mean now, of course. He has a wife and a daughter and a brand-new son."

He chuckled. "Good for him." The smile faded. "I hate rustlers."

"Yes, Bart told me about a run-in you had with some," she

replied, and her eyes twinkled. "I think you and J.C. would get along."

He chuckled. "Do you, now?" he teased.

The waitress arrived with their food, and they ate in a pleasant silence.

"This is good beef," she remarked.

"Not bad," he agreed.

She finished her piña colada with something like surprise. She hadn't expected the glass to be empty so soon. It was a huge glass.

"Want another?" he asked.

"I'd better not," she replied. She was feeling pretty good already. Unusually good. She sighed and smiled at him.

He raised an eyebrow. He remembered that she didn't drink at all. One piña colada shouldn't disinhibit her much, though. She was probably just relaxed.

But he ordered another. It had been a long week. He'd been helping Bart's cowboys with new fencing and it was harder work than he was used to. His muscles were aching.

"I never drink to excess," he said gently when he noticed her reticence. He knew how she must feel about alcoholics, having been victimized by one for so long. "If you eat while you're drinking, it lessens the impact. Besides," he added, stretching and wincing, "I'm beginning to think of it as pain relief. I've been helping the guys dig postholes."

"Say no more. I've helped with that on my place. I had liniment," she added, "but nobody to put it on for me. So it was aspirin and a heating pad."

"I hate the smell of liniment," he returned, making a face. His drink arrived. He lifted it in a toast. "This smells much better," he added on a chuckle.

She grinned at him. She felt lighter than air, as if she could fly. She had strange hungers as well. She looked at Cort and wondered what he looked like under his shirt. She felt like taking off her own shirt and smoothing her body against his. Heavens, she was losing her mind!

She flushed and almost overturned her glass.

"Oh, you're empty. Want another one?" the waitress asked, and took her silence for assent. "Be right back."

"I really shouldn't," she told Cort.

"Food lessens the impact," he repeated, grinning. "Live dangerously."

"I've been doing that a lot," she mused.

He laughed. How, he was wondering, by choosing a new knitting pattern or doing a new recipe in the kitchen? But he didn't say it. He was enjoying her company too much.

She finished her drink along with a delicious slice of cheesecake. She'd noticed that Cort was having one as well. It was a dessert she liked.

They went into the casino afterward and she played one of the slot machines, at least until she started feeling dizzy. She dropped to the floor suddenly just after she'd started a new round.

Cort was concerned. He propped her against his knee. "What's wrong?" he asked worriedly.

"Too many of those coconut thingies, I think," she said, embarrassed that her voice was slurred. "You're all blurry," she added, trying to get his face to focus.

"Oh boy," he said to himself. He motioned to one of the security people. "Can you stay with her for just a minute? I'm going to need to get a room so that she can lie down for a few minutes."

"Of course," the man replied.

She was floating. She felt lighter than air. She opened her eyes and Cort was sitting beside her on the biggest bed she'd ever been in.

"Did I pass out?" she asked. Her words were still slurred.

"Abundantly." He brushed back her hair. "Are you all right?"

"I think so. I'm not sure I ever want to have rum again as long as I live, though."

"It was my fault," he said. "I'd forgotten that you aren't used to alcohol."

"I hated it. Henry was always drunk. Always trying to take my clothes off." She stretched, her dark eyes on Cort's face. "I'd let you take my clothes off, though," she said, smiling a little hazily. "Gosh, you're so handsome. I never thought a man who looked like you would ever want to take out somebody as homely as me!"

"You're not homely," he said, scowling. "You have a pretty face." He looked down. "And beautiful little breasts. I get hungry just looking at them through fabric."

"You do?"

He was shocked that he'd said such a thing. He shouldn't have had so much alcohol, either. It had gone to his head. She was going to his head.

"I thought men liked women with big breas…breats…breasts," she said, getting it right on the third try.

"I like small ones," he replied. He moved onto the bed next to her. His lean hand went to the buttons on her blouse. "Don't let me do this."

She laid back with her arms beside her head. "Okay," she agreed, smiling dizzily.

"That's not helping."

She moved lazily. "What do you want me to do?" she asked.

"I want you to stop me."

She blinked as he got the blouse open and started on the front hook that held her lacy little brassiere together. "Stop you from doing what?"

"This," he said, pulling the edges away. He caught his breath. She was beautiful. Her skin was silky, glowing, perfect. Firm little breasts with hard pink nipples. It was as if he'd never seen a woman before.

"I'm too little," she began.

"Oh, baby, you're not too little," he whispered, bending toward her. "You're just right…!"

His mouth settled right over her breast. And while his tongue worked on the nipple, he suckled her suddenly. She came right off the bed with a husky little cry and caught his head. But she was pulling, not pushing.

"Oh my gosh…!" she cried out, gasping.

She made it all new for him. He was as inebriated as she was, out of control and having the time of his life. He was sixteen again, with his first woman. That was how it felt.

"You taste like candy," he murmured against her soft skin.

His big, lean hands smoothed up her sides, easing her out of the blouse and bra. They felt wonderful on her skin.

"It's…not like it is in books," she managed unsteadily.

"Isn't it?" he whispered as he moved to the other breast. "How so?"

She shivered. "I didn't know it would feel…like this," she whispered brokenly.

"And we've barely started."

She would have said something else but his mouth moved up to cover hers softly, slowly, hungrily, and while he kissed her, he unsnapped his shirt. Seconds later, she felt his bare chest against her bare breasts. She moaned so hungrily that whatever effort he might have made to slow things down went up in smoke.

He had her out of her clothing with an ease that should have set up red flags in her mind, except that he kept her at fever pitch the whole time. His mouth was all over her, exploring her, tempting her, teaching her, in a hot silence that went from pleasure to higher pleasure, each plateau leading only to another, better one.

She was dimly aware that he'd moved the covers and the pillows off the bed and that more bare skin than ever was now in

contact with her own. She thought that she should say something, protest, slow him down. But what she was feeling was
new and exciting, and her inhibitions had long ago been compromised by the unfamiliar liquor.

His mouth slid down her long legs, to the inside of her soft
thighs. Involuntarily, her legs moved farther apart to give him
more access. One big hand had moved right in between her
legs, his thumb pressing in a place that shocked and delighted
her all at the same time.

She made a sound, a tiny protest.

"Let me," he whispered huskily.

So she did. Her hips lifted to his hand and she shivered as she
felt a taste of pleasure that was like holding a live wire in her
hands, She cried out softly.

His mouth pressed down hard on her stomach while his fingers slowly, tenderly, invaded her. He felt her flinch, just barely.

He lifted himself so that he could see her eyes while he did
it. "Don't look away," he whispered.

Her lips fell apart in a silent gasp as she realized what he was
doing. She flinched again and her nails bit into his arms.

"I've never done anything this exciting in my life," he said
roughly as he watched her. "My God, it's…it's…beyond words,"
he whispered as he felt the whispery protection of her body come
away in his fingertips. He flushed as he looked straight into her
eyes. "Oh, baby," he breathed. "Baby!"

She was shivering. There hadn't been much pain, but she
was beginning to realize what she was doing—almost. Just as
she thought that maybe this wasn't such a good idea, his hand
shifted again and she moaned and lifted toward him in an arch.

"There?" he asked softly, and did it again.

"I… I…never…" she stammered.

"I know." They were only words, but there was a world of
emotion in them. He shifted over her, so that she could feel the
hard press of his skin all the way up and down her own body.

He shivered, once, as his mouth slid tenderly over hers and cherished it. Still, that expert hand taught her body new sensations, kept her in thrall, while he eased between her long legs and she felt the press of him at her innocence.

Her eyes opened wide and her fingers dug into his upper arms.

He took a long, shuddering breath and moved down, right inside her body. He stilled, and they stared at each other.

She flushed. It was so intimate. She couldn't have imagined anything more intimate, even more than what he'd already done with her. But she wasn't fighting him. She could feel him, inside her, warm and hard and tender.

He pushed a little harder. She swallowed, hard, but she didn't push at him or try to get away. Her eyes were still looking straight into his.

"All the way, this time," he breathed, and his hips pushed down. He let out the breath that had caught in his throat. "Okay?" he asked tenderly.

She shivered. "O...okay."

He eased completely into her and he groaned, harshly, his eyes dilating as they met her shocked ones.

"You're...inside me," she whispered shakily.

"Deep inside," he managed, shivering.

His big hands framed her face, on either side of her head, and he bent to her mouth, resting his weight on his forearms. He moved slowly. "Do whatever you want to do," he whispered. "Anything goes."

Her eyes searched his. "Anything?"

He smiled, tenderly. "Anything." His hand moved between them, and he touched her where they were intimately joined. He stroked her, watched her eyes dilate, felt her body jump under his. He laughed softly. "You burn me up inside. I think I dreamed you."

Her hands were on his chest. Fascinated, she moved them to his waist and looked up, hesitating, into his eyes.

"Touch me," he whispered. "Come on. Touch me."

She slid her hands down until her fingers encountered him, where he was touching her.

He shivered and laughed out loud. "Oh yes. Like that, baby. Just like that!"

"You like it?" she whispered.

"I love it. Do whatever you want to do."

She was fascinated. She'd never encountered anything like this in her reading, or even her own writing. She traced him and felt his body quiver, heard him laugh as he encouraged her to be adventurous. And all the while, he touched and traced and whispered erotic, shocking things to her.

The heat rose quickly in both of them. His hips began to lift and fall, and she shivered with every slow, deep thrust, her eyes looking up into his.

"I thought I knew it all," he managed, his voice choked as pleasure began to rise in him. "I knew nothing!"

She moaned, lifting up as he moved down, her eyes holding his. Her fingers were digging into his arms.

"Don't close your eyes when you come," he whispered huskily. "I want to see you when you feel this for the first time. I want to watch you."

The frank request should have shocked and embarrassed her, but she was still reeling from the effects of the alcohol, enjoying the first true physical pleasure of her entire life. She was beyond embarrassment, for the moment. She wanted to ask if he was accustomed to watching women when they reached a pinnacle, but he moved suddenly, unexpectedly, and she cried out.

There had been all the time in the world. Now there was none. He drove into her, his eyes holding hers the whole time while she gasped and clung to him and begged him not to stop.

He shifted his hips and his legs, moving hers even farther apart as the pleasure climbed and climbed. He came down on her with his knees beside her rib cage, her own beside his as he built the pressure and the pleasure whisper by whisper, moan by moan.

He shifted again and felt her shudder. "Are you ready?" he whispered huskily, and he moved down into her with quick, hungry, almost violent thrusts.

She couldn't even speak. Her mouth was open as she endured such a rush of pleasure that she thought she wouldn't survive it. She cried out, sobbing, her eyes dilating, her body convulsing.

"Yes," he ground out. "Oh... God...!"

His teeth clenched as he arched down into her and shuddered over and over and over again, until he thought his spine would snap. He actually sobbed with the force of a pleasure he'd never experienced in his life, with any of his lovers.

An eternity later he collapsed on her damp body, still shuddering.

"Are you all right?" he asked at her ear, his voice husky and urgent. "Did I hurt you?"

"No," she breathed. "Oh no. No."

He caught his breath and was about to tell her how glad he was when he felt the tears on his cheek.

He lifted his head and winced at the expression on her face. The alcohol had finally worn off, far too soon. She looked as if she'd committed a cardinal sin. And in her own mind, he thought grimly, she probably had.

"Oh...please..." she whispered, pushing gently at his chest. "I'm going to be sick...!"

He withdrew at once and watched her vault off the bed and into the bathroom. He could hear her dinner coming back up.

Almost boneless with pleasure, he got back into his clothes so that she wouldn't be any more embarrassed than she already was.

He gathered up her own clothing and went to the bathroom door. "I brought your clothes," he said. "Are you all right?"

The commode flushed. There was running water. She came to the door and only opened it a slit. She couldn't bring her-

self to look up past his chin. She eased one hand out the door
for her clothes.

"Get dressed," he said quietly. "Then we'll talk, okay?"

She didn't answer him. She took her clothing inside and
closed the door.

There was a minibar in the room. He got himself a cola and
pulled out a ginger ale for her. Probably it would be the only
thing she could keep down. He felt ashamed of himself. She'd
been compromised by the alcohol and he'd taken advantage of
it. Well, not really. He'd been compromised by it as well. He
couldn't actually remember how they'd wound up in this room.

While he was working on the memory, she came slowly out
of the bathroom and sat down on the sofa. He pushed the soft
drink over to her.

"Thanks," she said heavily.

"I don't even remember how we got in here," he said, pushing back his damp hair. "You got sick downstairs…"

She nodded.

He took a sharp breath and sipped his drink. "I'm sorry. I
don't…"

"I don't, either," she replied. She grimaced. "I've never had
a drink of hard liquor in my life."

"I have. But not enough to compromise me, until now." He
studied her quietly. "You were a virgin."

She colored furiously and took another sip of her drink, almost enough to choke her, because she remembered all too well
losing it in the most erotic manner she'd ever encountered.

He made a face. "I guess that's a memory you'd rather not
have. Sorry."

"We both had too much to drink."

He nodded.

"We should go home," she said after a minute.

He didn't need to ask if she'd been taking a preventative. He was sure she hadn't. And he wasn't used to being expected to provide protection, so he'd had nothing with him. Even if he had, they were both too involved too quickly for him to have thought of it.

Great, he thought privately, *now she'll get pregnant and she'll have it made until the kid graduates. All the money she's never had...*

He stopped abruptly. She thought he was a working cowboy. She had no idea who he was, really.

"You don't have to worry about...anything," she said after a minute.

"You're taking something?" he asked hopefully.

She hesitated. "Yes. I'm...taking something." She was. Vitamins. But he didn't need to know. He'd go back to Texas pretty soon and if she got pregnant, he'd never know. She thought about a baby and she felt warm all over. This was a complication she didn't need, but she'd wanted children all her life. She wasn't even upset about the possibility. But a roaming cowboy, well, he'd be worried that she'd want to garnishee his wages or something. She wasn't like that, but he wouldn't know it. He wouldn't need to know it.

"Oh." Odd, that he was disappointed. Because just at the last, he'd been thinking about babies. Mina, with her homemaking skills, would be a natural at taking care of a baby. He'd thought of a family, himself, but the sort of women he carried around with him didn't predispose him to fatherhood. He'd grown cynical, when woman after woman laughed at the thought of getting pregnant.

"So you don't have anything to worry about," Mina said.

"I wasn't worried," he said gently, and he smiled at her. It was a different kind of smile than he'd ever given her. It made her feel warm, protected.

She sipped more of her soft drink.

"You're right, though. We should get home. It's very late."

He got up and she followed suit.

★ ★ ★

She waited while he settled the bill and then they got into the truck for the long drive home.

He reached for her soft hand and tucked it into his as he drove. "Will it embarrass you if I tell you that I've never enjoyed a woman so much?"

She gasped.

"I guess it would," he said.

"You've been around," she began.

"Yes. Around. With sophisticated, selfish women who wanted pleasure but weren't disposed to give it without a lot of incentive." By which he meant, unknown to her, rich gifts. He glanced at her. "You gave me your innocence. I wasn't worthy of such a gift," he added quietly.

"I was drunk," she said.

He laughed. "I was drunk, too. That doesn't change what I said. You were meant for a different sort of man altogether. Not me."

Her heart sank. "There's never been anybody I felt that way with before," she said after a minute.

Pride glowed in him. "Not even McGuire?" he asked, hating his own jealousy.

"I don't feel like that about Jake. About anybody."

His fingers curled into hers. He was lost for words. He felt guilty and vaguely ashamed, but she was taking it on the chin, without blaming him, without tears. It made him feel even worse.

She turned her head toward him and said, "I know you like being free. Cowboys don't settle down, ever. They move from place to place and just enjoy where they are. So I don't expect you to start making me promises or apologies or anything," she added. "I'm the last person who'd ever try to tie you down."

His heart jumped. "Plenty have tried," he said before he thought, and he sounded as disillusioned as he felt.

"That's not right. You shouldn't let people use guilt to make you do things."

"You're very forgiving for a woman."

She smiled. "I've had a hard life," she said. "Hatred and anger just well up inside you, like a wound, and fester. They destroy people. I watched it destroy my mother. She hated my father. She hated me. She drank because she hated us so much, and in the end, it killed her. I don't want to end up like that."

"You're not like that," he said.

"Well, I did sort of fall into bed with you," she returned, flushing.

"You were inebriated," he pointed out.

"I guess so." She hesitated. "You know a lot about what to do with women," she added.

"I suppose I shocked you to the back teeth."

She smiled. "You did." She felt the heat rush into her cheeks. "I never knew…"

"Not even from reading all those torrid romance novels?" he teased.

"They were nothing like what happened," she said. "And they had scenes about how people felt, but, gosh, in real life, it's…" She swallowed. "I thought the first time would be awful."

"Maybe it is sometimes," he said. "Men can be cruel. Some are heartless."

"You aren't. You were…" She swallowed again. "Sorry. It's hard to talk about."

His fingers contracted gently. "You can talk to me about anything."

And she realized suddenly that she could. Anything at all.

"You don't think I'm like my mother?" she worried.

"Honey, you're not promiscuous. I came up on your blind side because we both had too much to drink. That said, I don't regret one second of what happened. You're an experience I'll never forget as long as I live."

"Until some new woman comes along," she laughed.

He didn't answer her right away. He was thinking about some new woman, and with absolute horror. He didn't want some new woman. It was a revelation that shocked him speechless.

"Did I offend you?" she worried.

"I'm not offended."

"You're very quiet."

"I'm thinking." He'd never considered abstinence. It wasn't even a word he knew. But when he thought about what he'd done with Mina in that hotel room, he couldn't imagine doing it with some social climbing gold digger. In fact, he couldn't imagine doing it with any other woman.

CHAPTER ELEVEN

Mina looked up at Cort with her heart in her eyes. It didn't take a genius to realize that she was falling in love with him.

That shocked him. He knew that she'd enjoyed him in bed. It had been her first time, and he wanted to make it something that she'd want to remember. But he'd assumed that two piña coladas had influenced her decision to sleep with him. Now he could see the real reason she'd given in, and it wasn't completely due to alcohol. Her eyes were soft, dark brown and soulful, as they met his. A woman like that, with principles, wouldn't fall into bed with a man just because her reflexes were dulled. She'd only do it out of love.

He touched her face gently. It was disconcerting to know how she felt. Women had loved him for years—for what they could get out of him. But Mina had been out of her mind with fear for him at the gas station the night before, when it looked as if Cort might be hurt during the holdup.

It made him feel warm inside, as if all the cold places the years had dug into him were thawing. It was like spring. He smiled.

"You really do look sweet," he whispered, and he bent his head.

She lifted hers for the slow, hungry descent of his hard mouth, clung to him as he grew hungrier and drew her body close against his. He wrapped her up tight, his mouth invasive now, tender, ardent. She moaned softly at the sensations that wound through her. All her senses were awakened, and she recalled with anguish the pleasure he'd taught her in bed. She wanted him now, as she'd never wanted anyone. She'd been unawakened before, with no desire for intimacy. But with knowledge of it came the craving, the aching need of possession. She pressed close to him, feeling his powerful body react almost instantly to the feel of her against him.

Cort was dying for her. He could hardly contain the hunger as he drew her closer in the shade of the cottonwood tree. It had been a long, dry spell, but his memory of the night before was driving him mad. In bed, Mina was everything he'd ever want. Even out of it, she was a constant surprise, a delight.

He groaned. His body was in agony, and there was no place they could go without being interrupted except a motel. His mind rebelled at the thought of treating her the way he'd treated women in the past. She was so innocent!

He drew back, grinding his teeth together when he saw her rapt expression. She was feeling similar things, having only just been awakened to physical need.

"Damn," he bit off.

Her eyebrows lifted. "Damn?"

His sensuous lips made a thin line. "There's not a soul in sight, but if I start undressing you, every cowboy in the county will suddenly have to ride this way!"

She gasped. "We couldn't…" she began.

He drew her hips to his and looked down at her sardonically as she flushed. "We damned sure could, if there was a private place."

She flushed. Her fingers drew soft patterns on his shirt under the shepherd's coat. "Well, actually, we…couldn't," she said, and couldn't look at him. She didn't want to mention that horseback riding was giving her some problems, although she'd wanted to go with Cort too much to mention that she was uncomfortable. But sleeping with him would be painful.

Cort sighed. It had been her first time and her body was reacting to it in a way he should have realized. She wasn't saying it, but he saw it in her embarrassed face. He tilted it up to his eyes. "Sore?" he asked gently, and without rancor.

She grimaced. "Sorry."

He drew her head to his chest and took a deep breath. "No, I'm sorry. I should have realized how new it was to you. And I shouldn't have taken you riding."

"I wanted to go with you," she said huskily.

He realized that. It made his heart swell. His big hand smoothed over the long, thick hair over her shoulders. "It's too soon." He smiled wistfully. "Even if it wasn't, where the hell would we go?"

She laughed, too. "I guess it would have to be a motel, because there's no privacy here at my place."

"Or Bart's. Not that he'd approve of me bringing you there," he added.

Which brought to mind what she'd heard about Cort asking Bart if he could bring Ida over for the night. Her self-confidence took a nosedive. He'd been dating Ida. Everybody knew that she was promiscuous. Did Cort think Mina was like that, too?

She looked up, concern darkening her eyes.

He shook his head. "We aren't going that route," he said quietly. "I respect you too much."

She felt elated at his expression, which was both protective and possessive.

He traced a pattern on her cheek. "I've never been much for emotional ties," he said haltingly. "It's pretty much been take them and leave them, when it came to women. But you're not like that, Mina."

She searched his eyes in the silence, unbroken except by the gurgle of the stream. "You were dating Ida," she began worriedly.

He put a long forefinger over her soft lips. "Ida isn't what she seems. And I haven't slept with her, regardless of how it might look."

She caught her breath. "I didn't ask…!"

"I wanted you to know the truth," he said, sketching her face. "People will think what they want to."

She bit her lower lip. "I guess you know what they think."

He nodded. "Ida encourages gossip. I'm not overly fond of it. Gossip can destroy lives," he added quietly.

"Yes."

He smoothed her fingers over his shirt. "We'd better get going, before the horses decide to leave us here," he mused.

She laughed. "Okay."

The next few days were like magic. Mina was in love and falling deeper as she spent more time with Cort and learned more about him. He borrowed Bart's truck to take her over to Yellowstone National Park and watch Old Faithful erupt with her. Big game was all over the highway, where many tourists stopped in the middle of the road and got out with cameras to film bighorn sheep and even a moose.

Mina laughed, delighted. "We had a moose come right up to the barn when we had our milk cow," she commented. "I think he was in love."

"What happened to him?" he asked softly.

"He broke down a fence trying to get to her, so we had to have him relocated by the wildlife people. And soon afterward, I had to sell the cow and her calf." She grimaced. "We have hard times occasionally. I missed the cow, but not the daily milking. It really hurt my hands."

He chuckled. "I tried to milk a cow once. I never could get any milk."

"There's an art to milking," she agreed. "Bill McAllister taught me how. I guess he's done a little of everything in his life."

"I guess." He was looking down at her curiously.

"What is it?" she asked.

"This." He touched the silver wolf pendant he'd bought her. He smiled tenderly. "I'm glad you like it."

"I love it," she said, smoothing her fingers over the cool silver. "I'll always wear it."

His heart jumped. A simple silver pendant, and she was overjoyed to have it. One of his lovers had taken a huge dinner ring sparkling with diamonds from his hand and put it on without even a thank you.

"You don't have expensive tastes," he said, thinking out loud.

"Not really," she agreed. "I've noticed that a lot of money doesn't make people happy or make up for what they don't have. Cousin Rogan lives alone. He has nobody, except me, and he spends his life traveling."

"He might be happy doing it."

She sighed. "I guess."

"There are a lot of things money can buy," he countered.

She looked up at him with an impish smile. "Like either of us would know," she chuckled.

He had to laugh. It wasn't true. He knew exactly what money could buy.

She slid her hand into his and he relaxed. Odd, she gave him peace. He didn't know that he'd ever experienced it with a woman.

"Mina," he said softly, and looked down at her. "What's it short for?"

"Oh, this is rich. Wilhelmina," she told him. "It was my father's idea. I was named for one of his ancestors."

"Somebody German?"

"I'm not really sure. I was so young when he left." Her face tautened. "I shortened it to Mina when I was still in grammar school. I took a lot of teasing about it."

His fingers contracted around hers. "My first name is Cortrell," he told her. "God knows where my mother got it from. At that, it's not as bad as Cash's. His real name is Cassius."

She laughed. "Really?"

He nodded. "He shortened it to Cash when he started in military school. Dad sent him away when he was nine, just after our mother died."

"That's awful," she said softly.

He shrugged. "He didn't get along with our stepmother. She told Dad something that made him furious. He packed Cash up and sent him off the same day. Cash never got over it. He and Dad didn't even speak until our brother Garon went to see him, just before he settled in the same town."

"Your father doesn't sound like a very nice man. Sorry."

"He isn't a nice man, and there's no need to apologize." He linked his fingers in between hers. "He was a rotten father. He never remembered birthdays or gave us much affection. He was gone most of the time, so our housekeeper pretty much raised us after Dad booted our stepmother out for cheating on him."

She sighed. "I guess we both had pretty rotten childhoods."

"Yours was worse than mine, honey," he said softly, smiling at her reaction to the endearment. "I had neglect. You had something a lot worse."

She nodded. She moved closer to his side. He let go of her hand and slid his arm around her.

"I'll be a better mother than mine was," she said quietly.

"I'll be a better father than mine was," he returned.

She drew in a long breath. "I forgot to tell you. I have to go out of town this weekend. I wouldn't go, but I promised."

"Where are you going?" he asked.

"My best friend is getting married," she lied. "I promised I'd be her maid of honor."

"I could drive you," he offered.

"I'd love that, but she lives in Miami."

He burst out laughing. "Okay. That's a little far to drive." He could have offered her a ride in the family jet. But she didn't know about him yet. He wasn't anxious to tell her. He was enjoying being just a man, with his best girl beside him. "I'll miss you," he added gently.

She pressed close to his side, just as Old Faithful shot water and steam up into the air. "I'll miss you, too. But it's only for a couple of days."

His arm contracted. "Okay."

She was crawling through the underbrush in Nicaragua with her small commando group. They'd adopted her two years earlier when she asked a local man—one who'd retired from duty as a mercenary soldier—a lot of questions about what mercenaries did. So he introduced her to his five old comrades. They were flattered by her curiosity, took her under their collective wings and began taking her out on missions with them through various insect-and snake-infested jungles. They'd taught her the ropes, and now she could handle military hardware right along with them. She learned about covert operations from the ground up, which gave her books a realism that many armchair adventurers couldn't manage.

Dan handled communications. Reg was their demolition expert. Harlan was the heavy weapon specialist. Ry was the leader and strategic planner of the group, with Craddock as his second in command and small weapons expert. Mina was small weapons backup, and she was proficient with a .45 auto.

On this mission, they were rescuing a small boy who'd been kidnapped by a poor relative of a very wealthy family. He was holding the boy for ransom, and the parents were afraid of local law enforcement. The father knew Ry and phoned him for help. He called in the group.

It wasn't the mission Mina had signed on for this weekend. She was supposed to observe the guys handling a military cleanup of a recent combat operation. Instead, she was on the front lines of a rescue. She didn't even hesitate. It was exciting. She loved the adrenaline rushes she got from participating in missions with these guys. They were like family.

Ry held them up just at the edge of the jungle. There was a shack in the distance. If their GPS was accurate, that was where the child was being held. Mina stood in awe of Ry's ability to dig out information from the locals.

"Crad, see what you can see."

Craddock shouldered his sniper rifle and looked through the telescopic sight. There was a long pause. "I see a man. The curtains are thick and they shelter the room." He swung the weapon around. "Only cover is a few trees just to the right of the shack. Open land getting to it."

"We'll need a diversion," Ry said at once. He looked at Mina and smiled. He was tall, with a light olive complexion, black hair and odd pale blue eyes. "Feel up to a little excitement, Bubbles?" he asked, using the group's nickname for her.

She grinned. "Always."

"Okay. I need you to fire at that caved-in barn to the left of the shack when I tell you."

"Will do."

"Reg, I think a few flash bangs might do the job."

"I'll need to be closer than this," he replied.

"Let me do it. I've got the ghillie suit," Craddock said.

"Don't need to ask me twice," Reg chuckled. "I hate crawling on my belly."

Craddock got into the ghillie suit and took ages to get in position. Ry signaled him. He tossed the flash bangs and the man came running out of the building just as Ry signaled Mina and she opened up with the .45 automatic toward the distant derelict barn.

Ry ran out, his semiautomatic leveled, and yelled at the man to get down.

Minutes later, they had the scared child in custody and the kidnapper tied up like a tangled kite.

Mina laughed with pure delight.

"At least you didn't get shot this time," Ry teased.

"Ah, well, that's the breaks," she said with a grin. "And what a great chapter this is going to make!"

"I want to be twenty and blond and handsome," Craddock told her.

"I want to be twenty-five, fabulously wealthy, dripping with gorgeous brunettes," Reg added.

She smiled. "I promise to do my best!"

She cuddled the frightened child while they made their way back to the truck they used for transport. Sometimes, she thought, the most unpredictable things were the most rewarding. It was a reminder that you couldn't choose exactly what experiences you got in life.

She was back in Catelow on Wednesday, a week and a few days before she was due in New York. She hadn't caught a bullet, but she'd had to take a course of quinine before, during and after the trip to ensure that she didn't come down with malaria, which was rampant in Nicaragua's rural areas. It was next to impossible not to get bitten by the mosquitoes that carried the disease, even with the best precautions. Poor Reg had forgotten to take his course of medicines and he'd come down with malaria just as they were all getting off the plane in Miami. Mina had felt guilty for leaving so soon, but she had to get home. Nobody blamed her. She also asked Ry if she could get back in touch with him about another mission they'd run in her absence. He said sure, just call him, and he gave her a new cell phone number where he could be reached.

She'd missed Cort. They'd been together almost every day

since they'd been to the casino. She couldn't wait to see him when she got home. But she was in for a shock when she called Bart to ask for Cort to call her. Cort was gone. "Gone?!" she exclaimed, devastated.

"He left you a letter," he said. "Want me to run it over there?"

"Would you mind?" she asked, her mind still in limbo. "I'm writing up our mission while it's still fresh in my head."

"I want to hear about that," he replied with a laugh.

"You can hear about it over coffee. I'll make a new pot!"

She read the letter while Bart sipped coffee. Cort had an emergency back home, he'd said. He was sorry he had to leave while she was out of town, but it involved a relative who was in big trouble and he couldn't turn his back on the man. He'd be back in a couple of weeks, he promised.

She put the letter down. Doubts crawled in. Was there really a relative in trouble, or was he just getting rid of an uncomfortable love affair that he didn't want anymore?

"He was torn up about it," Bart said softly, which was the truth. Cort had raised the roof. It seemed that his father and stepmother had hit a bump and separated. Vic was at the ranch roaring drunk and scattering cowboys. Cort had to deal with him. He'd asked Bart to make sure Mina knew that it wasn't from choice that he'd walked away.

Her dark eyes sought his and there was devastation in them. "Was he really, or was he just looking for a way out?"

He smiled. "He's crazy about you—couldn't you tell?" he teased. "I've never heard such language. He really didn't want to go."

She relaxed a little. She smiled. "Okay."

"He wanted you to know that he'd be back as soon as he could arrange things back home."

She relaxed even more. "I feel better."

He cocked his head. "What were you up to with the guys this time?"

"A rescue," she replied. "We saved a young boy from a kidnapper. It wasn't even planned—we just walked into it. I felt so good."

"Someday, you're going to have to level with Cort about what you really do for a living," he prompted. He didn't add that his cousin was going to have to do some confessing of his own.

She grimaced and sipped black coffee. "I know. I should have told him before now. I was living down to his image of me. It stung a little."

"I know. But your new book is climbing the charts. It's already made the *Publishers Weekly* list and it's on the *New York Times* list."

She nodded. "My agent called me early this morning to tell me that it was at number eight. She was over the moon. She says it will go higher."

"You bet it will. The reviews on Amazon are awesome."

She grinned. "It's so exciting! I never dreamed I'd get so far!"

"I did," he chuckled. "You have the talent. Not to mention some real solid research associates," he added. "I can't wait to see how Cort's going to react to that news."

"There may be fireworks," she sighed. "I don't lead a conventional life."

"You go to New York at the end of next week. That's a lot of travel."

She shrugged. "I'm used to it. Nicaragua was fun." Her dark eyes twinkled. "I love being part of the group, you know? It's the most exciting thing I've ever done." She laughed. "I've had requests from my team about how they want to be portrayed in this new chapter."

"Something along the lines of cosmetic changes?" he teased. "Some of them are pretty rough looking."

"But with hearts of pure gold," she replied.

"Speaking of gold, I'm going after a lot of new Angus yearlings. Want to come and look at them with me? You might want
a few for your own herd."

"Will it take long?"

"No. I'm going in the morning."

"Then I'll come, but just for the morning. I've got a lot of
work to do before I leave next Friday for New York. I've got
several meetings."

"I'll make sure we don't stay long."

She gnawed her lower lip. "You wouldn't lie to me, about
Cort not wanting to go home?" she asked in a worried tone.

His eyes were soft with affection. "Never about that," he said.
"He promised he'd be back in a couple of weeks. He always
keeps his promises." He didn't add one more thing; that Cort
had also said that he was going to tell Mina the truth when he
came back. He had long-range plans for her. Bart was delighted.
She'd had a hard life. It was time she had a little happiness.

The next friday morning before daylight, she boarded Jake
McGuire's private jet at the Catelow airport for the trip to New
York City with her bags packed, yawning.

"We have coffee with bagels and cream cheese," he teased
after they were airborne. "Hungry?"

"I could eat a small horse. I don't know what's wrong with
me," she added on a laugh. "I'm tired all the time."

"Still taking that quinine?" he asked with obvious concern.

She nodded. "I wouldn't dare miss a dose. One of our guys
came down with malaria just as we got off the plane in Miami.
I called Ry to check on him. He's doing okay, just trying to get
through the worst of it."

"Malaria is no fun," he said. "I had a bout of it many years
ago when I had to close a deal in Guatemala."

"I've never had it," she said. "And I'm crossing my fingers
that I never will!"

The steward brought coffee and a platter of bagels on a silver tray, with a dish of cream cheese and a knife.

Jake poured coffee into china cups and handed her one.

"Thanks," she said. "This is really kind of you."

He chuckled. "No problem at all. I told you, I have business in Manhattan, too."

"I dread the media tour," she confessed. "At least it's not like being in front of an audience. There's just me and the sound guy and the cameraman and the producer in the booth." She laughed. "It's so odd, not to be able to see the people who are interviewing me, except on camera."

"I can imagine. What was it like, in Nicaragua?" he asked.

"Hot," she returned, "especially in camo gear with a sidearm. But the guys have trained me very well. I'm not nearly the klutz I was in the first days they took me on missions."

He shook his head. "I still can't get over the danger you put yourself in. They take it for granted, but you've already been shot once."

"Just a flesh wound," she reminded him, and laughed. "I hardly felt it."

"You and your insistence on realism," he sighed.

"Next month I'm going out with a SWAT team in Dallas," she told him. "One of Ry's guys knows a guy who's going to let me do a ride-along."

"You're pushing your luck."

"It will be worth it," she said, grinning at him. "That realism is why I'm selling so many books."

"I suppose so. But it's still dangerous."

"Life is dangerous," she replied. "You can get killed in all sorts of ways here in the States without putting yourself in danger."

"True enough," he agreed. "More coffee?"

The media tour turned out to be a lot of fun. They filmed it at the studios of one of the major television networks. The staff had coffee and an assortment of breads waiting for her. They discussed her latest foray into mercenary work, although she never called any of her group by name, for their own protection.

She was still worried that Cort might see her on one of the broadcasts, but it was unlikely. He was in West Texas, and the only Texas interview she was doing was in Dallas. It lessened the discomfort. She wanted to tell him herself, and she'd have to do it pretty soon. If he was really planning a future with her, and Bart thought he was, she had to level with him about her true profession. She hoped he'd understand, and not object to her crawling through jungles with her research associates.

On the other hand, if she turned up pregnant, that was going to complicate things. It would mean an end to the missions, at least for a while. She smiled to herself as she wondered if there was already a tiny life growing inside her. It was much too soon to tell.

Jake took her to the Four Seasons for dinner late that afternoon, when she'd finished the media tour and made time to speak with her agent and her editor. The book sales were climbing, and her agent hammered out the details of the new contract with her. It looked good. There was going to be a considerable advance, which she'd already been told, and royalties would be sweet. She was sitting on top of the world, she told Jake, without mentioning Cort, or the possibility that she might be going to Texas with him in the near future, if she did turn out to be pregnant.

She wondered where they'd live. There was usually a bunkhouse for single cowboys, but there might be a small house they could rent from his boss. It was too early to concern herself with that, really. She still had the worry about what to do about her own ranch if she left Catelow.

She could put in a manager, perhaps Fender, her new full-time man. He seemed to be honest and trustworthy, and he was proving to be a competent worker. She allowed herself to dream of a future with Cort, of a baby in her arms and a happy marriage. Surely he wouldn't mind her profession. After all, the only things she needed were a laptop and an internet connection to pursue her craft. She could tell him about the writing without dropping the truth of her research into his lap until he got used to the idea of her profession. Surely he wouldn't mind.

"You're very quiet," Jake remarked as they finished dessert.

She laughed. "I'm working." She flushed. "Sorry, I tend to work out details in my mind before I ever put them down in a word processing program. It saves rewrites."

He chuckled. "Ah, the life of a writer," he teased. "You do love it, don't you?"

"It's been my whole life, for a long time now."

"I noticed."

"I can't tell you how much I appreciate what you've done for me, Jake," she said, her dark eyes meeting his. "I can fly commercial, but I'm nervous of planes, even with the guys."

"What do they fly around in?" he wondered aloud.

"This ancient DC-3," she said, shaking her head. "It's well maintained and it gets us where we're going, but I'm constantly amazed that it can get off the ground."

"They need something newer," he said.

She sighed. "I mentioned that. And they said that gear was far more important. They can borrow air transport if they need it. Gear, that's another thing." She grinned. "They even had a special suit made for me. I brought it home, along with the .45 auto they gave me." She whistled. "My hands aren't really big enough for a weapon that size, but I'm getting better with it."

"A smaller caliber might be a better fit," he ventured.

"It might be, but I like what I've got." She didn't tell him the real reason. A .45 could knock down a vicious target, something a lesser caliber couldn't do. If she and the group were in a really

dangerous situation—like the last time, when she'd been shot—
it could mean the difference between life and death.

He cocked his head and smiled at the picture she made in
her demure black cocktail dress, with her hair long and pretty
around her shoulders.

"You really are a dish," he mused gently.

She flushed. "Thanks."

He studied his coffee instead of her. "You and Cort Grier—
is it getting serious?"

She smiled and made a face at him. "Classified."

He burst out laughing. "Okay, I'll stop fishing. But if he ever
goes to the back of the line, you have to keep me in mind."

"You're one of my best friends, you and Bart," she said gently. "That will never change."

He sipped coffee. "Okay," he said finally. "But I'll never give
up hope."

He walked her back to her hotel. Even this late at night, the
streets were full of people.

"I love Manhattan," she said with a sigh. "It has to be the
most beautiful big city in the world."

"I've always thought so," he agreed.

"The lights are…are…" She stopped dead, her eyes on a battery of tabloids in machines near the hotel. She was staring at
the cover of one with shock.

Because there, in lurid color, was the man who'd seduced
her so tenderly, who'd said he wanted a child with her, who'd
stolen her heart.

Cort Grier was on the cover of the tabloid. The headline
was shattering. "Texas millionaire and Hollywood starlet dis-
cuss wedded bliss."

She looked up at Jake with sheer horror. She was almost shaking from the revelation.

He ground his teeth together.

"You knew," she exclaimed.

He bit his lower lip.

"You knew," she repeated, stopping under a streetlight as people filed by on their way to theaters or late dinners.

He shoved his hands into his pockets. "I knew. We sit on some of the same committees. I've known Cort for years."

"Why didn't you tell me?" she asked, as tears rolled silently down her cheeks.

"I couldn't. It was like playing dirty pool, to sell out a rival that way," he added quietly. "I mentioned it to Bart. He said his cousin was sick of being hunted by women for what he had. He just wanted to be an ordinary cowboy for a while."

"He's a playboy," she said, almost choking on the words.

"Well, yes, I guess he is," he told her with obvious reluctance. "His name has been linked with movie stars and debutantes and, once, with a princess. He's worth millions. He owns a big ranch in West Texas. He runs purebred Santa Gertrudis cattle and his family is heavily into real estate and oil."

She wanted to sit down, but there was nothing she could do but put one foot in front of the other and go toward her hotel.

"I am truly sorry," Jake said as he fell into step beside her.

"So am I."

She cried herself to sleep. The next morning, she got up and started to make coffee in her hotel room when a sudden uprush of nausea sent her rushing into the bathroom, where it felt like she lost two days' meals.

Great, she thought as she flushed the commode and washed her pale face. What a wonderful time to discover that she was probably pregnant, when the man she'd planned a future with turned out to be a two-timing snake!

She looked in the mirror. "You are a terrible judge of character," she told her image. "And just what are you going to do now?"

It was a good question. A termination, while it might be a solution for most women, was impossible for her. She couldn't bear the thought of giving up the tiny life inside her, even if she never saw its father again. Amazing, how hungry she was for a baby, even under the circumstances.

She told Jake she needed one more day to finalize some negotiations and later that morning, she went to a medical facility and had a blood test done. She was almost certainly pregnant, although they told her that sometimes it could be a false positive. Her symptoms, however, pretty much clinched the diagnosis. She walked out onto the sidewalk with her head in the clouds, enveloped in dreams.

She didn't tell Jake, for fear that he might share the news before she was ready. She still had to deal with Cort, and she wasn't certain how to do it. So she flew back to Catelow with Jake, her face as solemn as if she'd lost a member of her family to the grim reaper, even as the joy of her pregnancy welled up inside her.

CHAPTER TWELVE

Cort was furious. His father, drunk and disorderly, had fired one of the ranch's top hands in a drunken stupor. Cort had to find the man and offer him more benefits to come back. He hadn't wanted to leave Catelow in the first place. He should have had two more blissful weeks getting to know Mina. He wanted to marry her, whether or not she was pregnant. He'd never been so crazy about a woman in his life. And here he was, instead, babysitting a man who should have been plenty old enough to take care of himself!

"What the hell is your problem?" he asked his father, exasperated, as they sat down to dinner, served by their longtime cook.

"She kicked me out," Vic said, his voice still slurred. "I need another drink…"

"Over my dead body," Cort shot back. "Why did she kick you out?"

"I was just flir…flirting with one of her friends."

Cort's pale brown eyes narrowed. "Just flirting?"

The older man flushed. "I can't manage with just one woman," he said belligerently. "I've always slept around. I even told her, when we married."

"I know," Cort said coldly. "You slept around on Mom, when she was dying."

Vic had the grace to blush. He averted his eyes. "You don't understand."

Cort laughed coldly. "I understand, all right. You were a hell of a loss as a father. I guess you're even worse as a husband."

Vic gaped at him. "What?"

"Oh, come on," Cort said irritably. "You were never around when we needed you, especially after you split up with the stepmother from hell. Old Larry and our housekeeper took care of us when we had problems at school. They patched up the cuts and spoke to the principal when we got in trouble. They made Thanksgiving and Christmas for us while you were off philandering. God, if I turn out to be a father like you, I'll shoot myself!"

Vic stiffened. "I never wanted kids," he confessed.

"Then you should have learned about birth control!" Cort returned. "And shame on you for even admitting that!"

The older man had the grace to blush. He averted his eyes. He felt even sicker than he already was. He hated hearing those charges from his favorite son. Okay, he wasn't supposed to have favorites, but Cort had been with him at the ranch long after his other sons had scattered to the four winds.

"I was twenty-one and your mother was eighteen when we got married," Vic said. "She was the most beautiful woman I'd ever seen. A few weeks into the marriage, she got pregnant, and I felt trapped. She never looked at me the same way again. She loved having babies. All of you got the attention. I got nothing. I played around to get even with her, but she didn't even notice, or care." His face hardened. "So I found somebody who did. Or so I thought." He sighed. "I couldn't bear to see your mother when she was dying, because I felt it was my fault. I was never around when she needed me and I didn't realize it until too late. I loved her. I didn't realize that, either. I married your stepmother because I was grieving, not only for your mother, but for Cash. I let your stepmother's lies cause me to throw him right out of my life, and he hated me. I couldn't get him to come back." His eyes closed. "Then your stepmother started running around on me. I got a taste of my own medicine." He leaned back in the chair and his eyes were dead. "I've ruined my life, Cort," he said quietly. "Ruined yours, too." He met his son's shocked eyes. "Ruined all my sons' lives. Parker won't even come home unless he has to. Cash is friendly, but we don't have the relationship we could have had. Garon has a family and he's never been interested in the ranch. So there's just you and me. And your new stepmother, in Vermont. She caught me with one of her friends in a compromising situation. She said…" He hesitated, and his face tautened with pain. "She said I was the most worthless man she'd ever known and she was sorry she'd married me. She wants a divorce." He smiled ruefully. "She doesn't even want alimony. She just wants me gone." He sipped coffee he didn't even want. "I've been a fool. I don't know what to do."

"Take your yacht out and practice for the America's Cup trials," Cort suggested sardonically. "In a few weeks, you'll forget all about it. You always have."

His sad eyes met his son's. "It only seems that way. But maybe you're right." He got up from the table. "I'm sorry I've caused you more trouble."

"I patched things up." He cocked his head. "I'm getting married."

Vic stared at him. "To whom?"

"A sweet, guileless little Wyoming rancher who loves to knit and read romance novels. She wants kids. So do I."

"Wants kids, huh?" he asked. His smile was cynical. "Is she poor?"

Cort nodded.

"Is she marrying you for your money?" Vic asked sarcastically.

"She thinks I'm just a working cowboy who's as financially challenged as she is," Cort said surprisingly. "She likes to cook, too."

Vic sighed. "Just like your new stepmother. She was a newspaper reporter, but she's a homebody now. She likes to grow things. Oh hell, I messed up, big-time! She'll never speak to me again. I'm sorry for what I did to her, but she won't let me tell her. She said I was only sorry I got caught, but it's not true."

"Why did you cheat on her?" Cort asked.

He made a face. "She's thick with her family," he said icily. "It got so I hardly had any time with her at all. I thought she wanted me for what I had."

Cort cocked his head. He was learning things about his father that he'd never known. Vic needed attention, lots of it. When he lost it, he started doing things to make his wives notice him.

"What was your childhood like?" Cort asked abruptly.

"Hell on earth," came the curt reply. "My father was a drunk, who beat me every time I talked back to him. My mother was rich as sin and never wanted kids. She punished me because my father got her pregnant and she lost her perfect figure. She slept with anything in pants."

Cort was shocked to the back teeth. "You never told us anything about that."

Vic sighed. "I was never around to tell you anything," he said solemnly. He looked up at his son. "I'm sorry. You're right. I was a hell of a poor father." He shrugged. "Maybe I'll get on the yacht and go sailing. If your stepmother calls, tell her...tell her I'm sorry and she can have anything she wants in the divorce settlement."

"I won't be here," Cort replied. He smiled. "I'm going back to Wyoming to get married."

Vic laughed softly. "Okay. I guess I'll stay and meet your new wife before I head out to sea."

"Try to stay sober."

"I'll do my best."

"And don't fire anybody else," Cort said firmly.

Vic held up his hands. "I'm reformed."

"Sure you are," Cort murmured, but he didn't say it out loud.

Mina had cried herself to sleep the first night she was back home. But crying wasn't going to help her situation, so she got up and threw herself into her work. Writing had always been her solace. When the world fell in on her, writing pulled her out of her misery. It was the one great joy of her life. Well, next to the baby growing in her belly. That was easily on a par with writing as the happiest thing she knew.

She was working away when someone knocked at the front door. Impatient, and irritable at the interruption, she saved the chapter she was writing and went to the front door.

She opened it, and there was Cort.

He expected joy on that pretty face. He was smiling, his pale brown eyes alight with happiness as he studied her trim figure in jeans and a yellow sweater, with her beautiful blond-streaked brown hair soft around her shoulders.

But she wasn't happy to see him and made it clear without saying a word.

"How are you?" he asked.

"Fine. How are you?"

She hadn't opened the door an inch farther, and she wasn't inviting him in. Her eyes were as cold as the traces of snow in the yard.

He scowled. "Aren't you glad to see me? I thought we were going to talk about the future. I'm sorry I had to leave so suddenly..."

She cocked her head. "But you had a hot date in Manhattan," she finished for him.

He blinked. "What?"

She smiled. It was a cold smile. "Gossip is that you're marrying the starlet who's working in that new television show about medieval times. You look really great in a dinner jacket, by the way. Very expensive."

He could feel the blood draining out of his face. "Bart told you," he said roughly.

"Bart didn't tell me a thing. I saw your picture on the front page of a tabloid when I was in New York City. With Jake McGuire," she added deliberately.

It was too much to take in at once. "What the hell were you doing in Manhattan with McGuire?" he asked belligerently.

He had no idea what she did for a living and she wasn't sharing it. Not now. "I was having dinner at the Four Seasons," she replied, and it was the truth. "The food is really great. Jake pampers me," she added and sighed.

His face hardened as he looked down at her. "I should have told you. I didn't know how."

"A millionaire, playing at being a cowboy, and I fell for it. The tabloid was very informative," she added, and meant it, because she'd bought a copy of it despite Jake trying to discourage her. "Apparently there are only a few movie stars you haven't slept with."

He cursed under his breath. "Mina…" He spread his hands, desperate for words that would take that contemptuous look off her face. "Can I come in? I need to talk to you."

She bit her lower lip. She loved him. She was carrying his child. If she let him in the house, she was going to fall under that spell all over again and she couldn't bear to.

He saw that look on her face. Hope rose in him. He smiled tenderly. "Don't you think a man can change, if he wants to?"

She was weighing the smile and the words against his known relationship with Ida, Catelow's bad woman, and that starlet on the front page of the tabloid.

He moved a step closer, so that she could feel the heat and power of his lean body. "Okay, it's true. I've been a rounder. I've had women. You knew that already. But you didn't know who I was, and you cared for me anyway. Cared a lot. Why can't you believe that it works both ways?"

She was wavering.

"There hasn't been anybody since the day I met you, when you stamped on my foot and dared me to have you arrested." He smiled at her expression. "I never lie," he added. "I wouldn't try to fox you anyway. Bart says you're pretty hard to fool."

"Usually," she conceded.

"You make great coffee," he said. "We could have a cup and talk, couldn't we? I promise to behave."

She drew in a breath, conflicted. She winced. "Well, I guess I could make coffee."

His heart lifted. She wasn't sending him away. He felt young again.

She opened the door and let him in.

"You really do make good coffee," he said after they were drinking it at her small kitchen table. He made a face. "Even if it's decaf."

"Thanks." She couldn't tell him why she was drinking decaf. It might not be good for the baby to continue her strong caffeine habit. Amazing, that she felt shy with him, when they'd been intimate.

He saw that. It made him feel warm inside. The only dark cloud was her friendship with McGuire. He didn't like her keeping company with him, but he had no way to stop it. Unless, of course, he married her.

"Where do you really live?" she asked.

"At Latigo," he replied.

Her breath caught. Jake had mentioned that Cort owned a big ranch, but she hadn't known it would be that one. She'd heard of the huge Santa Gertrudis stud. Most ranchers had. "That's the biggest ranch in West Texas," she said.

He nodded. "I owned it jointly with my brothers and my father, but I bought them all out. I'm running it myself now. Well, my father's been helping me since his wife left him last week," he muttered.

"Why did she leave him?"

"He was cheating on her." He laughed hollowly. "He cheated on my mother when she was dying. He's cheated on all his female companions. It's the only way of life he knows."

She felt her face go numb. They always said, look at the father and that's the son in twenty years.

He could see the indecision in her face. "Our stepmother cheated on him, so he threw her out. It's the only time he really got it back. Until last week, anyway." He smiled sadly. "His new wife is an upright, moral woman. I liked her."

"Doesn't he love her?"

"Honey, I don't think he really knows what love is," he said softly. "Maybe he loved our mother, at first, but that wore off when she had the first baby and stopped giving all her affection to him." He studied his coffee cup. "Apparently, when he feels he isn't the center of attention, he does every bad thing he can think of to get noticed. He fired my foreman. I had a hell of a time persuading him to come back. And Dad's still at the ranch. I can't really leave him alone there for long, or I'll be replacing everybody. He's climbed into the bottle to drown his sorrows, and he's a hell of a pain when he drinks."

"And I thought I had problems with my little herd," she mused. She sipped coffee and peered at him over the rim. "So you have to go home soon, I guess," she added, and tried not to sound as sad as she felt.

He searched her dark eyes. It was like coming home. "I hoped you might go with me," he said after a minute. His heart raced. It was the first time he'd really tried to commit himself to a long-term relationship and he was uneasy. It didn't show.

"And stay until you get tired of me, like all the others?" she asked on a long sigh.

"Try to remember that tabloids run on gossip. The more lurid the story, the more people buy it. The real culprit was the starlet. Her series is ending and she needs publicity so that she can get another job." His smile was pure cynicism. "I never even slept with her, Mina," he added, his voice deep and very quiet. "She was just somebody pretty to take around town while I was there." He lowered his eyes. "I never thought you'd find out about it."

"Would you have told me?" she asked, with some of his same cynicism.

He drew in a long breath. "Probably," he conceded. "But not until you were more sure of me than you are right now. You don't know whether to believe me or not, do you?"

"Look, I live in a small town. I've been here all my life. The only thing I've really learned about men in all that time is that you can't trust them. Maybe I trust Bart, but that's a different sort of relationship."

"It is. Bart's just a friend. But you love me," he said bluntly, watching her color.

She really wanted to deny it. She couldn't.

"You'd like Latigo," he said hesitantly. "It's big and sprawling. We're surrounded by thousands of acres of land. But if you want city life, El Paso's not that far away. Hell, nowhere is that far away. We own a jet and two light aircraft."

She was weakening. He sounded as if he really wanted her there. But he wasn't talking about marriage. That worried her.

He slid his fingers over hers. "Okay. What's that sad face about?"

She looked up at him. "It would cause a scandal…"

His eyebrows arched. "How so?"

"I'm not worldly," she began, flushing. "People around here

are mostly conservative, and I'm still trying to live down my mother's reputation."

"Oh." His eyes twinkled. "I see. You think I'm asking you to come to Texas and live in sin with me," he teased.

She went red. She jerked her hand away from his. "You stop that!"

He chuckled, but his eyes were soft with affection. "Actually, I want to make amends, for what happened in Lander," he added quietly. "I rushed my fences. I feel guilty about that. You should have had the gown, the minister, the whole works. But there's still time." He pulled a box out of his pocket and pushed it toward her.

It was a jeweler's box. She looked at him with curious interest.

"Open it," he prodded.

She flipped open the lid and caught her breath. It was a canary diamond, a huge one, at least two carats, in a yellow gold setting. Beside it was a wedding band, also studded with canary diamonds.

"I thought it needed to be something that told a story," he began slowly. "You glow. You're like sunlight. It had to be canary diamonds."

"This is a wedding set," she said, her voice soft with wonder.

He nodded. "It comes with a jaded rancher and a lot of cattle." He shrugged. "But there's a lot of emotion behind it."

Her brown eyes glowed with the love she felt for him.

"I'm having a nervous breakdown over here," he pointed out. "I've never proposed marriage in my life. Would you consider putting me out of my misery?"

She laughed softly, got up and sat down in his lap. "Okay."

She kissed him with aching tenderness, and his arms closed around her, mirroring the emotions she was feeling.

He lifted his head, and his own pale brown eyes were soft and quiet with growing possession. "Is that a yes?" he teased.

She laughed. "It's a yes."

He held her close and kissed her with growing hunger. "Torment!" he accused.

She smiled under his devouring mouth. "I am not a…a…oh dear!" She pulled out of his arms and ran for the bathroom. She hadn't even had breakfast, so apparently last night's cheese and crackers were making a return appearance.

He was right beside her. "Should I call a doctor? Are you okay?" he asked, with real concern.

She swallowed down the nausea and rested her head on her arm. "I'm okay," she said huskily. A few seconds later, she felt confident enough to flush the toilet and get up to wash her face. He stood behind her, still worried and unable to hide it.

"Mina, what's wrong?" he persisted.

She turned and looked up at him. "Your baby doesn't like cheese and crackers, apparently," she said in a breathless tone.

"My…" The blood drained out of his face and then rushed back. There was utter glee in the glitter of his pale brown eyes. "You're pregnant?"

"The doctor I saw thinks so… Cort!"

He had her up in his arms, swinging her around, as he exhibited the most incredible joy he'd ever felt in his life. "Pregnant! And the first time!" He set her gently on her feet, his face jubilant.

"Well, at least I don't need to ask if you're pleased," she said softly, and love sparkled in her brown eyes.

"Oh, pleased doesn't come close to expressing it. I want to tell the world…oh God, we're not married!" he burst out.

"Now, Cort…" she began.

But he was already on the phone giving orders. An hour later, she was being hustled aboard the Latigo jet, which had just landed at the Catelow airport. The fixed base operator was talking animatedly with the pilot, who was doing the walk around before he filed a flight plan.

"Nick flies us," he told her as they strapped into their seats in the luxurious jet, which was even more elaborate than Jake McGuire's. "He was a combat pilot, but he didn't want to give up flying, so we got him. He's good."

"But where are we going?" she persisted.

"Las Vegas," he said. "We get married. Then we go home and plan a big, splashy society wedding. You can meet my brothers and their wives. Well, except for Parker. He's not married." He frowned. "If my dad doesn't sober up first, we'll hide him in the closet until after the wedding."

She laughed, caught up in his enthusiasm. "It really is unorthodox."

"Orthodox is for normal people," he chided. He leaned over and kissed her hungrily. "You and a baby. I've hit the jackpot and we aren't even on the way to Vegas."

"Will I be enough for you?" she worried. "I mean, that starlet was so beautiful."

"You're beautiful, you sweet little idiot," he chided. "Beautiful inside and out. I've never known anyone like you." He leaned back in his seat. "You'll have all the time you want to knit and read romance novels," he teased. "We'll find a good manager to take care of your place in Wyoming. We can spend summers there, if you like."

Knitting and reading romance novels. She grimaced, because she had yet to tell him what she really did for a living. She had to be honest with him. She opened her mouth, but Nick came aboard with another man, probably the copilot, and still a third man. She smiled and nodded politely as Cort introduced her to them.

"Marlowe—" he indicated the man with the pilot "—and that's Bib. He's our flight attendant. Want something cold and fizzy to drink?" he added.

"After we take off," she said.

He took her hand in his. "No worries. Everything's going to be okay."

She really hoped so. She'd have to wait until they had a quiet moment to tell Cort about her profession. She could do that when they went back to Catelow, because she'd have to have her computer and her flash drive. She used the flash drive to back up her files, just in case the computer ever failed.

They were married in a small wedding chapel, with Mina in her denim skirt and checked blouse, and Cort in his own cowboy regalia. He slid the wedding ring on her finger and kissed her when the official pronounced them married. Tears slid down her cheeks. She hadn't really believed that Cort was serious about marrying her, until she saw the rings. He was grinning from ear to ear, hardly the look of a reluctant bridegroom. It gave her hope for the future.

They got back into the stretch limo he'd hired and settled her beside him.

"What would you like to do?" he asked, smiling.

"This will sound stark."

"Try me."

She drew in a breath. "I'd like to go home," she laughed.

His eyes twinkled at her. "Puritan," he accused softly, but with affection. "No curiosity about the steamy side of life?"

She shook her head. "It's all very pretty," she said, studying the city lights and marquees as they passed them. "But I think a little Black Baldy calf is the prettiest thing on earth."

He drew her close and kissed her slowly. "So do I. Except in my case, it would be a purebred Santa Gertrudis calf."

"Semantics," she teased.

He chuckled. "Okay, then. Home it is. We'll pack you and then head south to Latigo."

Her breath caught. "I can't wait!"

"Feeling okay?"

She grimaced. "Just a little queasy, but the doctor said that was normal, even all the way through the first trimester." She looked at him worriedly, because they were newly married and she knew that he wanted her.

"Stop looking like that," he chided softly. "I'm not going to leave you alone and go hunting women just because you're sick. I'm not my father."

"Oh, I'd never think that," she said at once. "But I know you must want to, and I feel so bad about it."

"Honey, we have all the time in the world," he said softly, kissing her nose. "Besides all that, I'm going to be a father." He beamed. "Damn, I can't wait to tell my dad and my brothers!"

She laughed. "Why?"

"To see the look on their faces on Skype," he replied smugly. "I was the odd one out. Now Parker's going to be."

"I'm looking forward to meeting your family." She hesitated. "They won't think I married you because you're well-to-do?" she worried.

"You fell in love with a cowboy, Mina," he reminded her tenderly. "Not a cattle baron."

Her eyes softened on his face. "So I did. Fell hard, too, or I never would have ended up in bed with you."

"I figured that out on my own," he replied solemnly. "It's a big responsibility."

She frowned. "What do you mean?"

His fingers curled into hers. "I have to take good care of you," he said. "I've been responsible for the ranch and half the businesses for years. But it's another thing, to be responsible for a person. For a family," he emphasized. "It's going to be a learning curve."

"For both of us," she reminded him. "I've lived by myself for several years. It will take time for us to get used to each other."

He nodded. He smiled. "That learning curve I'm going to enjoy," he said.

She smiled back. But she was dreading the revelations he had yet to hear. She ground her teeth together. She'd been pregnant while she was crawling through the jungles of Nicaragua on her belly, risking being shot. How would he react, knowing that? And there was still the revelation about her research group and their deadly occupation. She was afraid to tell him, even more so now that she knew she was pregnant. What she'd done was a huge risk. But she hadn't known about the baby then. Maybe that would help her case. She hoped so.

They went back to her ranch and while she packed, Cort phoned his cousin.

Bart laughed until his sides hurt. "I don't believe it!" he told Cort. "You, married?"

"Married. Mina and I are over the moon. There's something else, too, but you have to keep it under your hat for a while."

"She's pregnant," Bart guessed.

"Oh yes. I'm the happiest man on earth," he confessed. "Mina, and a baby. What a combination!"

"And, you're okay with the other?" Bart queried softly, assuming Mina had told her new husband about what she did for a living.

"What other?" Cort asked pleasantly.

"The ranch," Bart amended quickly. "Are you going to put somebody in charge over there?"

"Yes. Fender. Can you keep an eye over this way?" Cort added. "Just to make sure he does things the way she'll want them done?"

"I certainly can!"

"Good man. I really appreciate it."

"Can I speak to her?"

"Sure. Mina?" he called.

She came out of the bedroom, where she'd just finished packing. She grinned up at Cort as he handed her the phone.

"Hi, Bart, guess what?" she teased.

"You're married," he chuckled. "Could have knocked me

over with a feather. I'm happy for you. He's a good man. He'll take care of you."

She looked up at Cort, her eyes brimming with love. "I'll take care of him, too," she said softly.

Cort flushed a little at the idea of a woman wanting to take care of him. He'd never had anybody offer. He had to swallow down the pincushion in his throat.

"You haven't told him, have you?" Bart asked.

"Well, no, not yet."

He heard the hesitation in her voice. "Don't wait too long," he advised. "Your book is rising on all the lists, and it has your photo on the back cover. You have readers all over, even in Texas. Don't let him find it out the hard way. Okay?"

"Okay," she said. "Watch out for Fender, will you?" she added. "And if he gets in a real tight spot, call Cousin Rogan. He'll know what to do."

"I will. Congratulations, my friend," he said. "I wish you all the happiness in the world. Cort, too. Tell him."

"I will. Thanks, Bart. We'll be in touch."

"I'll hold you to that."

Cort put away the phone. He was smiling when he looked down at Mina. "Okay, Mrs. Grier. Got your gear bagged up?"

She grinned. "Yes, I do. And my computer."

He frowned. "We have computers at the ranch, you know."

"I really need my own." She started to tell him, but she got cold feet. "I...game," she said. It was almost the truth. She had *Star Wars: The Old Republic* on her computer, complete with its distinctive icon. She'd played it a little over the years. It was a good enough excuse, for now.

"Oh, I see." He shook his head, laughing. "Wonders will never cease. My wife, the rancher and knitter and gamer."

"I can shoot a gun, too," she blurted out.

"In the game, you mean?" he asked.

She almost bit her tongue off as she forced a smile. "Of course!"

He chuckled. "I may have to learn, too, in my spare time. I don't have much of that lately, with roundup starting on Latigo. We've also got some labor disputes in one of our mining concerns," he added with a worried glance. "I may have to be away from home a bit. I'll try to make sure it's not excessive."

"That's okay," she said. "I can always…knit," she said, almost choking on the word.

"Fair enough. Let's get going!"

CHAPTER THIRTEEN

Mina's first glimpse of Latigo was a revelation. It wasn't what anyone would picture a ranch house looking like. The house was huge, two stories high, made of wood and brown stone in a design that melded into its landscape. There was a black wrought iron gate, which the driver opened automatically from a control panel over the windshield in the big Jaguar XJL that he was driving, with Cort and Mina in the backseat. The paved driveway led down through white-fenced pastures to a huge complex that featured the house itself, along with a garage, guesthouses, shade trees and a privacy fence made of stone, which surrounded the house complex. It, too, was gated.

"This ranch is unbelievable," Mina exclaimed.

He chuckled. "Thirty thousand acres," he said. "We have several thousand head of purebred Santa Gertrudis, on this ranch and another one in an adjacent county that we absorbed a few years ago, when its owner had to sell up."

"Your mountains aren't what I expected," she confessed.

He chuckled. "Well, they're not the snowcapped Tetons," he teased. "But they're mountains, just the same. We have miles of improved pasture here. The stables, and the barn, are farther out."

"The house is enormous."

"Ten bedrooms—each with a private bath—an indoor Olympic-size swimming pool, a conservatory with every sort of plant you can imagine and a kitchen with a walk-in freezer. It may look imposing," he added as the driver pulled up beside the front door. "But it's just home."

"Just home," she laughed.

There was a big gold Mercedes sitting at the steps, parked askew. Cort's face tautened. "My father's here," he said curtly.

"It will be all right," she said, putting her hand on his. "Don't worry."

"He can be a handful when he drinks."

She just smiled. "I never told you, but so can Bill McAllister. They used to come and get me when he went wild in the local bar. I'd lead him out like a lamb."

"Aren't you afraid of people who drink?" he asked softly.

"I was afraid of Henry because he was violent, and he hated me," she said. "Like my mother did. But it doesn't bother me so much when I know the reason. Bill lost his only daughter in a wreck a few years ago," she added. "He drinks because he hurts so much. I think maybe your father does, too."

He drew in a breath. "He's been morose since his new wife left him. But he's not hurting you—I don't care if he is my father," he said firmly.

Her heart lifted. She liked it, that he was protective of her. He brushed his mouth against hers. She touched his cheek and kissed him back.

The driver opened the back door for them. Cort got out and helped Mina out. He didn't let go of her hand as they moved up onto the porch, which seemed to go all around the house.

"It must be heaven to sit out here at sunset," she remarked, loving the wicker furniture with its deep cushions and the porch swing.

"I wish I had time to do it," he responded enigmatically. "Come on in." He hesitated as curses echoed from the living room. His lips made a thin line. "Damn it! Mina, it might be better if you wait here…" he began.

She ignored him and went right into the hall and, from there, into the elegant living room with its crystal chandelier and Victorian furniture and big, open fireplace. A white-haired man, tall like Cort, was trying to pick up a table which he'd apparently overturned. He was staggering.

Mina went forward and righted the table as he finally got it back in place. She could almost feel his pain. She'd lived with alcoholics for a long time, but this one didn't frighten her. She remembered what Cort had told her about his father. The older man looked down at her, his silver hair falling onto a broad forehead. Dark brown eyes met hers. He blinked. "Who are you?" he asked belligerently.

"I'm Cort's wife," she said softly.

He seemed disconcerted. While Cort looked on, spellbound, she reached for the elderly man's hand. "Wouldn't you like to sit down? You look very tired."

"Well…well, yes, I am tired. A little."

She led him to the sofa and waited while he sat down. She perched herself on the edge of a wing chair.

"You're the rancher from Wyoming," he said, slurring his words.

She nodded. "It's just a little ranch, though," she replied gently. "Not anything as big as yours and Cort's." She shook her head and sighed. "It looks as if you could ride all day and never leave Latigo." She frowned slightly. "Latigo. That's the leather strip on the saddletree that tightens the cinch," she mused.

He chuckled. "Well, the history of the ranch is in a book somewhere." He waved his hand in the general direction of a floor-to-ceiling bookcase in an adjoining room. "But the legend is that the first owner, a Spanish grandee, caught his hand in one while he was tightening the cinch and got dragged to the front gate. He had a grand sense of humor, apparently, because that's the name he gave the ranch. It's been Latigo ever since."

"I like it," she said.

Vic looked toward his son. "You never said she was pretty," he chided.

Cort chuckled as he joined them. "You never asked." He raised his voice. "Chaca, any chance of coffee and cake?"

A small, dark woman poked her head out of the kitchen. "Do you see that?" she asked, indicating a piece of equipment on an end table. "That is an intercom. You push the button and I answer."

"More fun to just yell," Cort retorted with a grin.

She threw up her hands. "You are the most troublesome man…" She stopped dead when she saw Mina. "Oh, excuse me," she said hesitantly and she moved farther into the room, wiping her wet hands on the long, embroidered apron she was wearing. "I am Chiquita, but everyone in the family calls me Chaca, for short," she said softly.

"Mina," came the soft reply. She shook hands. "I'm very happy to meet you. I'm Cort's wife."

"Wife!" Chaca gaped at him. "You got married? I am so happy! I never thought you would give up those horrible women and bring me somebody so nice!"

"Obviously, you underestimated my ability to attract somebody so nice," he chuckled.

"This is obviously true." Chaca sighed again and shook her head. *"Bienvenidos,"* she said to Mina. "I will bring coffee and cake at once, for you and Cort."

"And why not for me, too?" Vic demanded.

"Because you broke my best crystal serving dish this morning and I am not speaking to you," she huffed, and went off into the kitchen.

"I sat on it," Vic muttered, aware of amused glances. "Well, she had it in a chair cleaning it and didn't tell me and I sort of sat down hard. Damned thing. Could have ruined my new pants."

Cort just shook his head.

"So you got married." Vic smiled at Mina. "You remind me of Cort's mother," he added softly. "She had hair like yours, and a sweet, gentle nature."

"Mina likes to knit, too," Cort added, smiling at her. "She's a homebody. Oh, there's one other thing. We're going to make you a grandfather in a few months."

"A grandfather." Vic had to fight tears. "And this one will be where I can get to know him," he said quietly. "I've missed seeing my other grandkids. They live so far away. And they don't visit much."

"You're never home, much," Cort drawled.

"Well, I will be, when this one comes." He frowned at Mina. "He married you because of the baby?"

Mina laughed. "He didn't know about the baby until after he proposed."

"Well!"

"It's been the happiest two days of my life," Cort confessed. "I wasn't sure she'd have me."

"Silly man," Mina said softly. "I loved you the minute I met you."

"She stomped on my foot and dared me to have her arrested," Cort chuckled, telling on her.

She flushed. "He made fun of me because I was talking about how much I liked to knit."

"I swear that I'll never make fun of you again," Cort said, hand over his heart.

"You're only saying that because you don't want your foot stomped on again," she teased. But in the back of her mind was her profession and his misconception that she'd spend their married life knitting and raising children. Well, she could do both, of course. But she might have to depend more on her commando group to sit and tell her about adventures, rather than go with them. She had a feeling that Cort wasn't going to be understanding if he knew what she'd been doing with her life since she started writing books. And there would be the inevitable tours when she'd have to travel to sign books at the various venues, including independent bookstores where she already had readers who loved her work. In fact, there was a tour scheduled the following month. How was she going to tell him?

The coffee and cake were delicious. The coffee seemed to sober up Cort's father, who was quiet and even more morose and sober. He excused himself after one cup and went to his room upstairs.

"He needs to call his wife," Mina remarked.

"Good luck getting him to do it," Cort mused. "I tried. He said she'd been pretty firm about not wanting him back in her life, and she'd already seen the divorce lawyer." He grimaced. "When he gets served, he's going to go wild."

"We'll handle it," she said simply.

He searched her eyes. "There's something I didn't mention," he began. "Because you didn't know who I really was. But I've got business meetings in several states, starting tomorrow. You're going to be on your own for a while. I don't like leaving you here with Dad, in his present state."

"I like to write poetry, as well as play games," she said. Well, she had, in the past. "So I'm at my computer a lot. I'll just knit and compose and play video games and watch sunsets."

He chuckled. "Poetry, huh?"

"Yes." It was a lie and it was probably going to come back and haunt her. She had to find a way to tell him what she did for a living. It was going to be difficult, if she was totally honest. She'd work on it while he was away.

"I'm glad you have hobbies to keep you busy," he said. He leaned back on the sofa, studying her. "You look tired."

"I am, a bit," she confessed. "It was a long trip, even in a comfortable private jet." She touched her stomach. "I don't think the baby likes flying."

He grinned from ear to ear. The baby lifted his heart. He'd never imagined what it would be like to have a wife who was pregnant. He was discovering a family man hidden deep in his philandering heart. "He'll have to get used to it," he teased. "He'll inherit Latigo one day."

"And my little ranch," she replied.

"And your little ranch." He got up and leaned over to kiss her softly. "Come on. I'll show you to your room. I'll have one of the cowboys bring your bags up, too."

Her room was bigger than most of her little house back in Wyoming. The bathroom was twice the size of her bedroom. She was aghast at the utter luxury of it. Everything was done in shades of blue and beige, and the bed looked big enough for five people.

"This was my mother's room," Cort said softly. "I'm putting you in here temporarily, because I'm going to be gone a lot for the next few weeks. I'm really sorry," he added. "Things piled up while I was away. Now I have to play catch-up."

She turned and looked up at him. "It's okay," she said, smiling tenderly. "I love this room."

He moved closer and drew her against him to kiss her with soft, tender lips. "I'll sleep in here with you tonight," he whispered. "But I'll be gone before you wake, I'm afraid."

"Where do you have to go?" she asked.

"New York. Chicago. Miami. Denver. Los Angeles." He rattled them off and smiled ruefully. "The cattle are our main concern, but we own mining interests and oil interests, and a lot of real estate. It takes hard work to keep it all solvent, and I'm the point man."

She smoothed her hands over his broad chest. "It's an empire," she mused.

He nodded. "It is. I'm sorry that we won't get much of a honeymoon, but I'll make it up to you when I get things back in line. Where would you like to go? France? Italy? Spain?"

She laughed. "Let me have a little time to get used to being here," she said, "before we rush off to foreign places." In fact, she'd been in a lot of foreign places, most of them where sane people would never go.

"I can do that." He smoothed over her long fingers, resting on his chest. "Mina, you're going to have to learn a few things. Like how to organize business dinners, cocktail parties, stuff like that. And you'll need new clothes." He winced at her expression. "I'm not trying to talk down to you. Honest I'm not. You dress well for someone on a budget. But you're not on a budget here. I'll get you a gold card and you can fly up to Dallas, to Neiman Marcus, to shop. You'll need a whole new wardrobe."

She bit her lower lip. "Not right now?" she asked, almost pleading.

He let out a breath. She was tired, and this was culture shock. He could understand her reticence. "Okay. Not right now. I'll give you time to settle in before we go along, okay? You'll get used to it."

She recalled how much he'd been drinking at Pam Simpson's party and it disturbed her. She knew that many social parties involved drinking. She wasn't afraid of Cort's father, or Bill McAllister, when they had liquor, but she was nervous about strangers who had too much. How could she explain that to Cort?

She started to try when his phone rang. He pulled it out of the holder. It was a short conversation, but it caused him to brood.

"I have to leave today," he said, grimacing when he saw Mina's expression. "Honey, I'm sorry. There's a labor dispute at a company we own in Ohio. I have to go myself to negotiate with the shop foreman."

She drew in a breath. "You're a tycoon, so you have to do tycoon stuff," she translated. She forced a smile. "I'll be fine. You go and do what you have to." She didn't tell him that she was going to have to be on the road in a couple of weeks. She didn't know how, just yet.

"You're a sweetheart." He bent and kissed her hungrily. "Damn," he muttered as he put her away from him. "I'll miss you like hell."

"I'll miss you, too. Can you call me from time to time?"

"Of course." He smoothed back her hair. "I'll give you Parker's number. If Dad gets out of hand, you can call him and he'll come home and take care of whatever's wrong."

"Okay. But I think we'll get along," she added.

He chuckled. "That's my girl."

He was gone in an hour, after a rushed goodbye. Mina's things were sitting around her in the guest room. She unpacked her laptop computer first and set it up on a small desk by the window that overlooked the Davis Mountains, beyond the huge valley full of red-coated cattle. It would be a good place to write, she thought.

She put away her few clothes and grimaced, because most of them had come from low-end stores. She had the one good dress that she'd worn to Pam's party, but she was going to need new clothes not only for Cort's business interests, but also for her own. She had to dress the part of a successful author. And what about the guys, she wondered. How was Cort going to react to her commando friends? She rolled her eyes. Well, one disaster at a time.

She went downstairs, her cell phone in the pocket of her

beige slacks that she was wearing with a yellow sweater. Chaca motioned to her.

"The grande señor," she said, "has passed out in his room. He will probably sleep for the rest of the day." She made a face. "So I will feed him when he comes to. But would you like something to eat? An omelet perhaps, or a salad?"

"An omelet sounds very nice. Can I sit in the kitchen with you?" she added, after a glance at the huge, luxurious dining room. "I'm a little intimidated by all this," she confessed with a soft laugh. "I live on a tiny little ranch in Wyoming. I'm not used to fine things."

"Nor was I, when I first came to work here," Chaca laughed as she led the way into a huge kitchen with a small table and chairs in a corner. "It was hard to adjust. My people live closer to the border, in a little village called Malasuerte. We had fifty people and two Jersey milk cows," she teased.

Mina chuckled. "I have Black Angus cattle on my ranch. So does my friend, Cort's cousin Bart."

"You could have knocked me over with a feather when Cort introduced you as his wife." She shook her head. "So many glitzy women in his life, none of them with any character or any interests rather than money." She glanced at Mina. "And here he brings me a quiet, sweet woman whose eyes have no trace of greed."

Mina smiled. "I don't care about money. If I have enough to pay my bills, I'm happy."

"It is the same with me."

"Are you married?"

"Oh yes, for twenty years. My husband is the livestock foreman here, a job of great responsibility. The family has stud bulls worth millions and millions of dollars. We have full-time security guards here, and not only for the bulls. We have had problems with drugs coming over the border on the southern edge of the property. Not often, but the people involved think nothing of killing anyone who gets in the way."

"Good heavens!"

"There has never been a problem with safety here, at the house," Chaca was quick to add. "And we have the Border Patrol as well. Those people are very good at their jobs."

"That makes me feel better," Mina said.

"The baby, you are happy about it?"

Mina drew in a long breath. "So happy!" she said. "Every day is like a miracle. I can't wait until I'm really showing." She grinned. "I'm looking forward to maternity clothes. I guess that sounds sappy."

"It sounds like a woman in love who very much wants her child."

"It's like a dream, you know. I fell in love with a cowboy. I expected to live in a small house and do laundry and cook..."

"I do those things for you," Chaca said with a smile. "So you have time to sit and dream about the baby."

She laughed. "Well, I write a lot. So I'll be in my room a good bit, especially while Cort's away. Does he take these trips often?"

Chaca looked hunted. She didn't reply, busying herself with the preparation of the omelet.

"Chaca?" Mina prompted.

Chaca took the completed omelet off the stove and slid it onto a platter. She turned off the burner before she brought it to the small table where Mina was sitting. "He is almost never home, as a rule," she confessed, flushing a little. "It is a big responsibility, the business. When his father was home last, he took much of the burden off the señor. But since the talk of divorce, Vic has been helpless. He does nothing, so Cort must now do it all. It is a shame. When Parker lived at home, he also helped with the business." She finished setting the table and poured coffee into a cup for Mina. "It is too much for one man. I would like to say this, but I only work here."

"I'll say it," Mina promised.

"If he would only delegate," Chaca sighed. "He has competent people who run the real estate business, but he must involve himself in every part of it. Like this labor strike. He has negotiators and a business manager who could solve it themselves, but he trusts no one to do it except himself."

"I'll see what I can do," Mina promised.

Chaca smiled. "We will hope for change, then. Here, eat your omelet before it gets cold."

"The coffee is good," Mina said.

"It is decaf," came the dry reply. "Caffeine is not good for the baby."

Mina just laughed.

Vic came out of his room near bedtime. Mina was in the guest room with the door open, working away at the computer. It was a wonderful coincidence that she was working on a book set in Texas, and here she was in the best place to research it. Life, she thought, was funny.

She was deep in the middle of a shoot-out between rustlers and cowboys in the modern day setting when Vic paused at the doorway, frowning.

"What are you writing?" he asked.

She couldn't quite come out of the scene he'd interrupted. She turned slowly, her eyes blank as she tried to bridge the gap from fantasy to reality.

He came into the room, hands in his pockets, and frowned as he noticed the book on her desk. "Hey, I've read that book," he said, picking up the copy of SPECTRE. "It's really great!"

"Thanks," she said without thinking. And then she flushed wildly as she realized what she'd done.

He didn't notice her consternation. He was looking at the author's page on the back flap, the one that had a picture of Mina on it. "Willow Shane," he murmured. He looked at Mina with sudden realization. "That's you?" he exclaimed.

She ground her teeth together. "Yes," she said in a small voice.

"Well!" He let out a breath and laughed. "One of my sons bought it for his wife, and she went crazy over it. She shared it with her readers club and even sent copies to friends all over the country."

"I'm very flattered," she said, and meant it.

"So you knit and ranch and write books." He beamed. "You know, my wife always wanted to write a book." He trailed off. "She's a good woman. Better than I deserved. I cheated on her because she paid more attention to her family than she did to me. Her brother had just died of cancer and her family was grieving. I was an idiot." He smiled sadly. "Now I've lost her, and she's the first woman I ever really loved, except for my first wife."

She saved her work and got up from the desk. "Want to talk about it?" she asked.

He shrugged. "Well, yes."

"Come on downstairs. Chaca's gone, but I can make coffee." He smiled. "Okay."

He told her all about his wife, Sandra, and their explosive meeting.

"She was sitting at a table on the beach and I tripped over her purse," he recalled, his dark eyes soft with memory. "She helped me up, all apologies, and I looked into the bluest eyes I'd ever seen. I was hooked at once. She didn't know that I was wealthy. Kind of like you, with my son," he added with a smile. "She fell in love with a businessman. We got married and I brought her to Latigo. I thought she was going to faint. She'd worked as a newspaper reporter on a small weekly paper, but she was a stringer for one of the bigger papers in Vermont near her home. She was a good writer." He paused. "She wanted to write a novel, but she didn't think she had the talent."

"Most of us who write just sit down and get on with it," she said wistfully. "I never had great talent, but I was persistent and I had friends who believed in me. They pushed me to send a manuscript off to a publisher." She sighed. "It took a few false starts, but I finally sold a book. *SPECTRE* is actually my fourth novel, but it's the one that's getting all the attention. It's on the *USA Today* list and climbing, and it just made the *New York Times* list." She looked at him worriedly. "I've got to go on tour week after next…"

"No problem, we've got two airplanes and a jet," he teased. "We'll get you there and back."

"That would be nice. I hate flying commercial."

"So do I. That's why we have two airplanes and a jet," he confided with a grin. He sipped coffee. He scowled. He looked up at her suddenly. "I remember something from the book jacket. You actually slogged through swamps in Central America with a group of mercenaries to research *SPECTRE*?" he exclaimed.

She nodded. "A commando group adopted me after the first book." She laughed. "They put me through a training course you wouldn't believe. Then they packed me up and took me on missions. I'm only just back from Nicaragua. We rescued a kidnapped child. I'm still taking quinine tablets to make sure I don't come down with malaria."

"Did you know you were pregnant when you went to Nicaragua?" he asked worriedly.

"No," she confessed. She sighed. "I spoke to my doctor, before we left Wyoming. At this stage of the pregnancy, he said I should be fine. I'll have to find a local obstetrician, though," she added.

"We'll do that tomorrow," he said. He smiled. "And I'll stop drinking. For a while, at least."

She laughed. "Okay."

Vic was fun to be with. When he wasn't drinking, he was charming. He went with her in the Mercedes to a friend of his who practiced obstetrics, and got her in. He even sat and waited while she filled out all the forms and was examined by Dr. Truett.

"You're doing very well," Dr. Truett told her, "despite your adventure," he added with a chuckle, after she'd told him about her research trip. "Keep up with the quinine. I'm adding a prescription for prenatal vitamins as well. How about nausea?"

"I only have a little," she said. "It passes pretty quickly."

"If you have any problems, come and see me."

"I will."

"And try to stay out of jungles, at least until the baby is born," he added, tongue in cheek.

She laughed. "I'll do that. Thanks very much."

"Well?" Vic asked when they were outside.

"He says I'm doing great," she said. "I have a prescription for vitamins."

"We'll get that filled on the way home," he said.

"It's very nice of you to come with me," she replied.

"I'm sorry Cort can't be here to do it," he replied sadly. "I've been a drag on him lately. I'm going to get back into ranch business."

"It would help you," she said. "You need to keep your mind busy, so you don't have much time to brood."

"I wouldn't be brooding if I could get Sandra to listen to me," he sighed. "I really want her back."

"Give it time," she said. "You might consider writing her a letter," she added.

He pursed his lips. "I'm not much good at letters. But I could text her a poem and some emojis," he chuckled.

"It's worth a try."

"I suppose it is."

She laughed, remembering the hunter at Pam Simpson's party back in Catelow.

"What's funny?"

"I was remembering a party Mrs. Simpson gave for me, back home. One of my readers is a deer hunter. He takes my books into the woods to read while he's waiting for game to show up."

"You know, Sandra is one of your biggest fans," he mused. "Would you mind if I used you as a sort of bribe?"

She burst out laughing. "No. I wouldn't mind at all. Feel free."

"Then I'll do that, as soon as we get home!"

She phoned Bart to see how things were going back home, while Vic went upstairs to his room to text his wife in Vermont.

"Hi," she said. "How are things going?"

"Great! I checked with Fender. Your ranch is secure, no problems there. How's it going at Latigo?"

"It's nice. I've just been to an obstetrician with Cort's dad. He's very nice."

"Nice? Vic?" Bart exclaimed.

"Well, he's been nice to me," she returned. "He's sad because his wife left him."

"He was cheating on her!"

"He told me about that. He told me why, too. He's not a bad man. He has insecurity issues."

"Boy, there's a lot of that going around," Bart chuckled. "Well, as long as he's nice to you, that's the main thing. How's Cort?"

"I don't know. He had to sort out a labor strike at some company, then he's got to go a lot of places on other business. From what I understand, he's almost never home. I miss him. But I'm working on the new book."

"Told him yet?" he asked gently.

"Not really. His father read *SPECTRE*. He recognized me from the back cover."

"Mina, you really need to tell Cort before he finds it out the hard way."

"I know. I should have told him long ago. I just didn't know

how. He's not going to be happy about my commando group,
I just know it. So I've been putting it off."

"Listen, that book is in every major bookstore in America,
and it's climbing the charts. How long do you think it's going
to be before he sees your photo on the book jacket and makes
the connection?"

"The photo doesn't look that much like me," she said.

"In the circles Cort travels in, your book will be read a lot.
It's an expensive hardcover."

"I guess so. I'll tell him as soon as he comes home," she promised.

"You do that," he said. "And take care of yourself. I miss you."

She laughed. "I miss you, too, my friend. I'll talk to you
soon."

"Okay."

She started to put down the cell phone when it rang again.
"Hello?" she answered.

"Hi!" It was Ry, the leader of her commando group. "I
wanted to see how you were doing on the new book and if you
needed some help."

She laughed. "I do, I do!"

"We can come up to Wyoming..."

"I'm not in Wyoming, though," she said. "I'm married and
pregnant and I'm living on a big ranch in West Texas."

"Wow! Congratulations!" he said with genuine pleasure.
"Then, how about telling us how to get to where you are? Because we've got some new tales to share!"

"That's a deal!" she replied.

CHAPTER FOURTEEN

Vic came downstairs rubbing his hands and grinning.

Mina's face lit up. "Don't tell me. It worked!"

"It worked," he laughed. "You little doll, it worked! She said she'd do anything to meet you. Including discussing a second chance for our marriage."

"Oh, I'm so glad," she said on a sigh.

"So am I. Thanks," he added warmly.

"You're very welcome. Now I need a favor." She grimaced. "You may not like it."

His eyebrows arched. "Ask me."

"You know the commando group I hang out with, the ones I was just in Nicaragua with?"

He nodded.

"Well, obviously, I can't go crawling through jungles pregnant, but I need some insight into drug smuggling for the book I'm working on, and the guys have done interdiction in other countries…"

"And they want to come talk to you," he guessed. He laughed at her expression. "Tell them to come on. But wait until Sandra gets here." He rolled his eyes. "She'll go crazy when she knows they'll be here. She used to hang out with narcs and mercenaries and former mob members…"

"You're kidding!" Mina exclaimed gleefully.

"I'm not. You'll understand when you meet her."

"When is she coming?" Mina asked.

"Day after tomorrow."

"So I'll text Ry and tell him to come with the guys day after tomorrow," she promised. "It's going to be so much fun!"

He shook his head. "What a change you've made here already."

She smiled. "Thanks. I love Latigo. I'm going to be very happy here."

Two days later, Vic walked in the door with his wife, Sandra, fresh from the airport in El Paso. She wasn't at all what Mina expected. Sandra was little and wiry with amber eyes and brown hair and a smile that would stop traffic.

"Willow Shane, and I actually get to talk to you," she exclaimed as she hugged Mina. "I couldn't believe it when Vic told me! And you have a commando group for research. I thought I'd die of happiness!"

"I'm so happy to meet you. He—" she indicated Vic "—was very sad without you."

She turned her eyes on her husband and pursed her lips. "Yes, well, we have a few things to work out."

"A couple back home had those issues and they went to a psychologist," Mina said gently.

Vic sighed. "I'd go to a psychologist today if Sandra would give me another chance."

"You would?" Sandra exclaimed. "Honest?"

He nodded. He shrugged. "I guess I have more issues than I realized." He glanced at Mina and smiled. "I seem to have lucked out on daughters-in-law however. She's a wonder."

"She's my favorite author," Sandra replied. She took off her denim jacket. "I have about a thousand questions…oh dear…" Her voice trailed off when she saw Mina's face.

"Sorry!" Mina jumped up and ran to the bathroom in time to lose her lunch. She cleaned herself up and came back out with a wet washcloth, bathing her face on the way.

"Goodness, do you have a virus or something?" Sandra asked worriedly.

"I'm just pregnant," she confessed, and laughed.

"You lucky woman," Sandra said softly. "I'm too old to get pregnant, and I was too career-minded to even want to, while I was young. I've missed the boat."

Mina put an arm around her. "You can share mine. Would you like the morning sickness or the heartburn first?"

Sandra burst out laughing and hugged her back.

Meanwhile, Cort was just finishing up talks with the union to finalize a new contract and feeling guilty for leaving his new wife alone with his father at Latigo. He was miserable. He missed Mina. He wanted to go home. But there was a meeting he had to attend with some business leaders in Akron who were involved in the ranch's real estate holdings. It was a cocktail party.

In the old days, he'd loved mingling with beautiful women—and there were always beautiful women, married or single—and drinking until he felt pleasantly numb. But now, alcohol and other women had lost their appeal. He must, he mused, be getting old.

A gorgeous brunette he'd had a brief affair with latched on to him at the party and he became aware belatedly of the flash from a camera of some sort. But he disregarded it. Someone was always taking candid shots of other people, or selfies, and the room was dark.

A flash would have been necessary. He wondered why most of the affairs he attended were conducted in such dim light.

Probably, he said with a silent chuckle, so that some of the phi-landering went unnoticed.

He hoped his father was behaving himself. Certainly, Mina could call Parker if she needed help with him. But she seemed very capable of handling Vic, even when he was roaring drunk. It was a revelation, watching her do that, with her traumatic background. A lot of her life had been ravaged by the abuses of drunk people, including her own mother.

He'd called her the night before, just to make sure she was okay. She'd laughed and said that except for morning sickness, things were good. Vic had stopped drinking and was actually talking to his ex-wife. She didn't add that Sandra was there at Latigo, or that her commando group was due to arrive soon. She didn't have time, because he was interrupted by another urgent business call and he had to hang up. He was impatient with himself for that. He shouldn't have cut her off. Well, he'd be home soon, and he'd make up for his absence.

He watched one of the single women present trying to interest a very wealthy married man over martinis, but the man walked away. Her eyes lit on Cort and she moved toward him like a slinky predator. He laughed to himself. That type of woman no longer attracted him. He compared this pretty serpent with his sweet homebody of a wife who liked to knit and read romance novels. Mina would never do something like that. She'd never come on to another man at all. He felt good about that. She was just what he needed; a wife he could leave alone when necessary without having to worry if she was running around on him.

It was a good thing he couldn't see what was going on at Latigo two days later. Mina and Sandra were sitting in the living room with five men dressed in casual clothes. But they weren't casual people. They were Mina's commando group, and their delight in her marriage and pregnancy made her feel very good. Three of them had wives and kids of their own.

"When the baby comes," Ry said with a grin, "we'll teach him the fine art of stealth!"

Mina laughed. "I can hardly wait."

"I want to know all about that stint you mentioned in the Congo," Sandra said, with an apologetic glance at Mina.

"So do I," Mina laughed. "But first," she said, pulling out her cell phone and turning to the Notes Application, "I need to know about drug smuggling on the Texas border and interdiction strategies."

"That will be my pleasure," Ry said. His face hardened. "One of my men left to work in the Border Patrol. He was killed by a group of drug smugglers. Most of them are well armed and they have nothing to lose. They don't mind killing government employees, ranchers or anyone else who gets in their way."

Mina nodded, having already researched as much about smuggling as she could find on the internet. There was, however, no comparison with men who knew about it from personal experience.

"We're having problems with drug smugglers now," Vic interjected, having joined them with Chaca right behind carrying a tray of coffee and cups. "Thanks, Chaca," he added as she put it down, smiled and left them to it.

"Interesting," Ry said. "How so?"

"They're using the southern border of our ranch as a trade route, you might say," Vic replied. "We have good intel that they're part of the Zetas. Camo, military gear and weapons, the works. One of our cowboys got shot on my own land."

Ry pursed his lips and his eyes began to twinkle. He looked at his men and saw the same anticipation on their faces. "This is the sort of thing we truly enjoy interfering with," he told Vic. "Think of us as a pro bono ex-military group on a stealth mission. Nobody will know except us."

Vic whistled softly. "My son really wouldn't like this."

"Your son really doesn't have to know," Ry chuckled.

Mina groaned inwardly. This was going to be one more thing that she'd have to explain to Cort. But if it would help keep the ranch solvent…

"And no, you can't come with us this time," Ry told Mina firmly.

She made a face at him.

"How about me?" Sandra asked excitedly. "I went on a SWAT raid once. I can shoot a .45 auto."

"Not on your life," Vic said immediately, and gave her a look that could have boiled water. "I'm not risking you. Not for anything."

Sandra flushed a little and smiled. "Well, maybe I'll wait to hear all about it when you get back," she told them.

"Don't get killed," Mina said firmly. "It will look very bad in my book." She grinned.

"Okay," Ry said, and he grinned back.

"Oh, the people you know," Sandra said with a sigh, after Vic had called in his livestock foreman to show the men where the trespassers were giving them the most trouble. It was a huge ranch. Even with fencing, it was impossible to watch the border night and day. Well, for the ranchers. Ry had a solution for that. He and his men mounted remote cameras in unexpected places and sat back to wait for results.

Their third night in residence, there was a sudden flurry of activity on the border. Ry and his men, already in sand-colored camo gear, assembled their weapons with solemn faces and went out to meet the threat.

Mina and Sandra monitored the assault on a network of monitors with night vision and audio that Ry and the guys had set up in a spare bedroom.

Cort was at yet another business party, talking a trade deal with some men from Japan. Apparently, their hostess was another fan of Willow Shane, because she had a copy of *SPECTRE* on a coffee table, just like another businessman's wife he'd met days before.

"She's the most marvelous author," the woman rattled off to a woman standing near Cort. "She actually goes on missions with this commando group into the jungle. She can use any sort of weapon that exists, and she's a brown belt in Tae Kwon Do. In addition to all that, she runs a ranch of her own somewhere in the northwest."

"Amazing," came the reply. "I'd love to meet her."

"But you can," the other woman said. "She'll be signing books at the Silver Bookmark, here in the city in a couple of weeks on an author's tour!"

"She will? I'll mark it on my calendar."

"I can't wait," came the reply. The women moved away and Cort shook his head. He was lucky to be married to a woman who just wanted to knit and raise babies, not some wild-eyed author who risked her life for a story and went on tour to sell books. He wondered if the mysterious Willow Shane even had a home life. And she was a rancher? How the hell could she run a ranch and be on the road all the time, he wondered.

Well, it wasn't his problem. He looked at his watch. He was ready to go back to the hotel and pack. With any luck, barring any further problems, he could fly home in the morning. He'd missed Mina. He recalled their one long, sweet session in bed and looked forward to more of them.

Of course, there was the morning sickness. He knew she was having a hard time right now. But he could hold her all night, even if she didn't feel up to intimacy. He thought about the baby and smiled. What a happy difference Mina had made in his life already. He felt sorry for his father, who'd thrown away his own chance for happiness with the reporter from Vermont. Maybe someday the older man would stop philandering and really settle down. He didn't know what he was missing.

★ ★ ★

Mina was glued to her chair in front of the bank of camera monitors in the spare bedroom, with Sandra sitting in a chair beside her. Neither woman wanted to miss the confrontation. It was going to be epic; she just knew it.

"This is so exciting," Sandra confided. "I haven't been a reporter for several years. I miss it terribly. Those adrenaline rushes are hard to give up."

"I know exactly what you mean." She sighed. "I'm going to be stuck at home for the immediate future. I really can't go out with the guys when I'm pregnant."

Sandra patted her hand. "This is almost as good," she said, indicating the monitors. "Oh, look!"

As she spoke, a small group of men in military gear, holding what looked like automatic weapons, passed by the cameras. There was both night vision and sound, so what they said was audible. They were speaking in Spanish, in terse, angry voices. Fortunately they weren't rattling off like some people did, so that Mina understood almost every word. What she heard chilled her blood.

"They're talking about the ranch house," she said to Sandra, and her face went pale. "Two of them want ransom…!"

"Your guys are out there. They'll shut them down," Sandra began.

"You don't understand," Mina said urgently. "There are two groups! One isn't associated with the smugglers. It's run by two men who separated from the others and just want hostages. It's a big ranch and they know that wealthy people live here. They think it's easy money, compared to running drugs!"

Even as she spoke, she heard the front door open violently. Mina ran to the closet and unpacked her .45. She grabbed the full clip and shot it home into the gun and cocked it. She hoped against hope that one of the commandos was monitoring the audio from those cameras, so they'd know Mina and the others were in danger. But she couldn't count on being rescued.

"Get behind me," she told Sandra, and suddenly she was someone else. She was Willow Shane to the teeth.

Sandra didn't argue. She did what she was told.

Mina went stealthily to the door. She wanted to call to Vic, who'd gone into his room to watch TV, and tell him not to move. She looked over her shoulder and saw Sandra texting furiously. Sandra looked up and nodded. Mina nodded, too. Obviously the women had the same thought.

There were muttered discussions of who would remain downstairs and who would look for somebody to hold hostage. This was a big rich house. Whoever lived here would pay and pay well for anyone they could snatch. They sounded bombed out of their minds, Mina realized. That would make this harder. You couldn't really reason with someone whose brains were on vacation. Her hand tightened on the .45. Her mouth was dry. Her palms were damp. She laughed inwardly at those visible signs of fear. But fear was only a symptom. It needed control, and the guys had taught it to her. She moved closer to the door.

Footsteps sounded on the soft carpet. She closed her eyes and listened. Only one person, she surmised. Just one.

The man was trying to walk stealthily, but it wasn't working. Mina heard him. She had to act before Vic decided to yield to his protective instincts and pop his head out of his room. It would most likely be immediately fatal.

So she moved out into the hall in an athletic stance, legs apart, knees bent, facing the target, shoulders in front of the hips. It was perfect for recoil management and firing fast follow-up shots if necessary. The target was a small, uniformed man with a smirk on his face.

"Ah, so you have a gun," he said in accented English. "I have one, too. Let me show you how easily I can shoot it…!"

He brought the pistol up, and his eyes signaled that he meant to shoot her.

She shot him in the knee before he could pull the trigger. He cried out harshly, but before he could raise his gun, she jumped forward and kicked the gun out of his hand.

"*¡Alto!*" she said. "*Si le gusta continuar con su vida, no mueve.*" Her eyes, over the barrel of the gun, were cold as ice.

The downed man, obviously not in a hurry to die, complied with her request and lay still, groaning. Sandra almost clapped.

Vic came out into the hall, shocked when he saw the man on the floor and Mina standing over him beside Sandra.

Just as he started to speak, a second man came flying up the stairs with his gun leveled, but he never got a chance to use it. A bullet found him first. He stopped, made a half turn and fell down the steps groaning.

Ry came in the door, almost panting. It had been a very rushed trip back and he'd run all the way from the truck in the driveway up the steps.

"Are you guys okay?" he asked at once.

Mina laughed, feeling faint. "Yes, but there's a guy on his back up here who isn't feeling so good."

"I've got three others in the truck," Ry said. "We'll call the Border Patrol and make them a present of these five."

"Better call an ambulance for this one," she told Ry. "I think he's going to need some major repairs on his kneecap."

Ry nodded. "This one's going to need a medic, too," he said, indicating the groaning man at the bottom of the staircase. "Best call the sheriff's office as well. Don't touch anything. They'll have to process the crime scene so that they can press charges. You'll need to give a statement as well."

She nodded, letting the pistol hang at her side. "Gosh, I'm glad you put me through that training course," she said. "I'd be dead."

"They don't usually kill people they plan to ransom until after they get the money," he returned.

"Yes, well this *pendejo* is stoned out of his mind and I wasn't sure he didn't have other purposes in mind for me," she added with an icy look at the man on his back on the floor.

The wounded man was moaning. "I need a doctor," he said.

Ry was pressing in numbers on his cell phone. "I'm going to need credentials," he said, and looked toward Vic.

"I hired you all two days ago to help me with a drug trafficking problem," he said at once, with twinkling dark eyes. "Amazing, how fast you guys solved this part of it."

Ry chuckled. "Not so amazing. We've had a little more practical experience than these guys."

"I noticed."

Mina leaned back against the wall, still holding the .45. "This will make an amazing chapter if I change enough names," she said heavily.

Sandra, who'd moved into Vic's arms the minute he came out into the hall, was smiling. "I get to read it first," she said.

Mina smiled at her. "Of course you do," she laughed. She swallowed hard, turned green and handed the pistol to Vic. "Sorry," she began, and ran for the bathroom.

The sheriff arrived along with the Border Patrol and the ambulance. Into the mix came a limousine with a man whose horror was immediately apparent to the driver, who saw Cort Grier's face in the rearview mirror just briefly, before his passenger jerked open the door and ran toward the house.

Cort's first thought was that something had happened to Mina. But he passed a swarthy-looking man on a stretcher and another being carried out by two husky paramedics on yet a second stretcher.

When he got into the house, there were nine men standing in the living room. Three of them were in uniform. Five others were in casual clothing, but they looked as if they belonged in military uniforms, just by their bearing. The last man was

Vic, who stood with his arm around Sandra while the men in uniform and the men out of uniform spoke.

There was blood all over the floor in the hall.

"What happened?" Cort demanded anxiously.

Several people started talking at once, but he looked up and there was Mina, in a long jumper with a tank top under it, looking pale and out of sorts.

He ignored the people talking, skirted the blood and rushed up to take her in his arms and hug her close.

"My God, there's blood on the floor! Are you okay?" he bit off.

"I'm fine. Really," she said breathlessly, hugging him back. "I didn't realize you'd be home so soon."

He drew back and looked at her worriedly, searching for any evidence that the violence had touched her.

"You're sure you're all right?" he asked again.

She managed a wan smile. "Yes."

"Who are the men on the stretchers outside?" he asked then.

"They thought drug smuggling was too much work, so they sauntered in here looking for hostages. I got the one upstairs. Ry got the one down here. We had to call the sheriff's office and Border Patrol, because Ry and his men had the drug smugglers in custody."

The sheriff, a tall man with white hair and a mustache and dark eyes, joined them on the staircase. A team of forensics people had just come in the door, and the deputy was showing them where to collect evidence.

"You got one…?" Cort asked slowly, all at sea.

"Hi, Cort," Darly Coolidge said, pausing to shake hands. "Were you here when all this was going down?"

"No, I just got home from a business meeting," Cort said blankly. "I don't understand any of this!" He looked at Mina. "You shot a man? I didn't know you had a gun!"

"I have a .45 Colt ACP," she told him. "Well, the sheriff has it right now. It's evidence in a shooting."

"And we need a statement from you, if you're feeling up to it, Mrs. Grier," he added with a smile.

She smiled back. "I'm all right now. I just have periodic morning sickness, usually at night," she laughed.

"You have a .45 automatic," Cort was still trying to process the information.

She nodded.

"Talk about living your novels," the sheriff chuckled, shaking his head. "Come on down when you're ready," he added to Mina, who smiled and nodded.

"Okay," Cort said, pale brown eyes flashing as he faced his wife. "What's going on?"

She grimaced. "It's sort of a long story. Couldn't we sit down and have coffee and I'll try to explain it?"

He was tired and confused and ill at ease with strangers crawling all over his house. Vic and Sandra seemed to be having the time of their lives.

Cort drew Mina to his side and walked her around the blood and into the living room.

"Cort! What an adventure you missed!" Sandra exclaimed, pausing to hug him. "I still can't believe who you married. Honest to goodness, Willow Shane, of all people, and her book just hit number four on the *New York Times* bestseller list! Or it will, next week. Her agent gets advance notice of the postings."

Willow Shane. *SPECTRE*. His head seemed to turn in slow motion toward his wife, who loved to knit and read romance novels. She was flushing and looking very uncomfortable. Bart had a friend who was a successful novelist. There had been a party for her in Catelow. Willow Shane. The book jacket said that she went on missions with a group of commandos, that she could shoot a gun and had a high belt in a Korean martial art.

He just gaped at her.

The deputy had taken statements from the commandos and was talking to the sheriff. Vic and Ry joined Mina.

"Well, it will be a story to tell your grandchildren," Vic chuckled as he hugged his son. "What a night! We caught the drug smugglers who've been using our southern border for a freeway, and two would-be kidnappers are on their way to a long sentence on federal charges. What a night!" he repeated, laughing as he drew Sandra close.

"You two are back together?" Cort asked. His mind was whirling like a top.

"I bribed her," Vic said. He grinned. "With your wife."

"With my wife?"

"Mina's her favorite author. I told Sandra if she'd give me a second chance, I'd introduce her. The guys there were a bonus." He indicated Ry and the others, just joining them.

"You'd be her commando group," Cort said quietly, his narrow-eyed gaze on their leader.

Ry shrugged. "She wanted to write fiction that sounded authentic, so we trained her," he added with a grin. "She was a hell of a pupil." He didn't add anything about their latest mission, for fear of making a bad situation worse. Obviously, Mina's new husband was getting a few shocks tonight.

"I'm working on a new book," Mina told Cort, her expression hopeful. "Since I can't go on missions with them, they're educating me about drug interdiction."

"Missions. Drug interdiction. Kidnappers. Blood on the floor." His deep, angry voice was gathering speed and volume. "You never told me what you did for a living!"

Mina grimaced. "I didn't quite know how. The longer I put it off, the harder it got."

Under the wide brim of his dress Stetson, his eyes were glittery with rage. "You could have been killed!"

"I've only ever been wounded once, and it hardly left a scar," she countered, and then bit her tongue when she saw his expression.

Ry whistled under his breath. "Mina, I think the boys and I will go along with the sheriff to give formal statements. We'll be in touch."

"Thanks for what you did," she replied.

"Thanks very much," Vic added, and shook hands with Ry. "I won't forget you."

Ry smiled. "If you ever need us, we'll be around. Take care of that baby, Mina," he added with a smile in her direction.

"I will. I'll text you a photo when he's born. And I may need a little more information," she added without looking at her taciturn husband.

"Text me. Let's go, boys." Ry threw up a hand and got out of the line of fire.

Cort was fuming. He didn't dare upset Mina any more than she'd already been upset, so he'd gone into his own room and closed the door. His wife was a famous author. She'd been in firefights. She was on bestseller lists. She went out with a group of commandos. And she'd let him think that she was a shy, retiring little rancher who liked to knit.

He wanted to howl at the moon. He'd never had anything hit him so hard. Secrets. They were only just married and she kept secrets from him.

There was a knock at the door and before he could tell the knocker to go the hell away, his father walked in.

Cort was bareheaded, his suit coat off, his shirt unbuttoned. He looked outraged.

"Can we talk?" Vic asked quietly.

Cort drew in a breath. "I've seen that damned book everywhere," he muttered. "It was at the last two cocktail parties I attended. She's famous!"

"Very famous," Vic agreed. He smiled gently. "She got Sandra to forgive me. I guess I'll be going to a psychologist to find out why I want to cheat on everybody. Mina's special, and I mean that. She was probably afraid to level with you about what she did. You were so happy to label her a little homebody who knitted." He shook his head. "She's a hundred times more complex than that little Wyoming rancher you thought you knew."

"Complex." He made a rough sound and picked up the whiskey he'd poured himself. "I've had a hell of a night," he muttered. "I need some sleep before I try to cope with all this."

"That's exactly what Mina said," Vic agreed.

He drew in a long breath. "She went on commando missions." His heart stopped. He looked at Vic. "Recently?" he asked.

Vic moved restlessly. "She's still taking quinine tablets to prevent malaria. She went with the group to Nicaragua and helped rescue a kidnapped child."

"Oh my God," Cort burst out. "She's pregnant!"

"Yes, but she didn't know it at the time. I took her to Dr. Truett and he said she's fine. So is the baby."

"Anything could have happened to her," Cort exclaimed. "I thought she wanted to have kids and raise them. I didn't know that she came with a whole damned career!"

"Said the man who's never home," Vic murmured half under his breath.

Cort glared at him.

"Well, it's true," Vic returned. "You could have delegated that union mess, and you know it, Cort."

The other man shifted his feet and sipped his drink.

"Marriage isn't as easy as it looks," Vic continued. "Look at me. I've failed at it miserably. At least, until now. I think I have a fighting chance at saving my marriage." He pursed his lips. "You might try to save yours. I believe Mina's packing right now to go back to Wyoming."

Cort's heart jumped. But just for a few seconds, he thought

how it would be if she did go home. He'd be free again, to pursue beautiful women, to live the life of a playboy. Did he want that, truly?

CHAPTER FIFTEEN

Mina was miserable. Cort had looked at her as if he despised her. She should have tried to be honest with him. She'd brought this on herself. She knew it, but it didn't help. Cort was furious, and he was right to be. She should have told him at the beginning who she really was, not have him find it out in a traumatic way, like he had tonight.

She put the last few clothes in her suitcase and closed it gently. Well, she had a ranch to go back to, and she had the sweet baby lying snug in her womb. Many women had much less.

She sat down in her wing chair and pulled out her cell phone while she waited for the house to be quiet so that she could call a cab to take her to the airport. She'd have to get a ticket. She was on her way to a website to buy one when she chanced on an item in a digital newspaper she read.

Her eyes flamed. It was a photograph of her brand-new husband with his arm around a drop-dead gorgeous brunette at some cocktail party. He was nursing what looked like whiskey in a squat glass, and his smile was as brilliant as if he'd won the Nobel prize. She almost threw the phone across the room. Her husband! She'd convinced Sandra to forgive her own philandering husband, only to turn around and realize that she was in the same boat! And she thought, *forgive*, hell!

She picked up an ugly vase on the dresser in her room and started out the door with it, fury making her face red. She went downstairs and looked for Cort. She found him standing behind a chair while he talked to his father and Sandra.

"You snake in the grass!" Mina raged. She threw the vase at him.

He caught it handily and put it down on the end table before he moved toward her, "What are you talking about?" he demanded with some indignation. Surely he was the injured party here!

"This!" She pulled up the news item on her cell phone and showed it to him. "Explain that!"

His mouth opened. His cheeks had a ruddy flush, high on his cheekbones.

She glanced at Sandra. "Now I know how you felt!" she told the other woman. "He's only been married a few days, and he's already tomcatting around business dinners!"

"I wasn't!" Cort tried to defend himself.

"You had your arm around her!"

"I never!" he shot back. "Here. You look closely at that picture," he added icily. "I had my arm behind her. I was reaching for my drink on the table!"

She stared at the picture. It made her furious to see that he was right. He really didn't have his arm around her. It just looked that way. But the cutline was damning: Texas Millionaire Courts Oil Princess.

"Oh yeah?" Mina retorted. "Well, the headline sure is explicit!"

"She's married," he said belligerently.

"So are you!"

Vic got up. "Okay, now," he said, getting between them. "Listen. She had a career and didn't tell you," he told Cort. "While he—" he spoke to Mina, indicating Cort "—was apparently hanging out at business dinners with other women. It's done. It's over. You know about Mina's career now," he told Cort. "And you—" he indicated Mina "—know that he wasn't running around on you. It was just a headline and some journalist's attempt to start trouble. Everything's out in the open. You both have to make peace. She's pregnant," he reminded Cort gently. He smiled. "And this time, I'll get to know my grandchild, because you'll both be here. So will I. Sandra and I talked about it. She thinks I need to take some responsibility for Latigo and the businesses, so you won't be on the road so much, Cort. Now that her family is getting over its grief, she's willing to live here."

"Yes, I am," Sandra said. She grinned at Mina. "I can pump Willow Shane there for plots and such, and I can hang out with her commando friends. It's very exciting!"

"Exciting." Cort let out a breath. He glared at his father. He glared at Mina. "Maybe I'm the one who should pack and go back on the road."

"Why?" Vic asked.

"She risked her life and our baby's life, crawling through a jungle with a bunch of strange men carrying a .45 automatic!" Cort exclaimed, pointing at her. "The leader of the commando group said she actually shot at a guy! Not only that, she was wounded during one mission she went on with them!"

"I was not pregnant when I went to Nicaragua," Mina raged. "Well, I was, but I didn't know I was! And how do you think I can research a book on mercs or SWAT teams or feds without talking to them?"

"You can talk to them in the living room!" Cort shot back. "Or in their offices! You have no business in combat situations. You could be killed!"

Mina stared at him. He really did care. He was belligerent because he was afraid for her, and he didn't quite know how to admit it without appearing weak. It took the fight right out of her.

She went to him and smoothed her hands against his chest. "I'm tired," she said softly, and laid her cheek against him. "And sleepy."

His hands reluctantly went to her long hair and threaded through it. The unexpected fragility of her cut through his defenses like a knife through hot butter, and he sighed. "You've had a hard night," he said gently. "And I've been a fool. I'm sorry."

She smiled. "I should have told you. I'm sorry, too."

"That makes three of us," Vic added, his arm around Sandra. "But we were damned lucky that Mina's cohorts were around tonight. She might have been kidnapped, along with Sandra and me." He chuckled. "Mina threw down on one of the men who was threatening her and Sandra. She got him right in the kneecap. Hell of a shot."

Mina flushed and laughed softly. "I don't like killing people. In fact, I've never killed anyone. I was scared to death when that man came upstairs and I saw how bombed out he was. Men in that condition are on a hair trigger. He would have shot me."

"The sheriff agreed," Cort confessed. "So did your friend Ry. He said the men were high as a kite and hungry for money."

"It's not as bad as it seems," Mina said, snuggling closer to Cort. "You can get blood out of carpet. Honest."

He burst out laughing. "Okay," he said. "But no more shoot-ups next to the upstairs bedrooms," Cort said firmly as he pressed a kiss on her forehead.

"Okay," she said softly. She hesitated and a mischievous grin claimed her face. "Is downstairs all right for them, then?"

"I'll lock you in a closet," he threatened.

She laughed. "I'll pick the lock and get out. This master thief I know taught me how to break into any house...uh...oh."

"You know a master thief?" Sandra exclaimed. "Can you introduce me!"

Cort shared a resigned smile with his father over Mina's head. "Oh God, what have we let ourselves in for?" he groaned.

Vic chuckled. "Some exciting times, I'd venture." He paused. "Hey, it's not so bad. If we have any more incursions on the south border, we know who to call, right?"

Cort sighed. "Right."

Mina lifted her head and looked up at him with sheer delight. "They're going to teach the baby how to do stealth missions," she said deliberately.

"I will—" he began.

She kissed him, stopping the words. He hesitated only for a few seconds before he kissed her back. He lifted his head. "Not until they're in high school," he said firmly.

"They?" she asked.

He shrugged and grinned. "I have three brothers. Large families are nice."

She pursed her lips. "Well, I guess a handful, assorted, wouldn't be so bad. And I can knit, you know. They'll have unique sweaters, if I can ever learn to read a pattern, that is."

"I can read patterns, and knit," Sandra said surprisingly. "I'll teach you!"

"That's a deal," Mina laughed.

Cort moved Mina into his room, suitcase and all. She was worn-out from the violence of the night. He undressed her gently and slid one of her pretty new gowns over her head.

"I like this," he mused, fingering the pale yellow silk-and-lace garment.

"That's why I bought it," she teased, smiling up at him. "I thought you might."

He sighed. "My wife the commando writer." He shook his head. "Well, it does explain a few things. Although I'm going to thump Bart for not telling me."

"I asked him not to," she confessed. "At first it was because I

didn't like you, and I thought it would be fun to tell you somewhere down the road. But then I fell in love with you, and I
didn't know how to tell you."

He twirled a long strand of her hair around his fingers. "I
didn't know how to tell you that I owned the biggest ranch in
West Texas, while we're making confessions. I was afraid that
you'd back off if you knew I had money."

"I might have," she conceded.

"And I might have backed off if I'd known who you really
were," he confessed.

"I'm number four on the *New York Times* list," she said. "I'm
going to be very rich, at the rate my books are selling." She made
a face. "That's another thing, I'm obligated to go on tour week
after next. I didn't know how to tell you that, either."

"I'll go with you," he said easily, and he smiled down into
her surprised face. "I can work on the laptop while you're signing. We won't have to be apart."

"I'd love that," she said with genuine feeling.

He smiled slowly. "I would, too." He slid his lean hand over
her stomach. "I love this," he said very quietly. "I never thought
of myself as a family man," he added. "I played the field because
I didn't really want to settle down. But when you came along,
my whole attitude changed."

"What about Ida?" she asked suddenly.

He sighed. "Her first husband was gay and she didn't know.
He killed himself and left her a fortune. Her second husband
abused her in terrible ways. She didn't want to take a chance on
a third, so she developed this wicked reputation that puts men
off. She pleaded with me not to give her away and I haven't."

She relaxed. "I did wonder," she said. "She's so beautiful. I
never thought I could compete with a woman who looked like
that."

"You're beautiful to me, Mina," he said quietly. "It's what's inside you that makes you beautiful. I can't even describe what it is. But I'm damned glad that you found something in me to love."

She snuggled close to him. "You have more good qualities than you realize." She yawned. "I hope our son looks like you."

"He may be a she," he pointed out.

"You have four brothers," she returned.

"You do have a point."

"But we'll love whatever we get." She drew back, worried. "You don't really mind, do you? I mean, it's a big step just getting used to being married. Is it too soon for a baby?"

He shook his head, and there wasn't a trace of doubt or reticence in his lean face. He touched her cheek gently. "Vic and Sandra are going to love being around for the whole process. So am I," he added on a chuckle. "I'm looking forward to every minute of it."

"No regrets at all?" she prompted.

"Just one," he replied. "I wish I hadn't taken you to Lander. You should have had a proper wedding night."

"I don't mind," she replied, and meant it. "The way I felt about you, it was as natural as falling into water." She flushed a little. "It was the most incredible experience of my whole life."

He pursed his lips and looked down at her pert breasts, a little fuller from her pregnancy. "Want to see if we can manage another incredible experience? Or do you need sleep more?"

She shook her head. "I'm not really sleepy anymore."

He chuckled. "Neither am I."

Her hands went to his tie. She removed it and unbuttoned his shirt and pushed it away from his broad, hair-roughened chest. She removed his belt. But her hands hesitated.

"Chicken," he teased.

"Come on, now, I'm new to this," she chided.

He picked her up and put her gently under the covers. "Fair enough. I'll do the rest."

He took off the rest of his clothes and joined her on the bed, and her arms opened to welcome him.

It was a feast of the senses. There wasn't an inch on her soft body that he didn't touch with his hands and his mouth over the heated minutes that followed.

She caught her breath as the delicious sensations washed over her, lifting to meet his lips, hungry for more.

"You're getting better at this," he whispered against one taut little nipple.

"I'll get even better as we go along," she said, and then gasped as he found a very tender spot with his hands.

"The mind boggles," he teased huskily.

She tried to tell him that it was far more sensual than the first time, but she was suddenly overwhelmed by a flash of pleasure so intense that she cried out.

"Oh, you like that, do you?" he whispered. "How about this?"

She cried out again. Her harsh moan whipped the fire of his own hunger, and the gentle teasing gave way to a monstrous need.

"Tell me if I'm too rough," he managed as he moved over her.

"When were you ever rough?" she returned, shivering as she felt him moving slowly, sensually into her body.

"I'm starving," he whispered unsteadily. "I don't want to hurt you or the baby."

"You won't. Oh, you won't. Please, Cort, please, please…!"

His hips pressed hers into the mattress in a quick, smooth rhythm that very quickly brought her to ecstasy, but before she could relax, he started all over again. Each sharp movement of his body made her quiver with excitement. She looked into his pale brown eyes and felt herself begin to melt under him.

"It wasn't…this intense before," she choked.

"We weren't this involved before," he returned. He kissed her hungrily. "I love you," he whispered gruffly. "I'll never stop. Never…never…never!"

He ended on a harsh groan followed by a convulsive shudder that brought her own shivering body to another pinnacle. She cried out and her nails dug into his long back as she moved with him harder and harder until she thought she might pass out from the force of the pleasure.

"Oh… God…" he bit off, and actually went into convulsions.

She buried her face in his hot, damp throat and went every step of the way with him, shivering wildly as she followed him into the fire.

A long time later, he rolled off her and onto his back, still shivering in the aftermath.

"Are you sure I wasn't too rough?" he whispered.

"I'm sure." She curled up close to him, damp with sweat and throbbing with ebbing delight. "I never felt anything like that, not even the first time!"

"Me, neither," he confessed. He was still trying to get his breath and his heart was shaking him.

She lifted herself up on his chest so that she could look into his eyes. "Did you mean it?"

He traced her cheek. "Did I mean what?" he asked with a lazy smile.

"What you said."

"That I loved you?"

She nodded.

He chuckled. "Why else did I marry you?" he asked. "If I only wanted sex, I could have seduced you and walked away."

"I thought you might," she replied with a shy smile. "I mean, it was pretty intense, what happened in Lander, but I wasn't sure you really felt anything more than desire."

"You grew on me from the first time I saw you," he returned. "The women who passed through my life weren't interested in things like knitting and romance novels," he teased.

She made a face. "I can imagine what they were interested in."

He nodded. "Diamonds and fur coats," he said. "It was nothing but casual encounters. I never risked my heart. Not until I came up to Wyoming, disheartened and jaded, feeling more like a walking wallet than a man."

"Jake McGuire told me once that he felt that way, too. Don't look like that," she chided. "You know I only thought of Jake as a friend. If I'd known him a hundred years, I'd still have felt that way."

He sighed. "I wasn't as jealous of him as I was of Bart, until he told me that he thought of you as a sister."

She smiled. "He did. We never had even a spark of interest."

He rolled over and studied her flushed face. "I'm still amazed at what you managed to do for Dad and Sandra," he said.

She laughed. "They're very much alike. Your father just needs more attention than he thinks he's getting. If he goes to a psychologist, I think he and Sandra can work out all their problems. He really loves her. It shows, too."

"I guess it does."

"I'm just glad that the guys were here when the drug runners came over the border," she said. "I couldn't have taken on two of the would-be kidnappers."

He made a face. "I suppose your friends aren't so bad."

She grinned. "You'll get used to them. I have to have research associates, you know."

He sighed. "I guess so."

"I'll make sure you get adequate compensation," she said, drawing one silky bare leg against his.

His heart jumped. "You will, huh?"

"I truly will." She drew his face down to hers and kissed him slowly. "I can start right now, if you like."

He smiled back. "I do like…"

It was the last thing he said for a long time.

Cort flew up to Catelow to help pack the rest of Mina's things and bring them back to Latigo. Some would have to be shipped as well.

Fender was waiting for them when the limousine deposited them at the ranch house.

He grinned. "Congratulations," he said, shaking hands with Cort.

"Thanks."

"Everything going okay?" Mina asked as Cort helped her out of the car.

"Going fine," he said. "We had a small wolf issue, but Bart called the wildlife people and relocated two of them to the mountains." He grimaced. "I still feel guilty about that old wolf."

"Which old wolf?" Mina asked.

"Well, I was hoping for a job here and I saw the wolf attack the cow who'd just given birth. I tracked it and shot it. When I got to it, I noticed that it had been ripped open down its belly and the wound had never healed. It was pretty sick. I felt like it was more of a dignified end than letting it suffer."

Cort nodded. He'd told Mina about the condition the wolf was in. "I mentioned it to her and Bart," he confessed.

"It's not a big deal," Mina told Fender. "I'm just glad to know what happened to it and why. We never knew who shot it."

"Well, see, I wasn't sure what the law was about wolves and I didn't want to get in trouble in case it was illegal."

"We can shoot them if we have to, but the kill must be reported. In fact, Bart did report it to the proper authorities, and there was no action taken."

"I'm glad."

Mina smiled at him. "I hope you'll stay on here as livestock foreman," she told him. "Bill will work full-time as ranch manager, but he'll need help."

Fender smiled. "Ma'am, I'd be more than happy to stay. This is a good ranch."

"Thanks," she told him. "And if you ever need help and you can't find me, you call Bart."

"I'll do that. Anything I can help with?"

"I'll need to give you a list of things that I'll have to have shipped to Latigo," she told him. "But for right now, I'm just packing personal stuff."

"Just let me know. I'll be around," he promised.

"What about your father?" Cort asked when she'd finished getting her things together and making a list of furniture she wanted sent to Texas.

She turned. "What do you mean?"

"Your cousin said your father wanted to talk to you."

She hesitated. She drew in a long breath. "I'm not ready yet," she said after a minute. "One day, but not yet."

He touched her soft cheek. "Whatever you want, honey."

She smiled up at him. "Maybe when the baby comes."

He smiled back. "That sounds like a good time."

Their little boy was born just at Christmas, a month early, and he was named Jeremiah Riddle Grier, for his maternal grandfather and his father, whose middle name was Riddle. There was a crowd on hand for the birth, including all three of Cort's brothers and their families, along with the commandos and Bart.

Mina had never been so happy. She and Cort were over the moon.

Two months later, there was a christening, followed by a catered barbecue feast for the attending guests. The whole Grier family came back for it. Even Cousin Rogan and Jake McGuire showed up.

Cort was so pleased with his heir that he didn't protest the guest list. One unexpected addition to the group was Jerry Fender, who flew from Catelow down to Latigo for the event—minus his dog Sagebrush, who was staying at the ranch with Bill McAllister.

Mina was surprised to see him. She'd actually had Cousin Rogan invite her father to the event, so delighted with her new life that she was no longer holding the vicious grudge that had occupied her most of her old life.

Cousin Rogan smiled as she joined him while Cort held the baby and showed him off to Cash and Garon and Parker, his brothers.

"What is it?" her cousin asked.

"Fender's here," she replied. "I thought he was going to stay in Catelow to look after the ranch with Bill McAllister. And where's my father? I said you could invite him, but he didn't show up."

Cousin Rogan looked guilty. "Well, actually, Mina, your father's here."

She blinked. She looked around at the crowd, but she didn't see a single person that she didn't know. "Where?"

He took her by the shoulders and turned her slowly toward Fender, who was standing behind her, looking worried and apprehensive.

"There, Mina," Rogan replied.

Mina stared at Fender and images flashed in her mind. He was always watching out for her, checking to make sure she got home safely at night, taking an interest in who she dated. He had a big dog that he loved. Her father had loved dogs.

Her face paled.

"I'm sorry," Fender said quietly. "You didn't want to see me when Rogan first told you, and I had to try. So I signed on to work on the ranch." He drew in a long breath. "I tried so damned hard to get custody of you. I really wanted you with me. Your mother was too eaten up with spite and hatred to let me near you. I just…gave up. I was afraid she'd make up a story and have me put in prison. But not a day went by when I didn't love you or want to get you away from her. I tried several times over the years, through lawyers, to get custody. I failed every damned time."

"Why did she hate me so?" she asked miserably.

"Because you weren't hers," he said flatly.

She gasped. "What?"

"When we first got married, we found out that she couldn't have a child. I'd been briefly engaged to another woman and she'd gotten pregnant. She was dying and begged me to take you. I did, against your mother's wishes. She hated me for it, hated you, hated the world."

"So that was why," Mina said heavily.

"That was why. You're my daughter. But you're not your mother's daughter. The woman who gave birth to you was a kind, sweet woman who was frail and undemanding. Your mother was flamboyant and seductive and I fell head over heels for her. It was a flash in the pan. I paid for it, your real mother paid for it and you paid for it. One mistake, and you and I are still paying for it."

Mina felt a weight lift from her heart. She finally understood. "I'm sorry," she began.

"I'm the one who should be apologizing," he interrupted her. "It was my fault. All of it. I left your mother for another flash in the pan, although I didn't regret it except for losing you. The woman you thought was your mother was a greedy, cold, hateful woman, who poisoned every life she touched. She said she'd make sure I never got custody of you, no matter what lies she had to tell." He swallowed. "If you want to fire me, I'll understand. I didn't come here to ruin your special day."

She just stared at her father. She didn't know what to say. "I wish I'd known sooner," she said finally.

He shrugged. "You know now. That's enough. I'd like to get to know you all over again," he added. "I'm so proud of you."

She managed a weak smile. "I'd like that, too."

He nodded. He smiled. "So I've still got a job?"

"You bet."

"Then I'll get back to Catelow and do it."

She nodded. "You can write me. I'll write back."

"I'll do that. Thanks," he added huskily. "For giving me a second chance."

"Thanks for clearing up the mystery. No wonder she hated me. I was ashamed that I could never love her. Now I'm not ashamed anymore."

"No reason to be. She wasn't a lovable woman." He hesitated. "Well, I'll see you around, Mina."

She laughed. "I'll see you around. Dad."

He flushed. Then he beamed. "I'll work on earning that title." He shook hands with Rogan and smiled one more time at Mina before he turned away and had one of the ranch cowboys drive him to the airport, where Rogan's private jet was waiting to return him to Catelow.

"I think things are looking up," Rogan told her.

She agreed, smiling. "They are, indeed. Thanks," she added.

He shrugged. "My pleasure."

"Did you know that he was applying for the job at my ranch?" she added.

"No. That was his own idea. But if I'd known, I wouldn't have stopped him. He loves you, you know. He's carrying enough guilt of his own."

"I'll write to him. Things will work out. They just need a little time," she said.

He grinned. "They do." He glanced over at Cort. "I like your husband."

"I think he's amazing," she returned.

"I did notice," he drawled.

She laughed. Her eyes met her husband's across the distance that separated them. He looked back at her and smiled, too.

In that long, sweet look was a meeting of hearts as enduring as the land on which Latigo stood. Cort cuddled their firstborn close and started toward Mina through the crowd of family and friends. She met him halfway.

"Happy?" he asked her in a deep, soft tone.

"So happy that I can barely hold it all inside," she replied breathlessly. Her hand touched their son's soft tuft of black hair. "We have the whole world, don't we, Cort?" she asked.

"The whole world, and then some," he agreed.

She looked up into his eyes and sighed as she considered what a long road she'd traveled to get to this shared delight.

I'd do it all over again, she thought suddenly. *I'd go through every miserable bad day of my life, just for this.*

Just for Cort's soft eyes looking down into hers with love, as he held their son in his arms.

★ ★ ★ ★ ★